Praise for *If the Creek Don't Rise*

"The 1970s Appalachia of Weiss's brilliant first novel has a culture of moonshining, clan feuding, and enduring poverty that has kept an iron grip on generations of inhabitants... Writing with a deep knowledge of the enduring myths of Appalachia, Weiss vividly portrays real people and sorrows. A strong, formidable novel for readers of William Faulkner and Cormac McCarthy."

—*Library Journal*, Starred Review

"In this tender but powerful debut, Weiss paints both the bright and the dark in the lives of her fictional Appalachian community's denizens."

—*Publishers Weekly*

"Weiss catches and weaves together compelling voices from the haunted and haunting interstices of America. Each chapter is told from a different character's perspective, and they all add new pieces to the puzzle of Roy's dark soul, Sadie's bittersweet hope, and Darlene's mysterious disappearance. Part gothic, part romance, part heartbreaking Loretta Lynn ballad—Weiss's tale is a beguiling, compelling read."

—*Kirkus Reviews*

"An engaging page-turner...the characters who populate those pages [are] realistic enough for readers to passionately connect with, whether through an empathetic enjoyment, a delightful fascination, or a raging disdain. With its bewitching residents and rugged landscape, a journey to Baines Creek is a trip worth taking."

—*Shelf Awareness*

"This one nearly broke my heart. With deeply human characters I will not easily forget, Weiss captures the fierce pull of desperation and the formidable power of hope. An impressive debut from a talent to watch."

—Kathleen Grissom, author of the *New York Times* bestsellers *The Kitchen House* and *Glory Over Everything*

"Every page of Leah Weiss's debut, *If the Creek Don't Rise*, has a pulse as fierce and unyielding as its Appalachian setting. Told through an ensemble of narrators, men and women of all ages bound by the inescapable power of place and belonging, it is a lush exploration of the darkest rooms in the human heart, and the brightest fires of the human spirit. Weiss's remarkable gift for language left me breathless, and her characters, distinctive and unapologetically human, will haunt me for some time."

—Erika Marks, author of *The Last Treasure*

"Leah Weiss brings Appalachia to life in Sadie Blue's story. The setting becomes a richly developed character, and the hardscrabble tale satisfied this reader to the very last page."

—Ann Hite, author of the award-winning *Ghost on Black Mountain* and *Sleeping Above Chaos*

"This is for fans of Ron Rash, Wiley Cash, or Nick Butler. Simply fabulous writing topped by breathtaking characters who you will think about long after you close the pages of this stunning novel."

—Jessilynn Norcross, McLean & Eakin (Petoskey, MI)

if the creek don't rise

if the creek don't rise

a novel

LEAH WEISS

Published by Sourcebooks Landmark, an imprint of Sourcebooks, Inc.
P.O. Box 4410, Naperville, Illinois 60567–4410
(630) 961–3900
Fax: (630) 961–2168
www.sourcebooks.com

Library of Congress Cataloging-in-Publication Data

Names: Weiss, Leah, author.
Title: If the creek don't rise : a novel / Leah Weiss.
Description: Naperville, Illinois : Sourcebooks Landmark, 2017.
Identifiers: LCCN 2017001928 | (pbk. : alk. paper)
Subjects: LCSH: Country life--North Carolina--Fiction. | Domestic fiction.
Classification: LCC PS3623.E45554 I38 2017 | DDC 813/.6--dc23 LC record
available at https://lccn.loc.gov/2017001928

Printed and bound in the United States of America.
VP 10 9 8 7 6 5 4 3 2 1

For Paul, the brighter star

For Glo, the wind in my sail

For Dave, the honey in my days

CONTENTS

SADIE BLUE

I struggle to my feet, straighten my back, lift my chin, then he hits me again. This time I fall down and stay down while he counts, "…eight, nine, ten." He walks out the trailer door and slams it hard. The latch don't catch, and the door pops open. I lay on the floor and watch Roy Tupkin cross the dirt yard and disappear into the woods.

My world's gone sideways again.

"Sadie girl." Daddy's spirit voice comes soft from behind my open eyes. "You got yourself in a pickle this time. No two ways about it. That husband of yours won't stop till you and your baby draw your last breath. You don't even look like yourself no more. He broke bout every piece of sweet in you. You gonna let him break your spirit, too? You gonna do nothing?"

I'm tired, Daddy. Wore out. Roy Tupkin don't just beat me, he beats me down. Let me rest a spell. I don't know if I can lift my head just yet.

Now Daddy's voice comes from the yard where a lone wind rattles late-summer oak leaves and sounds like hollow bones. "If I could follow the bastard and kill him for you, I would, sweet girl, but it don't work like that." His voice drifts toward the rusty red truck up on blocks. "Don't lay there too long, Sadie. You don't need rest." His words fade. "You need…"

What, Daddy? What do I need? I listen but he's gone.

Percy scampers in from the hunt with a dead chipmunk. He drops his gift by my hand. When I don't move, he nudges it close till I raise a finger and touch fur that's still warm. Then he crawls on the rise of my belly and curls up. Purrs vibrate clean through to my spine.

I gotta get away, Percy, but don't know how. Gotta be careful.

Percy listens good but he's short on advice. I can't think what to do right off with my brain muddled from this morning's beating, so I gather strength to move. Shadows grow longer, and cold air glides across the doorjamb, giving me goose bumps. I roll over gentle to my side, scattering pieces of the green plastic radio I got working at Mooney's Rusty Nickel. Little Percy slides off without complaint. I put my palms on the floor and push to my knees. My arms tremble. My heart pounds in my ears. A bloody smear on the floor marks where my head landed. I brush sticky hair off my temple, hold on to the counter, and pull up, dizzy, one hand on my baby bump. I don't know I'm crying salty tears till they sting the cut on my cheek.

"You know what you gotta do." Daddy's voice is back burrowing inside my ear.

I do? Tell me and I'll do it.

"You'll figure it out. You got smarts you don't even know bout yet."

Daddy loves me better in death than he ever did in life. In life, when I was ten, with my hair in crooked braids, me sitting on a overturned bucket in a corner of the kitchen, watching the men round the table gamble, he throwed a night with me in the poker pot instead of five dollars he don't have. Granny and Aunt Marris never heard what he done, and I don't say cause they'd take a belt to him and take me away from him when he needs me. Daddy won the hand. Said he counted on it. But he woulda made good on his bet if he'd lost. He won't go back on his word.

Daddy hung bones on the walls inside our house like some folks hang giveaway calendars or pictures of Jesus. They was mostly bleached-out skulls he found hunting or tending the still. He ran twine through their empty eyes and wound the twine on a tenpenny nail high on the wall. He had the skulls of a fox, bear, bobcat, and panther, and the rib cage of a bear. Daddy even had a man's skull in the lot. Found it in a cave near a rockslide that pinned the poor soul down till he wasted away. Said it was likely a miner and a dreamer looking for rubies and stones. At night, under moonlight streaming through the front window, those bones glowed like pieces of ghosts.

Granny won't set foot in our house cause of Daddy's bones. Said it was a heathen thing to do. Said it won't natural. I asked Daddy why he brought such things inside when nobody else did. He grinned and said, "One time these bones was wrapped in flesh and muscle and brains. They mighta fought a good fight to the end. But in the end, even the smart ones is just bones with all the fight gone out. Looking at em makes me think different bout power and petty things."

I hear he don't start hanging bones on the wall till Mama left.

Some folks say Daddy was a peculiar soul. Some say he was a thinking man. He was funny, gentle, and always a pinch of sad the years I knew him, cause the pitiful truth is he got nothing from loving Mama cept me left behind.

I think it was a broke heart that killed him, mostly cause Mama left him with a baby girl who lately looked too much like her. I don't remember her face cept from a faded picture in a dresser drawer in a back room at Granny's. Mama had hair the color of mine, and she was built thin like me. Aunt Marris said she had gumption in her eyes and a slice of selfish that won't pretty.

That night Daddy ended up dead, he stumbled in my room on wobbly legs and fell on top of me sleeping in my iron bed. "Carly, my Carly Blue." He cried out Mama's name next to my ear, slobbering like a sorry fool. I never liked it when Daddy don't know me cause he tried things. So I pulled up my knees and pushed, and he fell off me and hit his head on the edge of the bed with a thud. I jumped over his body and run into the woods, wearing a thin nightgown that snagged on brambles that scratched my arms, a ghost girl on bare feet. I hid under the weeping willow at the creek, shivering till the moon went away and morning come shy on the mountain.

When I walked through the door, I saw death claimed Daddy. His body lay on the floor where I had left him. The color was drained, and his skin was like ash in a fire gone cold. His eyes stayed open, and a fly crawled on his cheek. He puked like drunks do, and it dried in his beard and over his ear and puddled at his neck. Daddy died cause I won't there to turn him over.

I wanted to stay at Daddy and my place on Bentwood Mountain, down the road from Granny and Aunt Marris, but

Preacher Eli said to move in with Granny so she could help me through a sad time. Granny don't do my heart any good, but when the roof on Daddy's house caved in the next big winter snow, I was glad to be outta the rubble. Then that summer, vines started to crawl up the sides and through the broke windows, and over and around those pointy teeth and skulls on the wall. Nowadays, five years since, the vines claim it all.

Now I stand on wobbly legs and whimper like a hurt puppy cause I can't help it. Today was beating number three since I got legal. I figure Roy don't need a reason no more. I close the trailer door against the chill, then shuffle to the bathroom to wash off the dried blood. The face in the cracked mirror shows another loose tooth, a split lip, and a eye turning purple. I don't see *me* no more in that slice of looking glass. It's a strange feeling thinking the face in the mirror is somebody else. I half think to see her lips move to talk and mine stay closed, or the other way round.

Wonder what Miss Shaw, that teacher with her pile of books and globe that whirls, would say now if she saw the fix I'm in. What would she think if she saw my life so different from hers? When I go see her next, I'll cover the bruises best I can. Don't need her pity.

Truth is, I been a sorry fool like Granny called me when Roy Tupkin, all charm and light, showed up every once in a while in early springtime. I'd be leaving Mooney's place with a sack of supplies or walking to see Birdie or Aunt Marris. Roy would come like fog or a wish with that sassy grin of his. One time he jumped from behind a tree to block my way and made my heart flip. Another time he sneaked up behind me and pulled my hair, him with his lanky frame and eyes locked on nothing but me for a spell. At the start he made me smile and my heart flutter. He made me hide behind my long hair so he don't see me turn twenty shades of pink.

Once, when the creek was high water, that man give me his rough hand to help me cross over, and don't let go of mine right away. When he did, I wanted to grab back his hand cause mine felt safe in his. That's how stupid I was.

Another time he carried my paper poke of supplies, and another time blackberries I picked. He walked me to the edge of Granny's yard but don't come close to the house cause he won't welcome. Granny give him the hard eye and pointed her shotgun at him from her porch and said, "I know how to use this here gun. It ain't for show. Now don't you step your sorry ass on my land."

Roy Tupkin backed away with his hands up, laughing at a big ole woman with stockings knotted at her knees and her cheek bulging with chew. When he left, I cried and run up the stairs to my room and slammed the door. Granny give me a strong talking-to outside my closed door, but that don't change things cause I was young and dumb. I was pulled by the raw scent of that man, not knowing the stink below the skim of sweet.

Granny said, back then, through pinched lips and squinty eyes and hissy voice, "You knock them fake stars outta your blind eyes, Sadie Blue, or you gonna lay with the devil and live in hell. When that happens, I can't help you."

I thought she was jealous cause I was happy. I thought I was smart and loved a bad man turned good. I've been on a losing streak a long time.

What was funny in the mix was the man Billy Barnhill, back bent, face pocked, hair greasy. When I'd see Roy, there'd be Billy a ways off, hands shoved deep in his pockets, mostly looking at his feet, waiting. I asked Roy what Billy was to him, and he said, "Nobody."

The first time I give myself to Roy, I was weak-willed after meeting up just three times. We sat close in the front seat of his truck on the shoulder of Good Luck Pass. One of his hands rooted up under my skirt, and the other pinched a nipple through my blouse to make it rise. Out the corner of my eye, through the rear window, I see Billy in the back bed with the canvas tarps and cement blocks and gas can. He leaned against the tailgate, legs out straight, one hand working inside the slit of his overalls. His mouth was loose and lips wet, him looking at me weird.

I told Roy that Billy was a creep and I wanted him gone for now. Roy laughed that day and said, "Let him have a little fun," and pulled me to him. When I pushed back, nervous, the cool coming off my skin, me sliding over to my side of the seat, pulling down my skirt, Roy's eyes dulled over. He waved for Billy to leave, and Billy jumped out the truck bed, lickety-split, and crossed the ditch. I scooted back into Roy's arms, but I could still feel Billy's eyes crawl over me.

The thing what got me married by summer's end was the baby growing inside me through four cycles and me still living with Granny. She got meaner every day when she knew I carried Roy's baby. She found new ways to hurt me and say I was a vile sinner—when she won't even a Bible reader. She don't answer when I talk. I walk in a room and she walked out. I step out on the porch, she goes inside. She cooked supper just enough for her and left me starting from scratch if I was to eat.

I hear ugly talk. Wherever two righteous souls meet up at the Rusty Nickel, God-fearing women standing at the counter with babies on their hips and a ring on their fingers, they whispered loud enough for me to hear, "She was a promisin girl who got ruint by a trashy man."

Prudence Perkins said in a hard whisper outside church, "The hellfires of damnation won't be good enough for you and that bastard you carry."

I flushed shameful at such hateful words, cheeks hot, heart bruised and breaking for my innocent child. Preacher Perkins and Mooney tried to stop the ugly when they was in earshot cause they are good men, but tongues let loose rattled on for spite.

I cried at night back then. Roy don't come round much, me carrying his flesh and blood, and I yearned for him in the summer dark. I was blind and dumb and slow to learn.

———

In the heart of the summer heat, it was going on day twenty-six since Roy been by. I was pining and not eating, wanting to up and die from the want of him, when his truck showed up in front of the house. He hit his horn for me to come outside, and I run to him. Without a hello or howdy-do, he said, "Get in," and I did, but I had to move tools to the floor so I had room to sit. Billy won't with him this time and I was glad.

Roy drove a short piece down the road, pulled into the woods, and turned off the motor. I let him have his way with me cause it won't nothing new. It was over quick, and after, with the truck windows down, and the smell of wildflowers on the air, and his wide hand on my white belly growing big, that teeny foot kicked my innards for the first time and made Roy and me jump.

Right then, with one baby kick, that man with the dark soul grinned, and it turned his face into something beautiful I never seen before. A light shined in his face on this cloudy day and wiped away shadows that lived behind his eyes. I brushed back the dark hair on his forehead and kissed it tender, over and over, cause Roy let me.

He looked up and said, "Let's get hitched."

I pulled back to see if he was fooling, and he looked different enough, so I fell into his arms. I was a fool hanging hope on a weak man I thought would stand tall if we got married.

That Thursday afternoon in late August, with soggy clouds squatting in the hollers, we drove the truck down the long, winding mountain, through countryside I'd never seen before or since. We crossed the county line, passed the cutoff to Burnsville, into the town Roy said was called Spruce Pine, with stores lining the main street on both sides and the North

Toe River flowing by like a wide creek. We found a justice of the peace by a sign in his yard, who answered the door with a napkin tucked in his collar, us interrupting his supper of liver and onions from the smell of it. I wore a off-white dress with a coffee stain on it from breakfast and a tear from getting caught in brambles. Roy wore a T-shirt and a tight grin.

After we said a quick *I do* and Roy paid him two dollars, we bought nabs and co'colas at the filling station when Roy got gas, then drove back home in the dusky quiet, not saying a word, shocked to see our names tied together on a legal piece of paper.

Back at Granny's, Roy waited in the truck, looking straight ahead. I rushed inside to pack a cardboard box of my things, hands shaking, part of me scared Roy was gonna drive off and leave me. When I called out to Granny I was married legal and leaving, she don't even come outta her bedroom to say good-bye or a fare-the-well.

Fifteen days has gone by since that piece of paper got signed. Roy beats on me pretty regular cause nobody stops him. I thought we got married for a mighty reason. I thought I was special to him.

I musta made it all up, cause none of it's true.

Daddy's spirit voice pulls me back from silly memories. He says, "Don't let your guard down, girl. Roy sold his soul to the devil long ago. Make sure the devil lays claim to it soon."

I nod and raise my nose to sniff Daddy's cigarette smoke

that's sometimes here. I rolled his cigarettes for him since I'm five, and I'm good at it. Today there's no smoke to smell, just mold in the corners and yesterday's fish.

I step back in the kitchen and start supper. It won't do for Roy to come home and find nothing to eat. I put on a pot of beans, heat the iron skillet, and drop pieces of rabbit flesh in hot lard. The smell of grease gags me, and I press my knuckles against my mouth so I don't throw up. Drop a dishrag on the floor and use my foot to wipe up the smear of blood from this morning. Pick up the plastic pieces of my broke radio and throw em in the trash. When food's ready, I keep it warm in the oven and sit on the sofa, working on a plan while daylight leaks outta the sky and the wind moans low through the cracks round the windows.

"You done right fixing supper." Daddy's words sound down the hall. "A hungry man's a mean man. Roy's mean enough with a full belly. What you gonna do now?"

Let me think for myself, Daddy.

When I don't say nothin right off, Daddy raises his voice. "Girl? You hearing me?"

I hear you. Don't yell.

"What's it gonna be?"

I don't answer and he goes away.

Fifteen days since the trip to Spruce Pine to get married, and there still won't a ring on my finger to cool the shame. I study the scorch on the tile floor where a skillet of fried chicken got dropped my second day as Roy's wife and smoked up the place bad. Roy won't happy one bit, but he don't hit me on my second day as his missus.

The thing what got me beat today was I got careless. I got used to acting easy the past week Roy was off at the still or Lord knows where, but letting me be by myself. When he was gone, I keep my radio out and sing along and bake blackberry cobbler I eat outta the pan. I fill a canning jar with wildflowers like Aunt Marris does.

I forgot to watch out for that man.

I was singing with my radio and got a wooden spoon in my hand, pretending I'm at the Grand Ole Opry standing right next to Miss Loretta Lynn in front of folks to please. Her and me is singing together like this was what I was born to do, me swinging my be-hind to the beat and my foot tapping. It's her hit "Don't Come Home A Drinkin' (with Lovin' on Your Mind)" we're singing, and I know every word by heart. That woman writes songs for me—even if I don't call what Roy does to me loving no more.

The first time I seen a picture of Miss Loretta Lynn was in the *Country Song Roundup* magazine a coupla years back. She was on the cover, and Mooney showed it to me cause he knows I love her so. His copy of that magazine was as dog-eared as the Sears and Roebuck catalog he keeps on the counter. He told me the words of Loretta Lynn's story inside while I looked at her pictures.

That's how come I know she was raised in a log cabin in a Kentucky holler just like Baines Creek. In that magazine picture, she was sitting on a sofa stacked high with fancy pillows. Her dark hair had thick curls spilling over her shoulder. She showed her dimple and had diamond sparkles on her fancy dress. Said she sang at more than two hundred shows a year, riding from one place to another in her own tour bus. She had four babies before she was eighteen and is already a grandma. Miss Loretta is rich, but she's my kinda people. She won't turn up her nose at a simple life like mine. She could be my friend if she ever knocked on my door.

———

This morning, Roy musta come up the trailer steps quiet while I was singing with the radio cause I don't hear him. He opened the door, sneaky. I feel a chill drift in and turned, still holding that silly spoon up to my mouth. When I saw him filling up the doorway, I stopped singing, but Miss Loretta kept on.

Without a hello or what the hey, that man pulled back his long arm and hit me upside the head with the flat of his hand. I grabbed my baby belly when I fell back against the sink, but, like a dern fool, I staggered back to my feet. He brought his arm down on my shoulder, and I dropped to my knees like a sack of feed. He kicked me in the back and rolled me over to my front with the toe of his muddy boot. Got down on one knee so I could see his devil eyes up close.

Roy drew back his fist clenched so tight the skin turned white, his temper trembling up and down his arm, and me trembling too. The smell that rolled off him was rotten. He held the terror there for me to see. I watched till I did something I never done before: I closed my eyes.

The place turned quiet cept for Miss Loretta ending her song and Roy breathing fast like a horse what's been run hard. Then he stood and, quick as lightning, picked up my prized

radio off the kitchen table, with the man saying, "That was
Loretta Lynn, folks, Queen of—" and it crashed against the
wall. That precious green plastic radio broke to smithereens and
rained down on me. I stayed down with my eyes closed while
he counted to ten to show he won.

Now, at the end of fifteen days tied legal to Roy Tupkin
and me beat up three times for no reason I can figure, his
supper sits warm in the oven and I'm working on a plan to get
free. I'll bide my time to make it right. When that day comes,
Roy Tupkin's gonna be sorry he ever messed with me and
Loretta Lynn.

GLADYS HICKS

What's your skinny ass doing here?"

"Wanna see if you was all right, that's all."

Sadie Blue stands at the edge of my yard and drags the toe of her sneaker in the dirt. A bright spot of sunshine holds her in its beam and shines through her skimpy dress. Her baby bump is the size of a honeydew.

"I don't need you checking on me, girl. This ain't your home no more."

She takes a step back, and I feel a pang of regret. Or maybe it's gas. I'm planted on my porch, hands on my hips and bun wound so tight my ears hurt. "I thought you was gone for good, now you legal and all."

As usual, Sadie don't say much.

"Well...you're here..."

With weak permission, my grandgirl steps in the yard, and I turn and open the screen door. Like always, it slaps my heels when I enter, and I head back to the kitchen and the smell of last night's collard greens.

Sadie comes in slow-footed, and I wanna hit her upside the head cause she's meek when she's under my roof. Instead, I slide the iron skillet onto the burner rough-like and slap in a mound of lard, then bark orders. "Peel potatoes and onions. Slice em thin. You slice em thick. I like em thin."

"Yes, ma'am. Thin."

I cut my eyes to see if she sasses me, but Sadie slices thin, then scoops up the pile of potatoes and drops em in the hot pan. She jumps back when the grease pops; her face stays empty. I plop down on the kitchen chair and my thighs settle over the edges. I sift through the thin stack of mail circulars with one hand and rub my knee with the other.

"Your joints ache, Granny?"

I don't bother to say. She sees how swoll my knee is. I sip sweet tea and watch Sadie turn potatoes and onions, slice ham, and wash yesterday's dishes. There's grace bout the girl. Like her mama long gone from here, in this plain place Sadie won't plain...and that galls me. I never got a speck of grace. I was born big-boned and grew tall in a family of runts, and I look down on folks ever since.

Sadie fills our plates from the stove and we eat without talk. Her eyes stay down, and mine stay righteous. When I'm done, I pull the chew outta my pocket and head to the porch glider like I always do to ponder troubles that stay too long. Sadie showing up jumped her to the head of the worry line. I sip on my jar of hooch I keep by the glider cause it softens my rememberings.

My grandgirl tied her hopes to a crappy man without a lick of promise. I could tell by the set of Roy Tupkin's eyes and jut of his jaw that he was the sorry kind. Sadie was blind to danger. She sneaked out at night when she thought I was sleep but won't. I looked out my bedroom window at her running cross the yard with her feet barely touching ground. For a stretch of time, she'd climbed into the front seat of Roy's pickup with the taillights out. I coulda told her he was looking for easy and a woman's life is hard, but she don't ask.

"Got me three dead babies... Then Carly comes along, a runty girl too strong-willed for her own damn good—"

"Granny?" Sadie sticks her head out the screen door, wiping her hands on a rag. "You say something?"

I'm talking out loud and don't know it. I look ahead and rock in the squeaky glider.

Sadie adds, "If you did, I didn't hear you, that's all."

I keep on rocking, and she goes back to the kitchen.

I don't like to look the fool. Truth is, sometimes I need to hear a voice even if it's mine. I'm not use to somebody in earshot to pay attention so I stop ruminating and head inside.

"You gonna stay?"

"That okay?"

"No...but you'll stay anyway."

My ruminating is all off with Sadie here. I grip the banister and heave myself up the warped treads. Have to stop midway to catch my breath. At the top I rest again, then head to the bedroom that's only changed for the worse in forty-one years.

This place belonged to my husband's family three generations back. A unpainted house on the somber side of Bentwood Mountain. When I come as a bride it was enough, but time's added a brittle coat of neglect. The feather bed sags deep when I climb into its valley.

While my body settles in, Sadie comes quiet up the stairs, steps over the loose board at the top, and closes her bedroom door with a soft click. Night sounds slide through the cracks in the walls. Sleep is gonna come. It always does, but so do rememberings. Sometimes they take me places I don't wanna go. Sometimes they take me places I don't wanna leave. I never know where I'm going when I climb in this featherbed.

"Push hard. You can do it," Birdie orders. "PUSH."

I push and push till I part the Red Sea, and out comes a tiny creature not meant for this world. Birdie's face is fuzzy, looking young way back then, and I know the little one's fate without her saying. She wraps it in a rag like leftovers, puts it on the floor, and starts to clean down there. A battle's been fought and I lost again. Birdie leaves and takes the leftovers. I wonder if she'll come back and don't care one way or the other.

My body stinks. My hair is limp on a stained pillow. I lay in my mess and study watermarks on the ceiling. One looks like a railroad track to somewhere else. I follow a crack cross the ceiling to where it meets the wall, then runs down and out the open window to the redbuds. It's bright outside. I squint against the glare.

Birdie comes back. She stands straight in midlife and gives me comfort words. "Gladys, let me clean you and finish up. Your work is done."

She set on the stool next to my bed a pan of warm water with the sweet smell of herbs and a clean rag. Like I'm the baby, she works my nightgown over my head. Takes long strokes down my arms, under my ninnies, cross my empty belly, down my legs to the calloused soles of my wide feet that got cracks in the heels. Rolls my tired body one way, then the other way, strips the soiled towels and sheet from under me and puts on clean linens. The sheets are cool and dry against my washed back. The scent of mint that grows beside the clothesline clings to my cotton gown and sheets. Birdie's face is smooth. Her hands are tender with sympathy and sadness. I appreciate the gift of her.

"You feel better now you cleaned up," she says, and at her kind voice, I squeeze my eyes and out squirt skinny tears. They slide cross my temples and into my hair and ears. She wipes my eyes and brushes my hair with her stubby fingers. The last thing she does is put a cool pillow under my head, then leaves me with my loss.

Walter would have heard and taken to his corn likker. I'll pay later for those nights he couldn't have his way with me and don't have a baby boy to show for it. For now, this clean space is mine to start to heal before he comes at me again. Tonight, this remembering don't make me wander. It stays put on a bed that smells of springtime.

I don't wanna leave.

———

At first light, I hear grandgirl Sadie in the hall outside my bedroom door, then she's gone back to where she belongs. I don't call out but let her and that baby inside her leave. I got to cause she's the only one who can clean up her own mess.

I get up slow, head to the kitchen, and pull down the can of Luzianne on the shelf. While it perks, I hear, "Yoo-hoo. Morning, Gladys. It's Marris!" My neighbor yells out like she always does when she walks into my house like the family she is and heads to the kitchen. She plops a bark basket of berries on my table, takes a chipped cup off the shelf, and pours herself some coffee before it's ready.

"It'll start a *purty* day, but a big rain's coming," she says, like I give a damn.

My anger spikes. "*Why* you do that?"

"Do what?" Marris asks, all innocent-like, and sips the weak coffee. She holds it with both hands with joints as gnarled and swoll with arthuritis as mine.

"Say your name every time you walk in." I imitate her high voice for spite—"*It's Marris*"—and watch her face fall. Then I add, "Like I don't know it's you coming through the door. How many times you been here? A thousand times? Ten thousand? I know who you is, for God's sake."

"I don't count the times." Her voice loses its lightness. "Don't wanna surprise you, that's all."

Her tone turns downright dull. I'm disappointed at the easy victory. Some days, Marris fights harder to keep her sunshine. Today won't one of em.

———

Marris is second cousin by marriage on Walter's side. Since she was a girl, she's lived around the bend, down the road, in a two-room house with a dirt floor she sweeps every day to clear out cobwebs. Marris used to have hair as red as coals cooked down in a fire. Walter would say in a rare time he was being funny, "You stick dough in hair that red, it woulda baked into a biscuit." Now it's gone to ash.

Not a thing's wrong with Marris cept most days she's more happy than a body has a right to be. Regular folks buckle under the piss and vinegar in this world. Not Marris. Her perky words irk me something fierce. Always have. Always will. I stand and pour myself a cup of coffee now that it's ready, then sit again.

"Since you brought them huckleberries and you standing there staring at the wall, why don't you fix a pie?" I throw at her, and the woman goes to work.

She sifts flour, cuts in lard, and adds spring water. She rolls out the pastry for the pie tin, adds the berries, sprinkles sugar on top, and is done lickety-split. While the pie bakes, she washes the bowl, the spoon, and her coffee cup and puts em away. Silence crowds the room. She hangs the apron on the nail, picks up her berry basket, and looks at me for the first time in fifteen minutes.

"Gladys," she asks, "why you boss me round like that and be so hurtful?"

She leaves before I answer and catches the screen door so it don't slam.

I stand and clutch the edge of the sink and look out the window at the garden that struggles in weak sunlight and sorry soil. The plot's gone to seed cause I don't bend the way I used to. My back and legs fail me most days. Few souls ever cross my threshold cept Marris…and she don't count cause of the aggravating she brings. Most of the time she don't even tell me gossip to lift my situation. What's a body to do when she can't care for herself no more and her house falls down? Just up and die?

When it's cooked, I pull the pie from the heat and set it on the window ledge to cool. Dern if she didn't put a four-leaf clover on top to throw the Scots Irish at me. I don't smile. No, sir. Life's too shitty. For a old woman, it's more shit than I can shovel.

I can't remember if I ever had a choice but to put one foot in front of the other and walk the line on a rocky road to nowhere. I pour more coffee, pick up a fork, and stab the heart of the clover. The first bite burns my tongue.

———

Marris was right. The rain comes late afternoon and settles in. The walls of the house get damp and stay damp, and shadows hunker down in corners and hide at the top of landings out of reach of light. I don't believe in ghosts, but they still come round and mess with me. Footsteps fade. Doors open and close. There's scratching in the walls.

I sip from my hooch that night and hope like a fool for a peaceful rest. Rain drums hard, and kitchen pots sit on the floor to catch leaks. Mad lightning and thunder howl through the holler, and branches lick the sides of the house. When I go to the bedroom, I throw a extra quilt on the bed to ward off the damp. There's no easy rest for the weary. I lay in my bed waiting for sleep when a raw memory comes calling instead.

———

"Woman, you got a lesson coming."

Walter stands at the edge of the bed, me waking up confused. I scoot back cross the mattress toward the wall, guilty, but don't know what for.

"What I do?" I ask.

Walter unbuckles his belt. The leather slides out the loops with a familiar hiss and wraps round his calloused palm with the buckle dangling. He leans his head hard to the right. "You think I don't know?" He reminds me of the mean rooster watching a worm he's gonna peck to death. "Bout the man in my house?"

"What man, Walter?"

The belt buckle strikes, and fat welts pop up on my cheek. I whimper and lift bare arms to cover my face. Pull my legs up to make me smaller.

"That traveling man?" he snarls. "You think nobody'd see him?"

WHAP!

"Think a good neighbor don't watch out for my welfare when I'm away?"

WHAP!

Baby Girl cries cross the hall. I try to stay quiet so the child won't worry, but the belt makes the sounds for me. I'm bleeding. One eye's swoll shut, and a finger's bent odd. One more strike and he drops the belt, stumbles over the threshold, and clatters down the stairs. The screen door slaps as he heads into the day's drizzle.

Through my haze I try to remember what could have riled Walter. Yesterday... Musta been that man in a dusty suit who knocked on my screen door. When I showed my face, he stepped back, polite. Asked if he could get a drink of cool water from the well. I said that be fine. He took his drink and left with a tip of his hat. I stayed inside the screen door the whole time with the lock hook in place.

That peckerwood don't know how much his sip of water cost.

I wake with my face wet with tears and my body weighed down. Feeling helpless does that to me. It would be years before fate and guts stepped in to stop Walter's beatings and save me and Baby Girl...but what for? Carly grew up in unhappy skin.

Swore she'd never walk in my shoes. Swore she'd travel a
different road. Find a better path. She likely ended up a fool
like the lot of us.

I hear sobs cross the hall. I don't go look. That room's been
empty a long time.

———————

Sunday morning, Marris comes on back to the kitchen and
don't shout out her name. Her face is flushed with excitement
when she comes in, but it goes plain when she sees me.

"You not ready?"

I butter my third biscuit and add a scoop of blackberry jam.

"What for?"

"That teacher that's come on board this year's gonna be at
church this morning. Thought you woulda heard."

"You know good and well I don't do church. And why
would I give a rat's ass bout a teacher?"

"They say she's taller than six foot."

"Hmm." I take a bite of biscuit, and the butter squirts out
on my chin.

"And pretty old, as teachers go."

"Uh-hmm." I wipe my chin with the back of my hand
and lick it.

Marris runs out of selling points but won't give up. She
says, "Well, it'd be something different to your morning,
won't it?"

I stand and say, "Let me get my hat." Scraps of last night's
ugly hang round, and going to see a giant old teacher sit in

Preacher Perkins's stuffy church and be stared at by the righteous might be the spice I need. I stick my black straw hat on my head, jam the hatpin in the top, and walk out the door.

Marris drives her truck with the muffler shot to hell so everybody hears us a ways off. Pieces of road rush by in rusted-out places in the floorboard; I keep my feet off to the side. We park at the Rusty Nickel and walk the rest of the way up the hill cause it looks like a homecoming crowd come to see the show.

"I ain't gonna stand," I declare to Marris, me huffing up the incline. "Need me a seat. I'll faint if need be."

"Don't get your drawers in a pinch, Gladys. Let's get inside first before you start to act pitiful."

Church is full. I set my eyes hard on the back of Ellis Dodd's puny head and make him squirm in the seat I wanna sit in. He turns, sees me, and gets up quick to stand in back next to Marris. Now I got a good seat on the end of the second row near the teacher woman in front.

Even when she sits, you can tell she's a big one. Bigger than me, and that says something.

On the other end of the front row is Prudence Perkins, Preacher Eli's sister. She sits upright like she swallowed a rod but not the divining kind. She turns her head and stretches out her chicken neck to cut ugly looks at the teacher on the other end. Prudence don't like nobody, but she must not like the teacher extra. I wonder how that could happen so quick? The teacher lady's been here little better than a week from what Marris told me.

Church always got a smell bout it that don't sit right with

me, and it gives me the itches. Maybe it's that fake hope that hangs in the air, frustrated cause nobody gets much back from praying. Maybe it's all that joy the preacher splashes on like toilet water when he tries to make the afterlife special when bout anywhere is special next to Baines Creek.

Preacher Eli still stands outside to say his hellos to folks coming inside, and we're packed tighter than toes in a shoe too small. I elbow Fleeta Wright so she scoots over and don't bump up on my sore hip.

We wait cause we got to, and everybody studies on the teacher. Her dull hair's cut too short for any respectable woman from these parts. She glances round, her eyes wide behind thick glasses, and wiggles her fingers at the Dillard girls, Pearl and Weeza. They grin and try to wave back, but their mama, Jolene, holds their hands down like it's a sin to wave in church.

Fleeta Wright leans over and whispers to me, "Been a long while, Gladys. You forget the way to the Lord's house?"

Her breath smells of garlic and onions, and I wrinkle my nose so she knows.

I answer back, "I know my way round all right. I come when it suit, not cause I have to."

Fleeta rolls her eyes and crosses her arms over her fat bosom.

Folks get fidgety now and clear their throats. They getting tired of waiting for the show to start. I look down at a glob of blackberry jam stuck on my dress. I pick it off and eat it.

Preacher Eli *finally* walks to the front, stands behind the podium, and looks round at everybody. He nods like he's surprised we're here when we just walked past him at the door.

"My fellow friends in Christ…" He starts the usual preacher

yammer and uses his loud church voice, which is silly cause the back wall ain't but thirty feet away.

I knew the two Eli Perkins preachers what come before this one, and they was all stumpy men who told poor-to-middling jokes like it was part of their job. They was okay as far as preachers go and not too pushy. I told em not to darken my door. I don't have need for the rules they sell, so they pretty much leave me be.

Like usual, Preacher starts with a joke.

"I went by Roosevelt Lowe's the other day."

He starts talking bout that old man what lost his leg in a hunting accident years back and don't have good sense to be pissed at his buddy who done the shooting.

"And the good man that he is, I overheard him talking to the Lord. He said, 'God, what's a million years like to you?' God said, 'Well, Roosevelt, it's like a second.' Then Roosevelt asked, 'What's a million dollars like to you?' And God said, 'It's like a penny.' Then Roosevelt got around to the point and asked, 'Well, then can I have a penny?' and God said, 'Just a second.'"

The teacher smiles and I hear Marris giggle in back, then the Preacher giggles too, but for the life of me I don't know why. Nobody's gonna get a million dollars, least of all Roosevelt Lowe and his wood leg. And what good is a second anyway?

Now the joke's over that's a waste of time, Preacher says, "I begin this morning's service with the glorious news that the Lord has indeed blessed us richly in the person of Miss Kate Shaw, who's come up from the valley to guide our children to read and write. Proverbs 22:6 says, 'Train up a child in the way he should go: and when he is old, he will not depart from it.' This is why we're here today, my friends. We train our children to be soldiers of the Lord, and Miss Kate Shaw has come to help."

When Eli says we're training soldiers of the Lord and puts teacher lady in the mix, she shakes her head *no no no*. She looks right at Preacher Perkins, but he don't pay her no mind. Prudence looks the teacher's way with a hateful grin on her face and I don't know why, so that gets my interest up just a bit, but I still nod off.

When I come to, that teacher lady stands next to Eli and makes him look pint-size, which won't hard to do. He sits down, and she talks about losing her job and looking for a new place to teach. What kind of god-awful news is that? We're used to crumbs up here. Now this here's a teacher who's crummy all on her own.

Baines Creek is getting the bottom of the barrel with this woman. She won't stay long. Marris was right for me to come today cause I'd be hard-pressed to understand what I see and hear if told from somebody else's lips.

Her and Preacher walk out first and wait at the door to say their good-byes. That's when I see Sadie in the back row looking extra pitiful. Haven't seen her since she showed up a week back, then slinked downstairs at first light. Forgot she goes to church from time to time. She's got on long sleeves and a skirt dragging the ground. One eye's swoll and her bottom lip got cut. What's outta sight must be extra bad, but her baby bump's still there.

Grandgirl's had a tough time of it lately and it's her own

dern fault. She don't have a ounce of gumption and her backbone's wormy soft. She's gotta look after herself better than
this. I can't do it for her. Nobody ever looked out for me.

Marris puts an arm round Sadie's shoulder. I elbow my
way through so I'm behind em in line, and I'm stumped when
the teacher takes the girl's hands and says, "So good to see you
again, Sadie Blue."

How them two know each other?

Then the teacher says, "Thank you for your help. I met
Jerome Biddle and he's agreed to chop wood and get me ready
for winter."

"This here's my aunt Marris," Sadie says, then they move
down the steps and it's my turn and I say, "Hello, Eli. Hello,
Teacher," and before I can even say I'm Sadie's granny, I get
nudged on down the steps and put out in the yard with Marris
and Sadie, all done.

I gotta stand there and wait while folks come up to Marris
and give her a hug and a pile a thank-yous for the supper and
the pies and the clothes she give em, when I know they take
advantage of her nature. All she gets back is a thank-you. It's
poor trade to me.

People head over to the soup pot that's been cooking
during service. I won't eat that slop, though it smells good
today. Heard tell one time somebody put a snake in it. Folks
ate it anyway.

When I finally get a word in edgewise from all the visiting,
I say to Sadie, "How you know that teacher?"

"Came to help Saturday last" is what Sadie says while she
cuts her eyes over to Roy Tupkin, who's got nerve enough to

stand in the tree line outside church land. Billy Barnhill, Roy's partner in sundry crimes, fidgets from one foot to the other while Roy leans against a tree, smoking a cigarette. Like always, his eyes are slits like a rattler's.

"Help do what?" I say and look back at Sadie, who still stares into the woods with a pull that won't natural.

"Get set up for school."

Marris sees Roy and Billy, too, and her face wilts. She pleads. "Honey, you come on home with us. Let us tend to you and give you a place to rest. You need to be with folks who love you. You and your baby need to be in a good place for a while. Right, Gladys?"

I don't pour syrup on Sadie and beg. Won't do any good. Plus I know when I'm not needed. Every time Sadie cuts her eyes over to Roy, he pulls her away from here with his stare. Sadie won't leave with Marris and me so I don't waste my breath.

She says, "I best get back to Roy," in a little-girl voice, then walks away and waves at the teacher and Preacher like she's leaving regular church and going home to a fried chicken dinner. That girl could break your heart if you let her.

We climb in the truck with the windows down, and when Marris turns the starter, it backfires like a gunshot. Only the teacher pays any mind. She ducks and laughs nervous.

"Well…" Marris says after we turn round and head down-hill, and I know I'm gonna get a earful about that tall teacher who wears britches and got hair chopped off, who nobody in the valley wants so she come up here to beg for a job, and we get leftovers like always.

All Marris says is, "Roy needs killing."

I sleep under a extra quilt cause of the nip in the air. I wake up with a stiff neck, a sour belly, and Walter on my mind, and the day goes down from there.

I put on my housedress, and when I put my arm through the sleeve, it rips. I add two sweaters against the chill, then open the bedroom door and the knob comes off. Wearing bedroom slippers, I stub my toe on a loose board and bleed like a stuck pig. When I reach the stairs, the top step tilts, and I bounce down the steps on my fanny. I land upright at the bottom, my legs splayed, my head dizzy.

What a nasty tumble!

I take stock, wiggle my fingers and toes, and turn my neck. Nothing's broke, though I'll have bruises the size of flapjacks on my backside for sure. I sit till I get my wind back before I stand. If I got killed or hurt bad, nobody'd find me cept Marris. Good thing she comes most every day. I grab holt of the newel post to pull up on, and damn if it don't almost give way. I bawl like a baby and can hardly catch my breath from crying.

I'm scared.

There, I said it, dammit. I'm scared.

My house is falling down with me in it. There's no two ways about it. Another leak in the roof, a window that won't open, one that won't close, a rotten step broke through. I wouldn't mind if I was to die soon, but truth be told, I still get round pretty good. Can shoot a tin can at ten paces, and my constitution's sound. The way things are going, my house will fall down before my time is up. Then what? I'd be in a pickle is what. This morning's put me in a bitter mood, and there ain't a quick fix for it.

Marris comes through my front door and yells out her name while I look out the kitchen window and don't move. She starts talking right off.

"Got your mail from Mr. Turner. He drive by delivering when I come, so I saved you a walk to the mailbox."

Last night's dishes are piled in the sink, and supper scraps are in the skillet. Marris reaches for the coffeepot. It's cold and the coffee's old. She looks straight at me for the first time, and her tone turns pitiful tender. "You okay?"

I don't say. Tender makes me close in on myself. I wait till she asks again like I know she will.

"Honey, it's me, Marris… You okay?"

"I know who you is, for God's sake. And no, I'm not okay. And there's not a damn thing you can do about it."

I bump Marris out of the way with my hip, ignore my body aches, rinse and fill the old coffeepot, bang it harder than need be, and make fresh coffee.

"I'm old and wish I was dead." I spit out the bitter words as I spoon coffee grounds into the basket.

"You don't mean that, Gladys."

"Don't tell me what I mean! I *know* what I mean."

The coffee perks, and I scrape last night's scraps into a bucket and chuck dirty dishes back in the sink. Marris waits. She sits like a schoolgirl with her hands in her lap. I feel her eyes follow my doings. When the perking's done, I fill two cups, then sit cross from her.

"It's this old house," I start, then add, "and Walter."

"Walter? Where'd that thought come from? Your sorry husband's turning to dust going on eighteen years."

"I know *that.*"

"He can't hurt you no more. Let go of that fear. He got what he had coming."

I hate that Marris knows some of my business. It's what she don't know that's the bad.

She don't know I locked Walter outta the house in the meanest thunderstorm these mountains saw in a long time. He had kept on drinking till he passed out in the mud.

She don't know I come outta the house and worked his limp body cross the yard and leaned him on the iron plow at the edge of the road, him loose and heavy, slipping from my wet hands so I gotta pull him by the very belt he beat me with.

She don't know I got the piece of tin from under the porch that went on a old doghouse long before. Laid it over Walter like a blanket and held it down with a felled tree branch, with him leaning on that rusty plow. The howl in the woods from that storm was like screams of a banshee let loose and the haints that live in this house of Walter and mine saw what I done and don't stop me.

I put him in the path of danger and turned my back on Walter, is what I done. Went inside my house, closed the door, and looked out that front door window at the storm that stirred the world into a frenzy. Rainwater dripped off me and puddled on the floor at my feet, and I shivered with a chill that rattled my teeth, but I stayed put.

I prayed hard to the devil cause my prayers to God won't never answered. I tried to find somewhere else to lay my eyes besides that tin blanket over Walter. I couldn't do it. Couldn't turn away for nothing. It's like my feet growed roots, and my eyes watched till lightning found him and lit up the night. The very next minute that storm turned tame and calm as you please, all the fight gone out of it now that the deed was done.

I went out to him, folded over a towel, and grabbed the edge of the charred tin that's hot. Dragged it off Walter's body and burned my fingers through the towel, but don't let go. Pulled that blackened tin in back of the house, cross the creek, and up the hill. Stashed it behind a felled tree and piled on dead leaves. Then I come in the house, climbed my steps, and crawled into my bed in all my wetness. Wrapped my quilt over my head and put my fingers in my mouth cause they burned something bad…but they don't burn like Walter.

Marris come up on him next morning.

———

Last night's wanderings back those years let me know sins don't go away. I don't want Marris to look clear through me to my weak spot.

I whisper, "Go home. I need time to myself," and my ragged voice bout tears in two. I've collected the same worrisome thoughts for so many years that they're stuck deep in my marrow, and today they hurt almost more than I can bear.

"You got time to yourself every day. I won't go nowhere just yet."

She sets her mouth in that way of hers that pisses me off, but today in a good way.

"Talk to me, Gladys. I'm your friend."

"I'll say what I wanna say when I wanna say," I answer gruff and take my time, surprised I let her stay in my house when I feel like this. I'm putting things together.

Times like these I wonder if I ever been happy. From the start there's been a film of dingy on my days. I've always done woman's work; man's work, too. Woke up with work to do and went to bed before it got done. I see some folks walk easy and carry peace on their shoulders, but I been chained to a iron life.

Marris stays this morning, and when I can't hold it in no more, out pours the bucket of broke-down things in this old house I can't fix. Marris listens careful while my fears fill the kitchen and my voice grows thick. I bout drown in my grief, and I let this woman see my insides. I tell her a lot of things cept I know when to stop.

"Gladys," she says. She reaches her hand cross the table to touch mine. I snatch my hands back. Put em in my lap, grip em closed, and hold on to the familiar hurt. Pretty quick, the heat goes outta me and I'm spent. Like on those three stillbirth days when I worked so hard, and the babies come out dead.

I say to Marris, "Can't change things, so don't pretend you can." I end with, "A body lives a life bout as good as she can. Then what?"

Marris stands and does what she does best: moves with purpose round my stillness. She slices vegetables and rolls the crust for shepherd's pie, and while the pie cooks, she washes my dirty dishes and sweeps the floor, then sets the table for two and opens the window for fresh air. She steps outside and brings back a bunch of ironweed and puts em in a canning jar on the table. Then she sits and delivers comfort.

"A body lives a life as good as she can, Gladys Hicks, one day at a time." She pats the back of my hand and I let her cause I like the warm. "And that's enough. You done all right up till now. You're gonna keep doing all right. And that's that. Let's eat."

We sit at the table and let the pie cool, and Marris says, "I can't believe I plumb forgot a piece of gossip you gotta hear. You was in such a mess when I come, I got distracted from it."

"Go on. Spit it out. You know you're dying to."

"Okay, let me get to my start place."

Got no choice but to wait for her to find her start place, when any place will do. I nibble at the shepherd's pie. It's good and I'm hungry.

"I was at the Rusty Nickel. You know how I like to go there on Wednesdays for Swap Shop Day. Mooney turns on his radio at noon, and whoever's there gets to…"

I got no choice but to wait while Marris rambles, and I sip on coffee, feeling better now with that load off my mind and food on the table.

"…nicest voice, so sincere. Eddie Broom's his name. I might make him a pie, but I don't know how…"

I roll my eyes and finish my helping of shepherd's pie. I use my fingernail to scrape dried egg off my vinyl tablecloth. Notice a new burn hole and wonder when it came to be.

"…Wednesday last, I sit there with Sadie and Fleeta and Jolene Dillard. Sue Sorrels showed, too, with a nasty case of hives…"

Marris talks to hear herself talk, and I spoon more pie on my plate. I switch it with her cause hers is cooled. It's strange how some folks tell a tale. They go round and round cause the story is a little biddy thing that needs a lot of fluff to make it big enough to be told in the first place. I hate this part of gossiping.

"...the girl gone missing. That's the mystery is what it is. Somebody say her name's Darla or Darlene. One of them *D* names."

What? I missed a piece of her talk cause my ears shut down.

Marris sips her cold coffee and puts the first taste of pie in her mouth.

I ask to buy time and get filled back in, "Who was her folks, this missing girl?"

"Nobody we know that I could tell. She must have been a looker. She worked in that hoochie place out at Danner's Cove."

"Well, no wonder she's gone missing. She hangs with lowlife. The girl got what she had coming to her."

"Well, that won't the big news, Gladys. The big news includes you."

I almost choke on my pie. "*Me* for pity's sake? I never even heard of this girl, so how do my name get sullied? Who spreads lies bout me?"

"It won't you, exactly. It's sort of your grandgirl, Sadie."

"Sadie! She a skinny thing turning mousy!"

"Well, it's really bout Roy Tupkin."

Marris stops to put a big spoon of pie in her mouth and chews, and I gotta wait. She swallows.

"The girl gone missing—Darla, Doreen, or Deena, nobody

knows for sure—somebody says she was hooked up with Roy Tupkin for nigh on a month."

What a day. All my tied-up worries that pulled me down this morning got let loose with that gossip Marris brought in my house like chicken shit on shoes, and my Sadie's all caught up in it. At the end of the day, I sit on the porch glider, washed in a different kind of sadness from the morning. I sip sassafras tonic and smoke dried ginseng root Marris give me to ease my disposition and let the evening chill seep deeper in my bones. Like usual, I ponder disappointments.

It won't Sadie I ponder, cause to do that scares me with a foreboding with this latest talk. It's her mama—my girl, Carly—what comes to mind.

Carly is the only piece of me strong enough to make it into the world. I ain't laid eyes on her since she left her baby, Sadie, behind with her husband, Otis Blue, and took off with a fancy man full of flashy promises and little else. Don't need to hear what happened. Carly woulda delivered good news if she had any. Thought she was special that girl. Said we shamed her with our homespun ways.

Lord, she had a mouth on her. Could sass you with the cut of her eyes. What I saw when I looked at Carly was *hungry*. Won't a thing in this place that could fill her up. Like she was starved for different and won't settle for usual.

She'd laugh mean-like now. Point her finger at me, jab the air, and say, "You got what you deserve, Mama. A Big. Fat.

Zero. And Sadie, left in your care after Otis died…look what you done to her. She's in danger cause you won't fit to be a mama or a granny. You a Big Fat Nothing."

Truth always hurts and it's extra hard to look at late in life.

What if Carly's right about me being a big fat zero? Is she something so special? Or just a different kind of nothing?

I say out loud, "You still hungry, Carly girl? You ever find *different*? Do it taste as good as you hoped it would?"

I lay my head back against the metal glider, tired from a day with a new worry bout Sadie and old worries bout secrets that time don't change. In a long-ago thought, I see Carly marching cross my yard, and she takes over my thinking cause she's a bossy thing. Always was.

"What's your skinny ass doing in my yard?" I stand on the porch, my young self, with hands on smaller hips and pissed as usual.

"Daddy here?"

"What's it matter to you?"

"Is he or ain't he?"

"Don't use that tone, girlie."

Carly marches right up to the porch, brushes past, and bumps my shoulder hard. She says in passing, "Need a place to stay, that's all."

"Well, it's not gonna be here!" I say and half believe my words. "You breeze in here like you belong when you don't. You done made your bed, girlie, and it won't here."

I raise my voice and follow after my only child, who heads straight back to the kitchen and noses around for something to eat. She finds a fried chicken leg on a plate under a drying rag. Leans against the corner of the table and eats it. She looks everywhere cept at me. The air between us is flinty.

When Carly finishes, she throws the bone in the sink, wipes her fingers on the rag, and says soft-like, "Mama, don't jump all over me. I be gone by morning," and heads upstairs to her room, and I hear the door close. She won't say bout that belly up against her dress. Won't say bout the muddy mark on her cheek or knot on her forehead at the edge of her hair.

Otis Blue don't do that. Gotta be somebody else. Otis got a tender spot for Carly, and he loves her like a blind fool, though he's twelve years older. I never seen a man push to please a woman like he does Carly. Maybe if he stood up against her strong will she'd settle down for a bit. That won't likely happen cause Otis is a soft man who loves in all the wrong ways. The bruises on my girl came from somebody hard.

No mama wants to see signs like these. Fear grows behind green eyes. Only got the clothes on her back and a backbone that won't bend.

I whisper, "Anybody can tell you about broke in two, Baby Girl. Nineteen years on this earth with promise already trampled down. You can starve in a world when you're hungry and won't settle for crumbs."

I don't follow her. I fix a pan of biscuits for supper to go with leftovers. Walter's gone for two days at the still. Mash is bout ready to bottle and money will come in soon, so it's me and Carly tonight. While the biscuits bake, I go upstairs. Stand outside Carly's closed door. Reach for the doorknob.

"Leave me be, Mama," Carly says strong, like she can see through the door. "You can't fix it, so leave me be."

I let my hand drop by my side. I don't go where I ain't wanted. Ungrateful girl, who looks for more when there won't no more. She's got lessons to learn, and life's one bugger of a teacher.

I call out as I head downstairs. "Supper's ready, girlie. Come if you want. Don't matter to me if you don't."

I musta dozed cause I wake up in the glider in the dark with a nasty crick in my neck, light-headed. I'm chilled clean through, and I struggle to my feet when my knees forget how to help. Then I remember this morning's nasty spill down the stairs. I clutch the doorframe and heave myself over the threshold and inch my way up the stairs, careful of the top broke step.

Carly's a puzzle. She wanted more than was her right to have. I tried to tell her. Tried to ease her road the way a mama should. I told her a woman's gotta learn to settle, stay in the middle, know her place. Carly never learned to settle, and it got her nowhere but gone. Now, after seventeen years, she forgot how to get home.

I settled for the middle all my life, swallowed my grief and kept it inside…and it got me nowhere but lonely. Marris is the only soul who tends to me, and for the life of me I don't know why I throw vinegar on her every chance I find. Maybe I want her brought to her knees once and the cheer slapped clear outta her. Maybe I wanna know she feels just once where I live all the day long.

And Carly's child, Sadie, is a different puzzle. She stayed close and settled too quick, and it got her nowhere but here. She had promise a while back, a sweetness she don't get from her mama, then it all dried up and blew away when she tied her tomorrows to a devil of a man.

Sadie's more like me than I wanna know. Like me, she got her a shitty man, but I did something bout my shit and keep the truth from the law. Don't blab to nobody.

Sadie won't made that way. She turns coward when Roy takes her down. Her weak will's gonna get her killed. She needs her own perfect storm…and a piece of tin.

MARRIS JONES

I never sneak up on Gladys cause her ears don't work good no more. When I walk in her front door, I call out, "Yoo-hoo, it's Marris," so she don't get spooked. I saw her jump a time or two when a sound come too quick and she won't ready. Old hearts like hers and mine don't need testing.

Today she says, "You sound awful spry for the sun just up and frost on the ground."

"Got reason to," I say back and get her attention. She plays like she don't care, but I see sorting behind her eyes, and she wonders what my reason is. I pour me some coffee and sit cross from her and grin.

"You look ugly when you grin like that," she says to stretch out her asking.

I hold on to my news and sip coffee.

"When you grin like that, your wrinkles puff up and your eyes turn to sinkholes," she says to get under my skin.

I stay easy.

"For Lord's sake, spit it out," she finally says. "You know you want to."

I scoot to the edge of my seat and put both hands round my coffee cup. "Skeeter's gonna come with his new bride for a visit on the first Saturday in October," I say, so happy I can pop. "They coming at noon all the way from Asheville. How I know is Skeeter called Mooney, and Mooney told Preacher Perkins, and the preacher come by here on his rounds last Monday, and that's how come I know."

My hands shake when I try to drink from my coffee cup cause I'm so discombobulated.

"Last two times Skeeter say he was coming, he don't," Gladys reminds me, and that's true. He got car trouble one time and had to work last minute the other, as I recall. Been two years since the last visit that don't happen. Three years before that when he don't come, but I don't count when it comes to Skeeter.

"What'd he do with his old wife? She dead or throwed out?"

"Don't rightly know. Preacher Perkins don't give particulars and I don't ask. I'll know on Saturday. I feel good bout this time.

"His *new bride*, Gladys! That's the best excitement. Getting to start again. Don't know her name yet. She gotta be special if Skeeter picked her. Saturday will be here before you know it and I'll get answers. I gotta cook chicken and dumplings for him or he won't feel like he's been home."

"Don't go killing no chicken yet on account of that boy, Marris."

Skeeter's coming soon to the only mountains he's ever called home, but when I was born, my folks don't live in Baines Creek in the highlands of North Carolina like now. Baines

Creek don't have coal to dig in its heart that breaks a man in two. When I come along, we live over Rock Bottom way in West Virginia, on the airish side of the mountain where coal dust sifted through slits round the windows, and spindly houses can't be scrubbed clean. Where we lived looked the same inside as it did outside. Gray.

It was in the year 1898 I come to be, and everybody in the world knowed the name Mother Jones. Some got to see that lady hero for real. Mama and Daddy saw her once when she come through on the train in the rain. She stood at the back of the iron caboose and looked down on a passel of coal mine families washed in the rain that don't stop, but the coal dust stuck to their skin.

Mama remembered everything Mother Jones wore right down to the line of buttons on her shoes. It got told so many times I thought I'd seen her myself. The long, black wool dress with a high bustle on her backside. A velvet fringed shawl worn bare in spots. A black straw bonnet tied with satin streamers. A thin leather purse hanging by a chain.

How she looked won't the story though. It was what she did and how she talked. That little woman could fire up weary souls, call burly men cowards for taking scraps, pull em down to their knees, then raise em up in hope with just her words. Mama and Daddy knew that for fact, not recollect.

Mother Jones don't like that coal miners put a pile of gold coins in rich men's pockets and nary a penny in their own. If daddies got hurt, boys got sent into the mines. When bills won't paid, then families got put out on the road—their stuff crammed in a paper poke. If a man was to say out loud *That ain't right*, he'd be gone without a trace. When Mother Jones says *That ain't right*, folks listen. For a pint-size woman, she got a gallon-size voice.

My daddy, Leland Earnest Jones, took extra pride cause we got the same last name as the bona fide champion of the work-ingman. "She's something, that Mother Jones," Daddy would say and shake his head and grin, his crooked teeth light in his dark face. "It won't take a flea fart to snuff her out, but she won't afeard of *nothing*. It's like Mother Jones got angels all round her so she can sleep at night and fight all day long for working souls."

Her Christian married name was Mary Harris Jones, and that's where I come in.

That name got put on me in a fit of birthing pride when Mama had herself a girl after three boys and a long stretch of in-between. Mother Jones's words—a woman's words, no less—was the rage in all the papers, and on flyers folded over and passed on the sly from hand to hand. She come from Irish roots like my folks. When she outright called herself a hell-raiser, all the men cheered and the women don't mind. Said she abides where there is a fight against wrong, and for sure that was living dark in the mines. She was a gift from the merciful Lord is what she was.

Everybody was poor in Rock Bottom, and no amount of work changed it. Even when my three brothers went in the mines with Daddy, we can't get ahead of the bills for medicine and sundries. They was grown men starting to court when Daddy was home with Mama and me cause of a broke arm. The mine blew up, and my brothers died, and so did all the men underground. Everything broke inside Daddy that day. He turned old and never found his strong self again.

Rock Bottom cut the heart outta folks and let em walk round thinking they was alive when they won't. We left there with my brothers still in the belly of the earth. We left the only home I ever knowed, and the hard rains came and followed us on that journey away. The dirt road we trudged along turned to mud, slippery then sucking mud. With the heavens opened wide, mountain gullies spouted water that gushed swift cross the road we walked. We plodded with our heads down, thin clothes soaked clean through, downtrodden as anybody there ever was. The creek we walked by grew wide as a river and carried branches and rocks and danger.

Dark come early and we took cover in a dry pocket under a boulder. We shivered and held tight to one another, me in the middle. After all the losses we suffered those sad days, I pick that night to cry.

Mama felt me shake from more than cold and wet. With little sting in her voice she said, "What you crying for, Marris? You made of tougher stuff than this."

I felt little in this storm that beat and battered my world gone strange. I whispered, "Are we gonna die?"

"From a storm? No, child. We're safe here. We'll head to Baines Creek soon."

Daddy added, "If the good Lord's willing and the creek don't rise."

I slept for a spell, and when I opened my eyes, the good Lord *had* willed the rain to stop and tamed the creek like we wished for. Then the warm sun came up on as special a day as I'd ever witnessed.

What I saw for the first time was *colors*. At ten years old, I had to learn my colors like a baby cause I don't know a single one. There was greens and yellows and reds. But it was the blue sky and white clouds that tickled me most. They was pure is what they was, and surely a peek at heaven. I wish my brothers coulda seen colors.

My folks told me they give me Mother Jones's whole name and hoped I'd grow a backbone straight and strong as hers. They hoped the red hair on my baby head was a sign I had spirit to spare.

Truth is, I won't much of a fighter. The good and bad of me is that I see blessings most every day in every way. Even when it's a speck that shines in a gray sea of sad. It's how my heart looks at things. My folks was kind not to let me know they was disappointed in me.

That hero, Mary Harris Jones, she's been gone forty years now, and folks still say her name *Mother Jones* respectful, like in church. On the day I take my leave, this Mary Harris Jones— who was lucky enough to marry sweet Willis Jones and don't have to get used to different, and whose name always got scrunched in tight to *Marris Jones* that fits me better—is gonna ride out on the next puff of wind. That'll be fine by me. I don't look for glory in this world.

We come to Baines Creek after a long walk part the way and rides from strangers the rest. Mama said *baines* is another word for *bones* so I thought I'd see a lot of bones on the ground, but I don't see any that first day. They must have been underground like my brothers.

We go to cousin Luther Hicks's place with our heads down low from loss and our bellies empty. They feed us beans and give us a roof outta the weather.

They got a boy named Walter who's twelve to my ten, and a nasty bugger. He tried to catch a look at me when I use the privy or wash at the creek or change clothes in the shed where we stay. I stay away from him as best I can, but he's a sneaky little snot with too much time on his hands.

One time, Mama asked me to pick blackberries before the critters eat em all, and I make a bark basket and go like I'm told, but I watch out for Walter. I pick as fast as I can when somebody shoots at me! I drop my basket and fall to my knees. I look round while my heart knocks like knuckles on wood. Then they shoot again and miss me by a foot. Dirt kicked up off the ground to the side of me.

Then I know it was ornery Walter. I pick up my basket and go back to picking berries. He shoots off to the side again to mess with me, but he gets tired after a while when I don't pay him no mind.

I think Mother Jones would have kept right on picking berries, too.

I got a handful of days to fill before Skeeter comes and it's chicken-killing time, and my Sadie needs tending to in the worst kind of way. I seen her a handful of times since Gladys and me went to lay eyes on the teacher, Miss Kate Shaw, at the start of September. What I saw that day was Sadie beat up and it tore me apart, her just married a few weeks back. I never feel more helpless than when I see Sadie watching Roy and following after him and that lizard Billy Barnhill who's more dumb than danger.

Now everybody's talking bout that *D*-name girl gone missing. That could happen to our Sadie if somebody don't do something. She needs to hear somebody loves her and that she's got a place to come to if she's inclined to leave.

I cook since sunup cause I don't visit empty-handed, specially for family. I put the huckleberry cobbler and potato bread on the truck seat. Add a jar of my watermelon-rind pickles cause they're Roy's favorite. He's got a sweet tooth, and them pickles is a peace offering if he's at the trailer and don't want to let me in. I don't think to ask Gladys to go with me this morning cause she already give up on the girl. Plus Sadie's life looks a lot like her granny's. I don't blame Gladys if she shies away.

The old truck starts on the first try so that's a good sign. I drive past Gladys's place. She's out in the yard looking down at the rusty plow that's been sitting useless in the weather for years. Her and me can't move that plow though we aimed to long ago. It's like it growed roots into the earth a mile down. It's where Walter got killed years back by the perfect storm sent by God. Gladys don't look up when I toot the horn and wave.

Walter's death was a miracle is what some folks called it, and I think a lot of halfway Christians studied their Bible more after Walter got smote for his sins. I hear moonshine was off for a spell back then. Everybody now knew for a fact that God slays sinners and strikes em down for their transgressions.

I was the one who come up on Walter the morning after the storm cause I needed to see if Gladys was okay. I saw Walter even from a distance down the road and could tell it won't right how he leaned on that plow. I could tell he won't passed out drunk in the yard like a hundred times before. This time puffs of smoke come off his blackened body.

From top to bottom, Walter Hicks was scorched. His clothes was burned clear off the front of him, and his skin was black as coal dust he never worked in. Even his pecker was shriveled like a burnt sausage. What little hair Walter had on his head was gone.

It was his face that was the clincher. It was the face of a man who saw the devil straight on and knew the forever fires of damnation waited for him: Walter's eyes was burned out. The skin on his nose, cheeks, and lips was burned clear down to the hard white of his bone. I guess he had so much hooch soaked in him that he lit up like kindling when lightning struck.

I looked down on that dead man fried by fire back then and wondered how many sins Walter Hicks carried to damnation in that charred, black soul of his. He beat on Gladys cause she stayed. He beat on Carly till she run away. He messed with me, too. Once. Almost. But I grew a backbone.

It's the same tired story these hills hear a million times. A nasty boy who can't keep his britches buttoned. A coward who sneaked his daddy's hooch to find courage.

The summer I turned twelve, me and Mama and Daddy moved down the road on Bentwood Mountain to our own place where Walter won't in my mind the way he was those years we was in the shed in the back of his house. When we lived there, I looked round every corner for his oily self being

sneaky. Here in our own place I got other things to worry
bout, like Daddy taken to bed and Mama grieving like he was
already dead. It won't a sunny time for the Joneses. If food was
gonna get cooked or a dish washed or wood chopped, I gotta
be the one to do it.

I took two buckets to the spring that day to fill. I come
back up the hill and the bucket straps cut into my palms. I set
down the buckets to give my hands a rest when Walter stepped
from behind a tree and blocked my way.

"Move outta my way, Walter Hicks. You got no business
with me."

"Marris Jones, why ain't you friendly to me? What'd I do
to you cept let you live at my place? This how you thank me?"

"*Your* place? Let your daddy hear you say that and he'll take
a belt to you." I lifted my chin a bit and stared at him like I
knew what I was doing.

He unbuttoned his fly and pulled out his limp dingdong,
grinning. Nothing was between him and me but two buckets of
water and whatever courage I could find. Mother Jones come to
mind when I needed her. Maybe her soul found me in a sad pickle
cause I said, "You step aside! I'm gonna pass, Walter Hicks."

I must have surprised Walter cause his jittery eyes settled
for a second.

"What you say?"

"You ain't gonna hurt me today or any day."

"And who's gonna stop me?" Walter looked round and slid
his belt outta the loops. "It's just you and me out here in the
woods—*girlie*. Your crappy daddy's bout dead, and your mama
ain't far from it."

I picked up the water buckets, squared my shoulders, stared him in the eye, and said, "Get outta my way."

"And if I don't?" His voice lost steam when his britches scooted down round his knees. He held on to a sapling to keep from tumbling backward.

"You don't want to know," I hissed and walked past him, determined to march on till I was safe at the cabin, even if the weight of them bucket straps dug clean through to bone.

When I got home and got over my shakes, I wondered what I meant when I said *You don't want to know*, cause I got no idea.

Walter never bothered me again. It was round that time Gladys come along.

I drive my truck slow, thinking on Walter Hicks, when I pass the Dillard place with a yard full of young'uns digging in the dirt. I yell out the window to four-year-old Eddie, "Tell your ma I'll bring supper for y'all later."

He runs in to do the deed and comes back on the porch and shouts, "Ma says you a angel."

I don't turn my back on friends in need. The Dillards is one and Sadie's the other, and she comes first cause she's family. I pull in Sadie's yard and don't see Roy's truck, so I leave the watermelon-rind pickles on the seat cause Sadie won't partial to pickles. I knock on the door and step back so it can swing open, and when it does, I see Sadie smile big like I've come for a party.

"Come on in, Aunt Marris." Her voice is brittle and hollow.

I step over the threshold, puzzled. "I brung you some pie and bread. You know I don't come empty-handed."

She leans over and sniffs too loud and too long. "It looks good. *Real* good."

I look close at Sadie and see her eyes is off. The dark parts are big as black dimes, and her hands shake when I give her the pie. I hold on to it so she don't drop it, and we put it on the table. I take both her hands and they're cold as winter creek water. We sit at the table.

"Sadie honey, what's got into you?"

The girl acts weird, and I can only guess why—and none of it's a easy fix. I look round for a jar of shine or some of that dandelion wine I give her awhile back but all I see is sweet tea.

"Everything's fine, fine, fine." She rocks on the edge of the chair and twists a strand of her hair. She's gone round the bend is what's happened. Ugly gossip and Roy is likely the cause.

I can't leave her here so I say, "Sadie, listen to me." I shake her by the shoulders gentle till she sees me. "I'm gonna take you home with me. I gotta keep my eyes on you till you come back round to yourself."

As I feared she would, she says, "No, no, no. I can't leave and have Roy come back to a empty place. You go on. I want you safe away from here."

Lord have mercy! This is bad and none of it's good.

"Here's what we're gonna do, Sadie." This is my no-nonsense tone I use to get Gladys to hear when she's hardheaded. "I need your help. I gotta tend to the Dillards and you gonna help me. I'll leave Roy a note. I even got him a jar of watermelon-rind pickles in the truck we'll put right on top of that note."

I talk calm and move out the door and down the rickety trailer steps as fast as my swoll knee will bend, grab the pickles from the seat of the truck, and go back inside, out of breath. I wanna be away from here before Roy comes.

I write: *Roy, Sadie gonna help with a sick ma. I bring her back in the morn. Marris.*

The pickles sit on top to keep the note in place. Don't want Roy to think I took Sadie and don't let him know.

Sadie still sits in the chair, looking at the floor and rocking without a rocker. I take her coat off the peg and wrap it round her thin shoulders. "Come on, honey. Let Aunt Marris love on you."

She stands and comes with me like a lost child, and I'm grateful I don't have to be forceful. The girl's had enough forceful.

When we get to my place, I help her outta the truck like she's sick and sit her at the kitchen table. I bend down and look her in the face so she hears better. "We gonna make pasties for the Dillards. Okay?"

I put the flour, lard, and spring water in front of her, and she lifts her hands slow, starts mixing the dough, then kneads while I peel and slice potatoes and onions. Don't want her handling a sharp knife just yet. She breaks the dough into pieces and rolls each one in a circle for the pasties; busy hands do a lotta good to settle a troubled heart. A story helps, too.

"I ever tell you bout my rosebush on the side yard? How it come to live in my yard?"

"I like that story," she murmurs, and her face gets soft.

"You want the long or short of it?"

"Long, please."

I pour us both a cup of peppermint tea that's been steeping in the teapot on the woodstove and drizzle in honey for sweet. She sips her tea and I start the story that winds round a bit but knows where to go.

"I love flowers. My Willis Jones couldn't pass a field of oxeye daisies or bluets or pussy willow without picking me some and bringing em home. He'd say, 'Marris, these flowers won't as pretty as you, but if they make you smile, then they can sit right on this windowsill.'

"That man was a pleaser and a smooth talker in a good way. He was gentle like your daddy, Otis. They both liked their likker too much, but they was what I called sweet drunks. They got all mushy-hearted on hooch instead of mean like your granddaddy Hicks."

Now that I've got Sadie's mind on something tender, I mound the thin slices of potatoes and onions on the dough she's kneaded and rolled. I add a slice of thick bacon and a dollop of butter on top for flavor, cause the Dillards don't get much flavor, and then pinch the circle of dough closed.

"Pasties are the best kind of supper for a passel of kids. Easy to pick up in their hands. Good to eat hot or cold," I say to keep sound in the room.

Into the oven goes the Dillards' supper and I top off our cups of tea. Sadie looks near normal. She even got a tinge a blush back in her cheeks from rolling pastry. I don't go on with my story right away and she reminds me like I hoped she would.

"You was telling bout the rosebush." She rinses her floured hands in the bucket and wipes em on a towel and sits back at the table.

"I was, won't I?" I add a log to the stove, then join her at the table.

"Now, I see a lotta flowers in my life grow natural on the mountainsides. Willis would hunt for new ones to surprise me. Once, when he was third day out hunting ginseng on Wolf Trap Ridge, he come up on a old farm he don't remember passing before. Windows all busted out. Floorboards rotted. Chimney crumbled to dust, he said. And in that yard, right by the door, choked by a patch of jewelweed, he saw a rosebush with one tiny bud on it. It had to be brung up from the valley cause it won't native to here.

"Willis dug the whole thing up, careful to keep dirt round the root ball. Then he put it in his sack beside the ginseng, it taking up space where more seng could go.

"Well, that evening, I was glad to see Willis get back from the woods safe. Hunting ginseng is crazy cause lazy fools do terrible things when the money plant comes in. They steal from the hardworking and don't think twice. I cooked possum stew and a pan of angel biscuits for him, and I sat right next to him while he scarfed down three bowls of stew and six buttered biscuits like a starved man. He tells me bout the hunt and the pretty views he saw that made his heart swell.

"After his belly's full, I go to spread out the seng roots to dry, and he said, 'Now hold on, woman. Don't you snoop in that bag yet. I got you a surprise.'

"Well, Sadie, I got tickled as a kid at Christmas to think

of Willis thinking of me when he's far off. When he pulled out that rosebush with one red flower, I cried at the beauty of something that come so far so I could see it.

"'Smell it,' Willis said. He looked as proud as if he made the smell in that flower with his own two hands. And I did. I sucked in that perfume till Willis said, 'Slow down! You gonna use up all the sweet,' and we laughed.

"Willis wrapped the dirt round that bush with a wet rag, and next morning he planted the little bush on the side of the house. He picked the sunniest patch of ground around. He got down on his knees and dug a hole in the loamy earth. We don't know if the little rosebush will like it here, but it won't from Willis not trying. He watered it. He put coffee grounds round it. Worked in manure. When cold weather come for sure, he piled wood chips on top to keep it warm. I never did know where he learned to do all those things for a rosebush from the valley."

I hold up my hand and say, "Hold on, sugar. From the good smell, the pasties are done and I don't want em to burn." I pull the golden-brown pies out of the oven and set em on top to cool. The house don't smell like roses, but pasties is good on a chilly day. This recipe come over from my Cornwall kin by way of Ireland and is good and filling.

Now I come to the tender part of the rosebush story. Sadie and me feel the sad grabbing us before I even start the telling.

"Willis died that winter, don't you know. I didn't see it coming till it was too late. A fever come on so fierce, and he throwed up blood and turned jaundiced. Some folks say it was yellow fever, but there won't no proof to speak of. It *was* yellow fever that got Mother Jones's husband and her children, too, before she turned hero, but I don't know what kinda fever got my Willis.

"We can't bury him right away cause the ground is froze. Since they was close, Walter and Gladys found a kind spot in their hearts and come to help ready Willis for his burial. They keep him in his pine coffin in their lean-to where me and Mama and Daddy lived once upon a time.

"One day next spring, after Willis got put in the ground in the Hickses' burial plot, I felt a lonely heartache and it won't stop. The heartache grabbed me with cold wiry fingers and *squeezed* hard. I prayed to the Lord for relief but feel guilty taking His time from important things. I prayed Willis don't look down from heaven to see me feeling sorry-assed for myself.

"Sadie, right then I stood straight up from this kitchen table filled with the light of hope. I walked out into the springtime I won't paying a bit of attention to. I walked round the side of the house to that patch of sunshine like I was pulled by the Holy Spirit. I don't have a choice cept to go where my legs carry me.

"The wood chips was still bunched round where that rosebush was, and I got down on my knees. I remember how bad my hands shaked over that bush cause I don't wanna find it dead under there after all the love Willis poured on it.

"But, hallelujah! What I saw was little nubs of life on them branches. Proof of the Lord's promise of salvation. Oh, Sadie, a piece of my Willis growed in my yard!

"Quick, I got chicken wire and put it over and round that bush so critters don't eat at it. I watered that bush. I loved that bush, and it loved me back. It give me roses every summer since."

My voice is raspy from telling the rosebush story. Sadie's boohooing and I'm boohooing, and we both gotta blow our noses on snot rags. It's a good kind of cry we do for all kinds of reasons, and we stand and hug each other, washed clean on the inside. Every woman needs to be loved like my Willis loved me.

I end my story like always. "There won't a speck of reason why that rosebush come up in the spring. Sun too puny. Winter too cold. Air too thin. It grew cause Willis and me loved it."

The light's come back in Sadie's eyes. "Can I see it?"

"Course you can, honey. Let me get my water bucket and you give it a drink."

In the autumn afternoon, the old rosebush is a marvel. I feel Willis here even more than where his pine coffin lies in the ground. The blooming's long done for the season, but there's one tiny bud showing off. Sadie gasps and clutches her heart, tender as I ever saw her. I say, "I think this here's for you, honey."

She whispers, "I wish I had a man who give me roses."

"Don't give up on that, sugar. You got a long stretch of living in front of you."

"I do?"

"Won't say if it won't true."

I break the stem, careful not to get stuck, and inside I put it in a blue milk of magnesia bottle.

"This'll come home with you tomorrow. It might open up if it's got a mind to. It's a late bloomer in the cold, so it's shy. Right now we gotta deliver supper to some hungry children."

When the Dillards get fed, and me and Sadie is in the truck heading back to my place for our own supper, I say, "Those folks got it bad right now and we brought merciful help. Horace Dillard can't do nothing on account of bad lungs from working coal."

Sadie stares out the window, likely pondering her own heavy load. Maybe she's thinking bout Horace's bad lungs from honest work and Roy's bad heart for spite.

Later, we finish supper of corn bread and pinto beans, and I pull down the tin of molasses cookies to go with our tea. This is what I miss bout my Willis gone. A body to spend evening time with. Sadie's quiet but got back that settled feeling bout her. I don't want to push. I let her be till I say, "Roy," and his name sits in the air.

Sadie says, "Roy Tupkin," and he gets bigger in my little room.

"You afeard?" I ask.

"I be lying if I say I won't."

I look at that precious face grown old and weary already. "What can I do, sweet girl?"

"What you do right now. Give me a place to be that don't hurt."

"Wish you stayed longer. You could live here if you wanted."

"It'd shame him."

But tonight she stays and don't pester me to go back to Roy's place. When it's bedtime, I blow out the oil lamp. The weak light of the woodstove pierces the dark. Sadie crawls into the featherbed beside me. She's light as a feather herself, so I don't hardly feel her there till she cries and rolls into my soft side. Ain't had a body lay this close for a lotta years. I fold her in my arms and she shakes and sobs, broke and empty, and can't hardly catch her breath. She loosens the hurt and sad that bout pulls her under.

If this be a night of wishing, then I wish Sadie was mine to keep.

I need Mother Jones's backbone—God bless her mighty soul. If she was in my place and worried about Sadie, she'd nail Roy Tupkin's sorry ass to the side of the Rusty Nickel so all Baines Creek saw his meanness. She'd show Sadie the truth. She'd help her break free from what's already broke.

All I do is hold her, pull the chill outta her baines, and comfort her with warmth.

Next morning, I don't wanna take Sadie back, but I do. Roy's truck is still gone. When we go inside, the note is where I put it under the jar of watermelon-rind pickles and the pie sits on the counter. Sadie puts her rosebud on the window ledge. I give her a hug, then pick up my pickles. Roy don't deserve no peace offering.

Before I head home, I make my way over to Preacher Perkins's place and tell him my worries about Sadie, and together we wonder what we can do to protect her. The look on his face says it all: not much.

———————

Today, Skeeter comes, and I got extra air in my lungs. Nobody brung word that he won't coming so I let myself think it might happen for real. Skeeter's my firstborn, a lot older now than when my Willis died at thirty-two years. No mama likes to say she's partial, specially when both boys she births is good, but when one of em comes out like his daddy she loves, it happens natural.

I pick a fat hen off her nest, step outside the coop, give thanks to the Lord, then break her neck. I chop her head off with my ax, quick scald the body in a pot of water, pluck her feathers for pillows, and put the body in cool water to rinse off the blood. Inside an hour that hen has gone from sitting in a coop to being cooked, and I start fixing dumplings.

I'm rolling out the dough when I stop and say out loud, "Lord, I hope Skeeter's wife can cook. A woman who can't cook good misses the best part of comfort." I set the table with my three plates and make sure I get the cracked one. Last thing, I fix a pan of biscuits ready to pop in the oven when they come. The extra can go home with em. I take off my apron, hang it on a hook, and check the clock.

It's ten past nine.

It'll be afternoon before Skeeter's car comes down the road. Last time he stayed two hours and looked itchy to leave every minute of it. He looked old that visit. I want to know city living agrees with him. I want to meet his new wife. I want to see him treat her special. Like Willis treated me.

I got time between ready and Skeeter coming, so I take my chair to the front yard to wait and think on my other boy,

Obie. Thirty-one years ago he come home for the last time in as fine a casket as these parts ever see.

Seemed after Obie went to soldier camp there was a accident. A uniform man drove up here with Obie in a long, polished box with a flag over it. That man stayed till we put Obie in the ground, then he pulled off that flag, folded it, and give it to me. I don't want to keep it but don't have the heart to tell him, so I put that flag in the bottom of the trunk Willis made me when I was a new bride.

It's odd birthing two good boys and then one of em leaves life before he could hardly grow a beard. Obie loved to hear me laugh. One time at supper, he stuffed six biscuits in his mouth, then he crossed his eyes till I snorted buttermilk out my nose.

Twenty-two years. That's all the time he got on this earth and I'm hard-pressed some days to recollect how he looked, and that shames me. The only picture I got of him is in his soldier uniform with his face serious and his eyes pretending to be brave. That picture is tucked under the folded flag.

Now there's only Skeeter.

———————

Mr. Turner, the mailman, drives down the road and sees me doing nothing and stops.

"Got a circular today, Miz Marris, my howdy for your Skeeter coming, and a little gossip, if you want."

"What kind of gossip? I don't like the mean kind."

"This one's funny. Bout Prudence Perkins."

Prudence is the preacher's spinster sister, and a more sour soul you'd be hard-pressed to find. "You got my attention. What happened?"

Mr. Turner shifts his truck into neutral and sets his arm on the window frame.

"Well, it won't what she done so much as what somebody done to her."

"Even better." I stand up stiff and bend forward to touch my knees, but only reach halfway. I stand back up on the dizzy side.

Mr. Turner won't a bit good at telling news cause he always blurts out the punch line before its time.

"Prudence Perkins got locked in her outhouse."

Now he could have done a lot with that news if he told it slow, but it's still funny.

"How long?"

"All morning, I guess. Preacher come home and can't find her in the house. He yelled her name and she shouted out, 'I'm in the privy!'"

"He tattled that kind of news bout his own sister?"

"Well, no. It was me who timed it right. I delivered mail when I heard her shout kind of weak and I heard the preacher shout back, 'Let me get my wire cutters. Hold on to your britches!' That struck me extra funny."

"Who woulda done such a thing?" I ask, knowing there is lots of folks who got reason for payback to that sourpuss.

"Don't know right off."

Mr. Turner giggles as he scoots back to the middle of his

seat and drives off. I'm glad he don't say bout that girl gone missing. There's enough talk bout that.

He passes Gladys's mailbox without stopping so today she won't even get a circular. I might take mine to her this evening…or maybe not. She'll likely think Mr. Turner missed her on purpose when he mighta forgot. Most days I can't win with Gladys. She thinks she knows everything bout everybody. Specially me.

But she don't.

Like the day Walter got killed by lightning.

———

I come up on Walter that time he was fried on top of the plow. His body was crispy like a skinny chicken, but I seen something else, too.

In the morning's light, there was wide drag marks cross Gladys's yard. They started at Walter's dead body, rounded the corner, crossed the creek, and went up the hillside where the trail showed clear as the path to damnation. Looking at it, anybody would be curious what laid that track, and they might have a mind to follow it. Gladys don't need curious right then.

Before the mud got hard in the day's sun, I picked up tree branches blown down in the storm. I zigzagged them leafy branches over those muddy drag marks that crossed the creek and climbed up the hillside. I found that piece of tin that used to live under her porch. It's got a burn hole in the heart of it. Lightning could make a burn hole like that. I pile the tree branches on top of that tin.

When I need to, I got the backbone of Mother Jones to do what's right.

———

I've been sitting on this kitchen chair near three hours, and my bottom's gone numb. I stand slow, hold my arms up, and bend one way and then the other, then pick up the chair.

And stop.

I hold real still. Listen careful.

It's a car engine a ways off.

It's coming this way.

I turn, holding my chair, and watch. A car rounds the curve. It's one of them little fancy cars missing a top. A man drives and a woman wears a long scarf that trails in the breeze. The car horn toots three times.

It's Skeeter!

He hits the brakes and the car stops beside me. My boy gets outta the car and hurries round back, and I think he's gonna hug me, but he opens the car door, and the woman who must be his new wife leans out and upchucks right at my feet and some of it splatters on my shoes.

I put the chair down and step back. Skeeter helps the woman outta the car like she's a invalid. Her lipstick's smeared. Her hair's a mess. The scarf on her head is cockeyed.

"Ma, this is Helen," he says without looking at me.

Helen holds out a limp, cold hand for me to shake, then she turns quick to hurl again.

I step back. "What's wrong with her?"

"Helen's constitution must not care for this thin air. We didn't know that till we got underway. That's why we're late. Sorry if we worried you."

"What'll make her better?"

"She may not feel like herself till we get back to the city."

Not a word has come outta Helen's mouth. I say, "I get a wet rag," and I get a rag and a glass of water. When I get back, Helen sits on my kitchen chair with her head hung low. She's pitiful is what she is.

I hand the rag to Skeeter and he looks like his daddy when he gets down on his knees, tender. He washes Helen's face gentle, then her fingers one at a time. He dabs at some spit-up on her coat, but when he comes to her flat bosom, he hands the rag to her. She cuts a smile at him. Reaches out and tugs his earlobe.

He whispers, "You are beautiful."

"Aw, Skeeter, you sweetie. I'm a *wreck*" is the first words I hear her say, with a little laugh.

I love her.

Just like that.

I love Skeeter's new wife.

She sips a little water, and my boy helps her to her feet, then turns her narrow shoulders toward me like he's showing off a prized blue ribbon. She's got crow's-feet round her hazel eyes and saggy skin on her skinny neck and not a speck of color in her freckled cheeks. She's older than I thought she'd be, but Skeeter's no youngster his self no more. Only that little car made em look young till they got close.

They look right side by side and I don't have to ask Skeeter if he's happy. He keeps one arm snug round her and tells me again, "This here's my Helen," and says her name extra special.

"Helen," I say and get all mushy inside thinking of the sweetness Willis and me had that belongs to them now. "Glad to meet you." I sound stiff like I'm sitting in somebody's parlor on a horsehair sofa when my insides are about to pop and my throat closes up with too much happiness.

Just when I think this moment can't get any better, my new daughter, Helen, loved by Skeeter, says, "I'm so glad to meet you at last. May I call you Mother Jones?"

ELI PERKINS

D addy took me to see the devil when I was nine years old. Mama didn't want me to go, but Daddy said, "If the boy wants to come, he comes," so I did.

The sun came up in a blue-sky morning and took some of the scare out of the day. Daddy carried his Bible clutched to his chest with one hand, and he held my hand with the other as we walked without talk through the woods to see the devil.

Granddaddy crossed the creek and came up beside us and walked. He took my other hand in his, so I was held tight by muscle and bone to my two heroes. I didn't know who this serious Granddaddy was who came this time without a joke or penny candy like he usually did. He wore his black fedora low and carried his Bible like a small shield, like Daddy did.

Then the brother deacons came one by one from their places in the woods till they were four strong. They followed behind Daddy and Granddaddy and me, and their hard leather shoes walked on soft ground riddled with roots and rocks and fallen leaves. Above us, crows followed from tree to tree. They swooped low and cried soft.

"Daddy?"

"Yes, Son?"

"Where we gonna see the devil?"

"He's taken up residence in the body of Pharrell Moody, God bless his soul."

I'd heard about Pharrell Moody from grown-ups, in scattered whispers, with wringing hands and worry, and none of it was good. Folks had given up on him and wanted him gone.

Not Daddy and Granddaddy. They don't give up on Pharrell Moody.

"What you gonna do?" I whispered.

"Help's on the way, and we gonna cast out the devil and send him back to hell so Pharrell Moody can get back to living."

Daddy gave my hand a squeeze of confidence, and we turned quiet and walked on.

That was a day I'd never forget.

———

I wake soggy brained, back in my aging body, stiff from a nap in my worn easy chair. I wonder what in the world pulled that devil of a day from my youth to the front of my mind. Back then when I was young, the name Pharrell Moody was folklore around here, part demon and part redemption. Pharrell Moody's long gone from this world, and his flesh has turned back to dust.

I'm parched from my dream about the devil, so I get up and sip water from the ladle in the bucket, standing at the window looking out upon the valley. Good folks and sinners scratch out a life here in Baines Creek, but the devil works overtime, so my work as a preacher will never be done.

I leave the warmth of the house and head out to my workshop to busy my hands and think on my memory.

Pharrell Moody was the teaching moment forty-six years back that confirmed my call to serve God. What nine-year-old boy would not be changed for good at the power of God's words that cast out the devil and sent him back to hell? It was one thing for me to want to serve the Almighty, Powerful God. It was entirely another to believe I was worthy of the calling. I still have moments when I think God might smite me for my nerve to call myself a preacher and step into the giant shoes worn by my daddy and granddaddy.

Some days I can't believe God entrusted souls to my care. I doubt my strength. I doubt the Lord's plan. That I live in the peaks and valleys of the oldest mountains on earth is a metaphor that never eludes me. The golden and the dank days, and the string of in-betweens meander like an old goat trail—my old goat trail.

"Brother, you out there?" Prudence calls flat-voiced from the back porch and stands in the shadows as usual, arms folded across her chest. Washed sheets hang under the eaves and sway in a chilly breeze.

I wave out the window over my workbench, then hold up five fingers to let her know I need five minutes. The screen door slaps shut, and I sand more wooden toys. When the cold comes in earnest, Christmas won't be far behind, and these gifts must be ready. I turn wood scraps into trucks and dolls and bears, and the stack of toys grows. I write the child's name on the bottom of each toy so they know they're special. For now, here at the end of August when the seasons change, I don't feel much pressure, so I tinker in my shop more than work.

Unlike Daddy and Granddaddy's good fortune, I never found my life's companion and have settled into a routine with my spinster sister, Prudence, twelve years my junior. Despite a kind upbringing and a decent education, she came into the world with a sour disposition that taints the sunniest of days. She's a martyr who wears poverty intentionally, even though we can afford adequate clothes and proper shoes with attached soles. Prudence takes *sacrifice* to unwieldy heights.

I choose to believe her heart has some good, though there's little proof except her devotion to me. To everyone else, her words sting and her giving is stingy. She knows what we sow we reap, and her return can be pitiful. That doesn't change her; Prudence lives in the shadows, and no amount of coaxing brings her spirit into the light.

I shake the sawdust off my carpenter's apron, hang it on the nail, and head in to the kitchen for lunch. The kitchen smells good with a simmering skillet of rabbit stew, dense and lean, made from Jerome Biddle's gift of two varying hares. We know to watch for random buckshot pellets that can crack a tooth.

On the pine table, crusty bread sits beside a large bowl of stew for me and a modest one for Prudence. She's sliced an apple and left on the red skin. Against white flesh, the crimson looks decadent inside this plain place with hardly a speck of color, except for the fancy green woodstove Mama got as a surprise long ago. I used to pick wildflowers to bring cheer indoors. Prudence would turn right around and throw them out. Said, "If God wanted flowers in a jar, He'd a planted em there."

We bow our heads to pray, then eat.

"The new teacher comes tomorrow," I say between spooning stew and sopping bread. "The one who answered my letter and our prayers."

Prudence nods.

"You going to meet her, take her to the cabin, and get her settled?"

She nods again.

"I think this one's a keeper, don't you?"

Prudence puts down her spoon and places her hands in her lap, as if ordered to stop eating. "No. She's old. Won't last."

"Old? She's not young, but she's close to my age, for heaven's sake! And what gives you the idea before you meet her that she'll quit on us?" I feel my bushy eyebrows spike up in a question.

"Why you think this one's different, Brother?" Her brows naturally crease into a frown. "She's the same as the others cause she come from the valley, all uppity…cept she's old. Like you."

I sigh. This would have been a good place for some levity about my age, but Prudence doesn't tease. I've got to preach a burial tomorrow or I'd meet Miss Kathleen Shaw and see her settled in myself. I've read her papers the Asheville education office sent, and it's true she's fifty-one and might not get around as well as these mountains require, but she has exceptional teaching experience.

I'm drawn unabashedly to a mind that works well, and my limited library helps only so much. There's no one within two days' walk who enjoys dissecting issues of the world and

politics. For that reason, I venture into the valley once a year
for convention to soak up conversation. On this mountain I
often reel in my words for fear I'll offend a limited soul.

We've scared off more teachers than the law should allow.
The last two teachers were young and full of the wrong kind
of hope. They barely knew the classics and didn't get my jokes.
They were too young for this remote post. When the last one
left after the teacher's cottage burned down, I wrote a letter
to the school board to explain why we need a teacher with
experience. An ethical and morally strong individual, one up
for a challenge. Miss Kathleen Shaw answered my letter.

Now, I worry. What good will we be to her? These clois-
tered families don't easily welcome jaspers. I worry Miss Shaw
may not understand my people's shyness and see only their
inadequacies. I've studied her letter of introduction and can read
little between the lines except that she's taught at fine institutions.
Sadly, I fear Prudence might be right: Miss Shaw may not last
long if she's infirm or set in her ways. That will be a loss for our
children and their future. It'll be a loss of wishful thinking for me.

We're running out of options.

When I was eighteen, Daddy walked me up to Rooster's Ridge.
He was strong enough that day and determined to walk, though
cancer crumbled his edges. It was a slow trek that morning on
the familiar trail, but we made it to the top. A cool breeze lifted
his damp hair and dried the sweat on his pasty face while the
kind sun hid behind clouds to make the light more tolerable. I

stood next to him and realized I was taller, or else he'd shrunk; Daddy usually made five feet seven feel like full stature.

That day he held on to a gnarled dogwood tree and said, "Eli, I never had regrets about the path or place I've chosen to live my destiny. Your granddaddy didn't either, and we were lucky. Up here is a little world, and you've got a big curiosity. You think a lot in that head of yours. If you aim to follow in my footsteps—"

"I do!"

"—then you have to go explore before you can settle here and know peace."

"How can I leave now?" I looked away, not naming the sadness that tainted my daddy's life. "You need me. Mama needs me. I need me...here."

"We'll do fine. Folks will help out like always. If I can, I'll take my time leaving this earth. I'll write every week and keep you up on things. Don't want you to fret your time at seminary about home matters. Besides, Son, this isn't about my life; it's about yours."

I was caught in a painful place. Daddy was the smartest man I'd ever known, and his advice came from a deep well of wisdom primed by hard life on this mountain. My mind struggled with the gift I was being given. Then, like always, I did what Daddy thought best.

In the fall of 1937 I came down off the mountain and rode a Greyhound bus for the first time. The bus took me to seminary in Louisville, Kentucky, riding across state lines on the Dixie Highway. Five hundred and eighteen miles separated me from the home I wouldn't see for two years.

I lived at Miss Vader's boardinghouse and cut her grass in exchange for meals. Walked to class on sidewalks bordered by trimmed green lawns. Seminary classes were free back then, and I worked a library job to pay for extras I'd need. Besides Bible studies taught in sixteen weekly lectures, I read the likes of James Joyce and Dostoyevsky, mixed with the wisdom of Misters Twain and Will Rogers.

Daddy sent news every week, and I didn't borrow trouble when I read his words. I got plumb drunk on book learning is what I did—though I never lost my appreciation for a good joke. Every joke I heard reminded me of Daddy and Granddaddy's penchant for humor to ease the hard.

Daddy waited for me to come home, then he died.

———

There were forty-one men from the state of North Carolina attending seminary the year I entered, and Henry Clayton was one of them. He had the spark of the Holy Spirit and sass about him that resonated in me. You'd have thought Henry and I were brothers the way we got on from the first. To the chagrin of our professors, we collected church jokes like ladies collect recipes or poems, and we learned the important key to good storytelling—add real people to the mix.

Henry's eyes always sparkled extra when he had a new joke to share. "Eli, you hear what Reverend Brooks told his congregation last Sunday?" he asked when he caught up with me as I headed to class on Revelations.

"No, Henry, what?" I played along.

"He said, 'Next week I'll preach about the sin of lying. To help you understand my sermon, I want you to read Mark 17.'"

"You don't say."

Henry delivered a joke like a pro. Straight-faced. He didn't get ahead of himself.

"Well, next Sunday, when it came time to deliver his sermon, Brother Brooks stood stately in his pulpit and looked down on the faithful. He asked for a show of hands. 'How many found time in their busy week to read Mark 17?' Several hands shot up, and he said, 'Well, the gospel of Mark has only sixteen chapters. I will now proceed with my sermon on lying.'"

At the punch line I already knew, Henry slapped his bony thigh and laughed that donkey laugh of his that got both of us in trouble more times than I care to admit. He's now the long-time pastor at Reedy Branch Free Will Baptist in Winterville in eastern North Carolina, and we've stayed in touch.

We trade jokes and meet up at the annual convention at the end of September. In between, every few months, Henry sends me a box of brain food holding back issues of the *New Yorker*, *Time*, and *Life*, and in recent years, back issues of the full-color *National Geographic*. Henry cuts out the suggestive pictures, like the bare-breasted native women, in case Prudence looks at the magazines. She would have thrown them in the woodstove embers, given half a reason. I'm proud of the stack of them on my shelf. It's a source of admitted pride for me, but I rationalize it this way: I believe the mystery of God's great and varied world is captured nowhere better than on those glossy pages. If you don't believe in God Almighty, Maker of Heaven and Earth, before you read *National Geographic*, you will after.

Prudence and I finish eating, and I pop the last slice of apple in my mouth and stand and stretch. I say, "Why don't you take some apples for Miss Shaw's welcome tomorrow? I think she'd appreciate the thought." I push my chair under the table.

"Didn't do it for the others," Prudence states.

"Maybe a better start will mean better results. We're running through teacher candidates faster than the law should allow. Second Corinthians 9:7 says, 'Every man according as he purposeth in his heart, so let him give…'"

Prudence quickly retreats to her room and slams the door before the next words grate against her selfish nature.

I raise my voice and finish the verse. "So let him give; not grudgingly, or of necessity: for God loveth a cheerful giver."

I have no choice but to give up but say before I turn away, "At least invite her to church so she can meet her neighbors."

Prudence doesn't answer.

Two days later, on Sunday, when the horizon turns pink with a new day, I head to church to start stone soup. An iron pot stays in the yard covered with a piece of plywood to keep out dirt and bugs during the week. I light the kindling under the pot, fill it with spring water, and throw in a smooth stone. Stone soup has been a weekly tradition here since my granddaddy's days. Baines Creek Baptist Church feeds more than souls with an idea birthed five hundred years ago.

That tale involves a stranger who declares he could make soup from a stone. While the water boils and the stone cooks, he regales the villagers with tales of travel—much like a preacher regales his flock with the holy truth. When the stranger declares the soup ready, the people sample it and say it tastes like water! The stranger says, "We forgot the herbs, didn't we? A sweet onion, perhaps?" The entertainment softens the crowd, and in the spirit of teamwork, the soup grows into something nourishing.

In the case of my little congregation, the recipe is simple: share what you can spare. Prudence no longer complains about the potatoes and onions I slice every Saturday night, nor does she offer to help. Others arrive at church and add wild mushrooms, a piece of venison, or ramp and chard. The soup simmers while I preach, and I start with a joke.

"My friends, many of you have asked me what's the best way to get to heaven, and I am here today to remind you of the one, true answer."

I pause for effect.

"Turn right and go straight."

I get a few chuckles, a sprinkle of smiles, and some dull faces, Prudence among them.

When church is over and soup is eaten, bodies and souls drift away, satisfied. I stay behind to wash out the pot. I've taken off my jacket, rolled up my shirtsleeves, and am bent over scrubbing the insides when I hear a voice I don't recognize.

"Preacher Perkins?"

I push up on my knees to stand upright, conscious my face is flushed from exertion and strands of limp hair have fallen to my forehead. This must be Kathleen Shaw, who stands tall, ten paces away. Short salt-and-pepper hair, freckles across her nose, glasses, tan trousers, a long-sleeved shirt, and a lovely smile. The picture of health and intellect in an oversized body.

She offers her hand and I wipe mine on a rag before I extend it. Her shake is firm. Her gaze solid behind round, wire-rimmed glasses. She is formidable in so many ways, and unlike any woman I've ever seen. For starters, she has me by seven or eight inches. Her stance says confident. Her clothes say polished.

"Miss Kathleen Shaw, at last we meet." My voice is extra cheerful.

"Please call me Kate. I hoped I'd find you here today." She laughs easily. "Is this a good time to catch up?"

"Yes, it is, Kate. Yes, indeed."

Miss Shaw follows me into church and down the aisle as I unroll my cuffs, button them, and slip on my coat to recover some dignity. There are ten pews on each side, and we sit in front. Other than the cross on the wall and the pine lectern built by my granddaddy, there are no trimmings here. I turn toward her, rest an arm on the back of the bench, and notice a dribble of soup stain on my tie. I cover it with my hand, surprised at my vanity.

"Are you adjusting to mountain life?"

"I'm making progress." She runs fingers through her short hair, then adjusts her eyeglasses.

"Is your cabin adequate?" I intentionally don't talk about

the teacher's cottage that burned down. I am embarrassed when I see the remains every time I come to church. It burned in the night two months back. Thank goodness it was empty. Nobody's talking about the culprit, but I suspect the reason for the fire: they hoped to stop outside teachers from coming to Baines Creek. I had to scramble to find an alternate place to house the new teacher. Pickings were slim and it is almost a mile walk up the mountain to her cabin.

"It'll do fine. I'm staying mostly warm and dry."

"Well, those are the basics, aren't they? It must pale in comparison to your last post at Ravenscroft. I've never ventured that far east in the state, but I've heard it's beautiful."

"It's different there. Flat as a tabletop."

"And here is…breathtaking?"

Her laugh is part giggle and grin, a young girl's laugh in a mature woman's frame. Delightful. And she catches my inference to thin mountain air!

"Ravenscroft has a different kind of beauty. Up here, I'm challenged in a good way. I confess at this early stage I prefer to walk *down* the mountainside, but that won't get me where I need to go, will it?"

"You're right there," and we chuckle together. This kind of easy exchange bodes well.

"Did you like teaching at Ravenscroft?"

"I brought good memories with me."

Because I am incessantly curious, I wade smack-dab into the deep end. "Why'd you leave your last post…if you don't mind me asking?" I work to sound natural, although I'm being nosy and know it.

Kate Shaw pauses slightly and looks down at her hands in her lap. "I was dismissed."

"Oh my…"

She adds, "It was personal. Unrelated to classroom skills. It won't affect my teaching."

I want to know more, but I'm at a crossroad and must decide to trust or doubt. "Well, Miss Kate Shaw, I take you at your word. I can't speak for everybody in these parts, but *I* believe we're lucky to have you with us. Thank you for answering my plea. Our children need structure, empathy, and, above all, hope. I want them to know they can have a more promising future."

"I want the same thing."

I'm so relieved at first meeting to see that Kate Shaw is all we need her to be. I add, "Can you join us on Sundays? Service starts at eleven."

Miss Shaw shakes her head. "I'm not a Christian. I don't believe or disbelieve in your god or your devil. I simply have little use for church dogma and man-made rituals that stifle people through fear and superstition. I've never seen any proof to support the teachings of your Bible." She looks me in the eye. "Nature makes a pretty strong case for its own evolution."

I'm taken aback. It is apparent Miss Shaw never met the likes of Pharrell Moody, nor has she seen the likes of her closest neighbor, Birdie Rocas. Miss Shaw's world hasn't been complicated by raw truths that defy science or logic, and can only be understood by faith. Few have put their lack of belief as succinctly as Kate Shaw just did, but she needs to attend church to satisfy the curious. I drop a different line to reel in my fish.

"Well, you might consider church a social vehicle up here, a place where your neighbors come together as a family to touch base and to offer help. They're all curious about you. In truth, it won't make you popular if you keep to yourself. I want you to work out, Miss Shaw."

"Kate."

"Kate." I say, and grin. "I want you to feel welcome here, Kate. You need to get to know these folks, and they need you and don't even know it yet. Could you do that for us? Come to church to get to know us?" For effect, my head tilts to the right in a plea.

She nods at my logic. "I'll come a time or two. For now, I've taken up enough of your day."

Kate Shaw stands, looks down on me, and ends our conversation before it got started. I follow her out and note her polished boots with the rim of mud on the bottom and the confident strike of her heel. She is not of this place and a moment of truth crosses my mind as I realize there are dangers up here that could harm her if she became too curious.

"Kate, I don't want to be a naysayer, but please tread cautiously on the mountain. Don't stray off the path. Don't be too curious."

She turns, standing on the second step down. I continue gently. "You're an outsider in an insulated community that has ways vastly different than the valley. There are moonshine stills in more places than I can count. Those men are edgy and skittish with revenuers and set traps to catch people as well as animals. And this is ginseng hunting season, too."

She looks puzzled, and I say, "You haven't heard of

ginseng? It's an herb that grows in specific places on the steep, shadowy sides of these mountains. To tell the truth, I've never seen a patch, but people off the mountain pay a lot of money for that fleshy root."

"What good does it do?"

"Some people believe it holds the key to well-being. It relieves stress and headaches."

"Headaches, you say?"

"Helps the heart, too. Sounds like a panacea for whatever ails you, doesn't it? Whatever the case, the root of that little plant pays big money to people around here willing to hunt for it in late summer and early fall. They guard where their patches of ginseng are like they guard their moonshine stills. They set traps. Carry guns and don't hesitate to use them. They'd shoot first, then ask questions later. You understand why I tell you to be cautious? Please don't explore on your own."

Kate's face tightens in a good way. "Yes. I understand."

"It'll help when you meet your close neighbors and they meet you. Some of them will come to church, and those who don't, we will visit. Does that sound like a plan?"

"I'll be here next Sunday," she says, and shakes my hand once more.

She's walking away when I remember to call out, "If you don't mind, I'd like to drop by sometime." I feel like a schoolboy with hope in his voice. "I'm partial to good conversation."

She says, "I'd like that, Preacher Perkins. My door's always open—especially since it doesn't have a lock," she adds easily, and makes me smile.

"Eli. Please call me Eli," I say as she turns and waves in

the air. I say a little louder, "And we can remedy that lock on your door."

"We'll talk about it—Eli." She laughs that young-girl laugh and walks on.

I feel a quick shot of pride abide in hearing my simple name spoken with a cultured tone. She thrusts her hands in her coat pockets, and her loping strides take her into the woods and out of sight. I'm surprised to hear Kate Shaw whistle as she walks, a secure woman who at first glance appears to be sufficiently suited for mountain life.

Still, she has secrets. And a flaw of faith. Education to sell. Prejudices to overcome.

On Mondays I check in on the sick and lapsed Christians who could use a bit of attention and a friendly voice. After breakfast I get my Bible, walking stick, and a rucksack of supplies and walk well-worn paths and rugged hollows to the souls in my flock that live on Bentwood Mountain and in neighboring hollers.

Mentally, I've mapped out my route to pass the school last because I'm curious and want to check on Miss Shaw's first day of teaching. Yesterday, at the close of service, I reminded families about the importance of education and the gifts Miss Shaw brings us. With the recent run of teachers we've had, they need proof before they believe. I hope someone shows up at school for curiosity's sake.

Roosevelt Lowe is my first stop. Beanie and Weenie smell

me before they see me and start their hound-dog warbles. The old man's home is a lean-to on the north side of the mountain. Moss grows up the sides, and there's a hole in the roof for woodsmoke to escape.

Roosevelt sits cockeyed in a saggy aluminum chair next to the doorway. An army blanket is tacked to the frame to keep out the chill. He wears his trademark grin and rubs the stump of his right leg with his arthritic fingers. The peg leg he wears to get around lies next to his chair. He lost that limb in a hunting accident a dozen years back. However, by all accounts, he didn't lose his good disposition. Didn't even get mad at his buddy for his carelessness. I envy Roosevelt because he appears to never harbor trouble. He is a soul at peace.

"Preacher, I sit here this morning and study on them two crows over there."

He points and I look.

"Only seed the two of em. You know a bunch of crows is called a *murder*, don't you?"

I nod. I first heard about a *murder of crows* at seminary. I came upon many poetic and odd phrases found in literature and mentally filed them away: an ostentation of peacocks, a parliament of owls, a knot of frogs, and a skulk of foxes. My favorite is the crows.

Roosevelt delivers the punch line: "I think them two fellas on their own is attempted murder—get it? Attempted murder..."

Roosevelt cracks himself up and that cracks me up, too.

"That's a good one. Might have to borrow it."

"It's yours if you want it."

"I got some good news/bad news of my own for you."

"Knew you wouldn't call with no new material."

"Well, you might have heard yesterday the good news that I baptized five people in the river. The bad news is that we lost two of them in the swift current."

Quick as a wink, Roosevelt says, "I know which two I hope you lost."

We chuckle again like cohorts.

"How can I lift your spirit today, my friend?"

"Preacher, you done it when you come. Got a extra squirrel skinned and ready to cook. Tattler Swann brought two. Don't need two. What you got in your bag to give me instead?"

"Cornmeal, dried beans, molasses…"

"I'll take beans, if you don't mind. Just run out. That's the meal that comes with its own music, don't you know."

After more uplifting chatter, I leave with a smile and Roosevelt's skinned squirrel that ends up in Miz Marley's cook pot, and she gives me sassafras root that I give Susie Ward.

When I near Roy Tupkin and Sadie's trailer, I sense the twisted heaviness that lives there when Roy is home, and my stomach tightens. Ugly talk follows Roy like fleas on a mangy dog. He's a spiteful, small-minded man who drinks hard and plays for keeps. Sadie Blue did herself no favor taking up with Roy Tupkin.

There are women in these hills whose men beat them because they misconstrue Ephesians 5:22–23 as saying they can. They twist God's holy words: "Wives, submit yourselves to your own husbands, as unto the Lord. For the husband is the head of the wife." They stop short of the truth that continues, "Even as Christ is the head of the church: and he is the savior of the body." They conveniently ignore the fact that neither God nor the law gives husbands unqualified dominion over their wives. Men like Roy Tupkin don't hide behind the Bible when they beat their wives. They beat them because they can and no one stops them. I've talked often to Sheriff Loyal Sykes about this kind of crime, and every time he says, "The law's pretty helpless in private matters like this. Nobody talks or presses charges, and our hands get tied."

So the beaten women stay. Sadie stays. That staying makes it harder to change things.

I look for Roy's truck. It's gone so my stomach knot loosens. I see Sadie's face in the kitchen window and wave. She waves back and turns to come outside.

I've known this sweet girl all her life. Her daddy, Otis Blue, was good-hearted and generous like his daughter and loved a good joke. When he was up in years, past the time men usually go courting, Otis fell in love with pretty Carly Hicks, an antsy girl with wanderlust that ran through her veins like her daddy Walter's white lightning. She looked for a step up and a way out, and for some reason, she picked Otis to help change things.

With stars in his eyes, he married Carly Hicks and turned her into Carly Blue for a while. He acted like he'd won the jackpot. When Sadie was born seven months later, Carly up and left the two of them for a traveling salesman who likely promised more than he delivered.

For the baby's sake, Otis tried to clean up and not drink as much. He took her everywhere strapped to his back when she was little. When he went hunting, she was with him. When he set traps and sold skins, she was with him. But he was flawed like the lot of us. For one thing he wasn't good at math or he chose not to count up to nine months when it came to Sadie being born. I found that commendable. He died four or five years back.

Today, Sadie comes out with a jar of jelly from her stock to add to my rucksack.

"Mighty good of you, Sadie. You want a trade?"

"No, sir. Them that got, give."

"You understand that truth better than most."

I look for bruises and breaks in her delicate frame, but the girl looks good today. There's a brightness in her eyes. Being pregnant agrees with her. I hope it begins to agree with Roy.

I say, "I'm going to school next because I want to hear about Miss Shaw's first day."

"I seen her."

"Did you? When?" I'm pleasantly surprised Sadie took the initiative to greet our teacher.

"Last Saturday. Went to help her set up the school." She looks pleased with herself.

"What do you think of her?"

"Got her a globe that spins."

"That's a good thing, isn't it?"

"Gonna teach me to read." Sadie's cheeks flush with pride.

"That's a *real* good thing."

"Don't even have to come to school." Sadie pulls from her apron pocket the *Country Song Roundup* magazine with her beloved Miss Loretta Lynn gracing the cover. She never tires of hearing the words in this article and the different one Mooney has at his store.

"Ah…Miss Loretta Lynn still lights a fire in you."

"You brought this one up from the valley just for me."

"I remember it well. Picked it up in a bookstore on Harrison Street. Knew you loved her music. You know Miss Loretta's a lot like you. Smart. A problem-solver. She figures things out."

Sadie blushes at that compliment like she always does. I've been planting seeds a long time to help her believe in herself.

"How many times have you heard this Miss Loretta's story? Three?" I ask, knowing the answer.

"More like twenty." Sadie grins. "That woman's not afeard of nothing. She writes songs and sings, and folks line up and pay to listen. Want to read her words myself someday." She slips the precious magazine back in her apron pocket.

"Then that you will do. Fingers crossed we can convince Miss Shaw to stay. I could use your help to make her feel welcome. She'll be at church Sunday and we need to show our support."

"I'll come if I can."

———

In the afternoon, like I planned, I pass the one-room schoolhouse and stick my head in the door and find the small cluster of desks empty. Miss Shaw's name is written in chalk on the blackboard. I hear voices outside and follow them around back. The children—little Lucy Dillard and her younger sisters, Weeza and Pearl, and Grady and Petey Snow—and Miss Shaw sit on a quilt at creek's edge. I'm relieved to see some children remembered school starts today and a few had a mind to show up.

"Afternoon, Preacher Perkins," Miss Shaw calls out. "After story time, we brought our lunch and lesson outside and the children have turned teacher. They've kindly enlightened me about local flora. We're almost done for the day."

Kate Shaw has made the children feel important and I'm overwhelmed with tenderness. I worry I'll tear up, sentimental fool that I am, especially after so many young teachers tried and failed. I look down at the tips of my shoes to regain composure.

They stand to leave, and young Weeza gives Miss Shaw a shy hug. I swallow the knot in my throat and say a little louder than necessary, "So the teacher is the student today."

"Always," she laughs. "One's never too old to learn." She shakes leaves off the quilt, folds it neatly, and tucks it under her arm.

This is a perfect teaching moment this place rarely sees. "I don't have to ask how your day went. The children's faces tell it all."

"It's a good start, don't you think?"

Kate is a magician, a pied piper who has absconded with our children's hearts. Mine, too.

I don't see Kate Shaw until Sunday although I keep an ear to the ground for news. School attendance increases and as far as I know no pranks have been done to scare her away—at least none she talks about. The other young teachers endured snakes, bloody entrails, manure, and other crass antics left in the teacher's cottage or schoolroom. They wilted under the pressure. I think Miss Shaw is made of stronger stuff. I do know this: Baines Creek needs Miss Shaw more than she needs us.

Soup is on and my sermon set. Curiosity and novelty mean attendance will be as high today as Homecoming Sunday. I take extra care with my attire this morning and Prudence notices.

"Why you act prissy, Brother? You tried on every tie when you only got three, and all of em blue. And you sponged that jacket front so much the stripes gonna come off."

"Let me be. I'm getting ready for church, that's all." My voice stays soft, but my hands shake.

Prudence squints looking at me. "That Miss Shaw messes with your head. It's her come to church that's doing this. She's a big, old woman who don't fit in nowhere else, that's all."

My sister finishes the dishes and takes off her apron, picks up her thin purse, and stands by the door, impatient. I slip on my jacket and stuff a paper in the pocket. She notices.

"You write out your sermon? You don't do that. You like to wait till the Lord moves your words."

"I need the start. That's all."

"Brother, ain't you the fool…" She shakes her head in admonishment.

There's pity in Prudence's eyes and extra starch in her backbone. She threw in *ain't* to spite me. She was home-schooled better than that.

Suddenly I turn on her like a cur riled with a prod. "Prudence! Keep your thoughts to yourself."

Instantly I'm shamed by my outburst. "I'm sorry, I'm sorry," I mumble and try to corral the guilt that always lives beneath my human skin. I raise imploring eyes toward the door to ask for forgiveness because I am the weak one. She's already out the door.

———

This start of Sunday bodes poorly and I can't seem to right it. On the walk to church I humbly pray, *Lord, fill my being with your wisdom and help me choose my words wisely.*

As expected, the pews are packed fifteen minutes before service starts, and I'm a nervous ninny with a knot in my belly because I want the teacher to love us. Men stand in back so women can sit. The small ones are pulled up on their mamas' laps. I saved a seat for Miss Shaw in front at the opposite end of Prudence because I don't want my sister's snippy attitude to rub off.

Sadie slips in at the last moment and squeezes into the last row. *Merciful heavens.* Roy has battered her sweet face since I saw her Monday. I work to keep my face neutral. God only knows what injuries are out of sight under long sleeves. It angers me to see she likely paid dearly to be here today. Her Granny Gladys sits on the middle pew with a crooked straw hat on her head and her usual sour look on her face. I guess curiosity brought her here like it did a lot of folks who don't practice church regularly.

Miss Shaw wears trousers and polished boots, and along with the absence of a hat and a thin purse clutched in rough hands, she is set apart from the women here today. She is incongruous. She is our blessing. I worry we'll lose her before she's even in our grasp.

I stand at the podium dizzy and don't quite know why. I pull the folded paper out of my pocket and the words swim in front of my eyes, unreadable. Nerves. I open with a joke, then quote from Deuteronomy 32:2: "My doctrine shall drop as the rain, my speech shall distil as dew, as the small rain upon the tender herb, and as the showers upon the grass."

It's a lovely, poetic opening meant to honor the teaching gift of Miss Shaw, but sadly, I fail to tie it to the sermon very well. No one looks at or listens to me anyway. All eyes are on the back of the head whose eyes are on me. I ramble on, then frustrated, I cut short my sermon and talk about what's on everybody's mind.

"Today, we welcome Miss Shaw into our family. She has come to us in good faith and with a willing spirit to teach our children reading and writing and important lessons. The gifts she has given us in her first week are remarkable. Your children are more eager than ever to use the brains the good Lord gave them."

I look straight at Kate. "I speak for everybody here when I say *thank you*, Miss Shaw, for coming to Baines Creek."

Just before I dismiss the crowd, Miss Shaw says, "Reverend Perkins?"

There's a unified intake of breath at her boldness.

"May I address your congregation?"

"Of course." I gesture for her to stand at my podium and I sit, straightening my tie. I'm mildly conscious of the fact that few women have ever stood in front of this church, and I think it's a shame.

"Thank you." She looks around and I hope she sees

humble souls, not tattered clothes. She speaks. "I lost my last teaching job because I stood up for what I believed was right."

She pauses, runs a hand through her short hair, and clears her throat. I've never seen my congregation so still. They're mesmerized by language, appearance, and behavior foreign to their ways.

"When I lost my last post, I saw it as a chance for a new beginning. One that would test me. One that would matter more than what came before. An index card on a church bulletin board asking for a teacher looking for a challenge brought me to the education board, then to Baines Creek. Preacher Perkins's letter made it easy for me to decide. I hope this community might benefit from my love of learning. In turn, I hope to find renewed purpose."

Folks start to squirm in their pews. They're confused. They don't understand everything Miss Shaw said, but they did bits of it. She did something wrong that got her fired, then she came to Baines Creek.

"I'd like to stay to teach your children. I believe I'm where I'm supposed to be."

Kate Shaw sits and folds her hands in her lap.

Awkward tension strains the walls of my little church. No one knows what to do with this odd turn of events, so I say, "Soup is served."

Outside the church door, Kate stands one step down from me, and I introduce her to the parents of her students and to her close neighbors. Widow Jolly lives to the right of the school. Lila Moon, Mooney's reclusive sister, lives to the left. Both are old and feeble, and neither one comes out except to go to church and the Rusty Nickel. The others I introduce are equally shy and don't want to say the wrong words. They look at their feet, at Miss Shaw's trousers and short, gray hair, and raise a tepid hand to hers, but for the most part, they muddle through.

When Sadie steps forward to introduce her aunt Marris to Miss Shaw, I want to fold the child in a hug and cry for her. She casts a glance across the clearing into the shadow of the tree line and to Roy Tupkin. He leans against a tree and smokes a cigarette, his sights tight on Sadie. He tips his hat to me and I want to throttle him. No surprise that Billy Barnhill is there, too.

What I really want to do is send Sadie home with Marris, to her tender care, but I can't make decisions for the girl. The line between duty and what's right isn't always clear-cut. All I whisper today is, "I'll keep you in my prayers, child." I know that's not enough.

Twenty minutes later, only Kate Shaw and I remain in the churchyard. She stayed behind and now faces me and fills in the missing pieces without me asking.

"I helped a girl get an abortion," she starts. There's a hard glint in her eyes, defensive. "She threatened to kill herself if I didn't. Even without the threat, I would have helped. Women have a right to make their own decisions about their bodies. The law on the books is archaic."

I look to heaven before I give the standard answer. "God and the law know killing an unborn baby is wrong. It's murder."

"I disagree." She shakes her head both in sadness and fatigue. "Anyway, that's the action that got me dismissed."

Physically we stand four feet apart, but ethically and morally, a million miles. One long moment rolls into two as we sort the deliberations before us. Lord knows Baines Creek has its rash of babies born to girls too young, in some cases fathered by incest, but the issue with babies is clear when I trust the Bible's law: killing a helpless fetus is murder.

"I won't sanction abortion, Kate," I say, knowing full well that pennyroyal and blue cohosh grow on these mountains and can end early pregnancies. I'm not naive. I am consistent.

"I'm not asking you to sanction it, Eli." There's respect and compassion in her tone. I see in Kate's eyes she'll never change her mind, but neither will I.

We call a truce and lay it to rest.

ELI PERKINS

Today, on a Saturday lit with the gold of autumn, I sit in Kate's cabin and she pours tea. Her first three weeks of teaching have gone well and attendance numbers are up. I drop two sugar cubes in my cup and stir with a teaspoon. There's a brightness to the air here in her cabin where thoughts breathe and expand. Despite our differences, I'm content here like nowhere else.

"Well, Kate Shaw." I clear my throat. "I can't quite tell from the bits and pieces I've collected about you. Are you an atheist or an agnostic?"

"To the point, Preacher Eli Perkins," she counters with an easy smile as she drops two sugar cubes in her own cup and stirs. "I call myself an agnostic. From as early as I can recall. I never saw the need for blind faith, nor am I patient with man-made rules."

I lift my bushy eyebrows. "That's self-evident considering your history, don't you think?" and we laugh as easily as the friends I want us to become. "No formal religion in your background? No miracles? Spiritual quests? Moments of wonder? Cries to God in your dark hour of need?"

Kate says, "I understand the relief your faith provides. You think it is the foundation for hope and comfort. The cause and effect you believe in are sin and reformation. Fear plays a big part in encouraging people to take the high road. I don't believe faith or fear lifts people to a better life. The cause and effect I believe in are education and opportunity. Those actions and goals elicit positive change. A god monitoring my days seems naive at best and dangerous at worst."

"Kate. Oh, Kate." I chuckle at her heartfelt tirade, and blessedly, she's not offended. "You are a seeker whether you admit it or not. An angel of God. I've watched the miracles you perform. Your faith in these children's possibilities brings about change. Sadie Blue is overjoyed you're teaching her to read. The knowledge is secondary to your faith in them. *You* lift them up. Not education. Whether you believe in God, He believes in you."

"I love to teach, and I love to learn."

"And God is Love."

Kate laughs without judgment and pours more tea in our cups. "Eli, we're not on different sides. I just don't *know* what you say you *do* know. You believe in the purity of a god and the evil of a devil, conjured creatures that serve your need."

"Kate"—my voice turns stern—"don't speak lightly of these things you know little about. I've witnessed battles between God and the Devil, and I'm here to tell you those battles are real."

Her bright face settles into serious, and she props her chin on the palm of her hand to listen. "Tell me, Eli. Tell me what you know."

This unguarded spirit of exchange has cemented our

friendship so easily, yet these are inky waters I will wade in today and carry Kate with me—if she wants to come.

"We need another pot of tea."

"I was nine years old when I met the devil face-to-face."

As expected, Kate's eyes widen, and she leans forward. I take these as good signs.

"You never forget something like that. I went with Daddy and Granddaddy to call on Pharrell Moody. The devil had crawled right into his skin.

"Pharrell had been a peaceful hermit until the day his eyes turned red and a foul smell filled his body. Hair dropped off his scalp, his arms and legs. His skin was bare, and he looked like a newly shed snake wet with a tinge of green. Some folks think he sold his soul the winter before when the blizzard blew long and trapped men in desperate places, caught between life and death. Whatever the reason, when his frightful story filtered down to church, Daddy went to check on this struggling soul."

Speaking of the devil always dries me out. I down my tea and Kate fills my cup.

"When Daddy got back from Pharrell Moody's place that day, he walked in, gripped Mama in his arms, and whispered long in her ear. Her backbone went rigid and she clutched Daddy tight while he whispered. When he stepped back, she dropped to her knees and started praying, her lips moving, her body keening, but no sound came out. Daddy said, 'Everything's going to be okay, little Eli. Stay with Mama while

I get Granddaddy and the deacons for a talk. We got the Lord's business to tend to in the most urgent way.'

"Mama stayed on her knees until the pain of kneeling made her cry out. When Daddy came back, he helped her to her feet and told her a stranger was coming to drive the devil out."

Kate breaks in. "Eli, are you talking about exorcism?"

"Yes. I've witnessed others since Pharrell Moody. He was my first and the most sinister."

"In what way?"

"It's what I saw when Daddy, Granddaddy, the deacons, and the stranger arrived with me in their midst. Pharrell Moody, a man in his late fifties with old-man ailments, was on the mossy roof of his hut, naked, coated in mud and blood. He howled like a panther. His fingers were claws. He moved to the edge of the roof and urinated a long blue arc to mark the stranger, then cackled and hopped from foot to foot in glee.

"Confident we were no match for him, Pharrell leapt off the roof and landed in our midst. I stood behind Daddy, shielded from the devil. The foul air around him stung my nose. The beast rumbled with cunning. The seven men encircled Pharrell Moody, Bibles open toward the devil. They spoke in unison. 'Yea, though I walk through the valley of the shadow of death, I will fear no evil: for thou art with me…'"

"Psalm twenty-three," Kate whispers, captivated, eyes wide behind glasses.

"Yes." I steeple my hands in prayer with fingertips to my lips. "Simple, sweet words everyone says often without knowing their power. The devil hates those words. Those words are acid poured on the devil's brain. Do you want to know what those words did to the demon?"

She nods like a schoolgirl.

"The demon inside Pharrell Moody was trapped in this circle of seven believers armed with the Holy Word. The stranger raised his voice. 'In Jesus's name, I command all demons to leave at once! In Jesus's name, I command all demons to leave...' Pharrell Moody clutched his head, writhed in pain, and fell to the ground while the seven holy men drew closer, chanting tirelessly. The creature cried red tears. He clawed at his body. I didn't think anyone could survive what I saw."

I drink more tea and take out my handkerchief to wipe my brow. Kate stays respectful and quiet.

"The sun set when Pharrell Moody lay on the ground emptied. Daddy turned him over so we could look upon his face. The fight was out of him. The devil had departed for easier prey. We watched Pharrell Moody heal, and right before our eyes his muscles knit back together and skin grew over wounds. Hair grew back as white as chestnut blossoms. The claws retracted and his humped back melted away. We stepped back, and Pharrell Moody sat up, dazed and liberated."

I end wearily with, "That day, I answered the call to serve God the rest of my days."

Kate sits back in her chair with her arms folded across her chest. She takes a deep breath and lets it out. I worry I've gone too far in my ancient tale of good versus evil, but she surprises me and says, "I understand. You wanted to be on the Good Guy's side, right? I don't blame you."

The end of September grows close, and against my heart's odd hesitation, I decide to go to the Baptist Convention. I rationalize that my new knowledge will give Kate and me something different to talk about. How erudite I'll sound with altered perspectives to old debates!

I'll spend time with Henry Clayton. We'll stay at the Howard Johnson Motel and I'll eat my fill of hot fudge sundaes. Henry and I always share a room to be frugal and to feel like boys again. It is four blocks to the convention center, and the walk to and from is when a lot of stuff gets sorted out. I need to talk to my old friend. He's a good listener. He knows me better than anybody.

The day before I leave for convention on Sunday afternoon, I go see Kate. The stray dog that came and stayed is at her side with a grin on his face. I'm thankful he is here as company or to protect her in my absence—as if me staying ever protected her.

The dog and the woman have come down from the summit. Her face is flushed and open and happy. When I didn't find her home, I waited. I didn't want to leave a note. I wanted to tell her firsthand I'd be away for five whole days.

"I head to the Baptist Convention tomorrow after church," I say, like it's a regular commute for me and she cares. "I'll be back Friday. Need anything from the valley?"

"Would you like tea while I make a list?" she asks and heads inside with me right behind. I'm used to the long shadow she casts. While the tea steeps, Kate checks her few cupboards, tears a page from her journal, and makes a list, writing in bold strokes. The sun finds the silver strands entwined in her dark hair growing on the head that holds the brain I admire.

"This should do." She hands me the paper. "The big thing is my supply of penny candy. Don't want to run out. And, if you find a new *Country Song Roundup* with a Loretta Lynn article in it, I'd love that as well."

I fold the list and put it in my shirt pocket over my heart.

"I envy you walking through a grocery store with stocked shelves," she says, laughing.

I almost say *I'd love you to be with me* but stop myself from sounding silly.

————

Henry never changes. He walks across the parking lot toward me, long strides, coattail flapping, toothy grin, old leather briefcase clutched under his arm because the handle broke long ago. He's the same height as Kate, and I mildly wonder about my comfort and attraction to tall people. We hug and clap each other roughly on the back, and grin like the boys we used to be.

"Made it another year, brother," Henry says. "Lucky for me when I consider the people I'm around. I opened my mail last week and found an envelope with a single sheet of paper in it. It had only one word on it. FOOL."

"You don't say…"

"So last Sunday, I said to my congregation, 'I've known

people who've written letters and forgotten to sign their names. This week I got a letter from someone who signed his name, then forgot to write the letter!'"

That's how it always is. Henry and I pick up where we left off, easy as pie. Henry supplies the entertainment and I give him my good ear and file away the wit.

It isn't until later that evening, as I enjoy my first hot fudge sundae while we sit in a Howard Johnson red leather booth and I babble on about Kate Shaw and inspired students, that he asks, "Is there something I should know, buddy?"

"What do you mean?" I'm puzzled. I wipe whipped cream from my chin with my napkin.

"Come on, Eli. You can confide in your oldest friend."

When I shrug my shoulders and keep eating, Henry sits back, lays both palms on the table, and studies me. "I got it." He slaps the table. "You're in love."

Whoa! What did he say? "*Love?*" I put my spoon down and shake my head at this ludicrous thought while Henry laughs and nods.

"No, no, no," I say, completely out of my comfort zone, pushing away my empty sundae glass. "Why in the world would you say that?"

Henry studies me like I'm an insect trapped under a magnifying glass until I squirm. I don't know what I've called these weeks with Kate. Intellectual? Stimulating? Marvelous? But in love? That's too priceless a gift for me to receive or give or even name. I'm too old. Too set in my ways…

"If you could see the look on your face, Eli Perkins. It's a first for you. Talk to me."

Henry holds up his hand and signals to the waitress *another round*, and I get a second hot fudge sundae and he a Coke float. We skip the lecture "When Hell Freezes Over." Convention lectures can be predictable.

Where to start? When Kate first said my name and I had my head down in the soup pot, unprepared for a flush of dizziness? When I saw her sitting on the quilt in the sunshine surrounded by children? Or when she argued the misplacement of women in religious history?

"She's tall," I say.

"Uh–huh…and?"

"Old."

"Uh–huh."

"And fifty-one. Name's Kate. She's tall…"

"Eli, I'll clock you side the head if you tell me one more statistic that could apply to half the people in this restaurant, considering you're a runt."

"No, I mean she's *really* tall. Okay. Okay… She's that teacher I told you about from Ravenscroft. The one who saw your index card. She got fired and came to Baines Creek. She's fifty-one," I fumble, completely bad at this and truly unaware of my repetition until Henry stops me.

"Well, you're sweating, your sentences have been reduced to repetitions, and you haven't touched your second hot fudge sundae. Therefore it's official: you stink at love."

I laugh halfheartedly, feel sick to my stomach, and think part of this is a joke and part of this is serious and all of it will end poorly if I allow myself to dream. A preacher's life isn't about dreams. It's about garnering strength to face an arduous life, to prepare souls for the afterlife, and hold people's hands on the rough rides when it all tumbles down.

"Henry, you've got to talk me out of this. I'm too old to court. I'm a preacher to Kate, one who comes by to talk. That's all. She's never even been to my place. Prudence thinks poorly of her."

Henry roars at that declaration, and people turn to look. "Your sister thinking poorly of Kate is a huge plus in my book. But let me get this straight." Henry actually wipes tears from his eyes with the palms of his hands he's laughing so hard. "This Kate's tall and fifty-one, and love isn't possible for an educated woman who's never been to your home, and of whom your sister doesn't approve. I get it," he chides me. "You came all the way down off the mountain and carried this as a burden, didn't you?"

He turns serious on me, and I feel my lungs have collapsed and I'm a puddle of hot fudge oozing out onto the table without a vessel to hold me together.

"I'm lost, Henry. Hopelessly, totally lost...and sick inside."

"No, you're not. You're a novice. You'll flounder like all mortal men, ill-prepared. That's part of the initiation." His voice turns to preacher comfort. "I remind you of Deuteronomy 31:8. 'And the Lord, he it is that doth go before thee; he will be with thee, he will not fail thee, neither forsake thee: fear not, neither be dismayed.'"

"How can I not?" I wail on low volume. "Kate Shaw's an *agnostic*!"

While I was in the valley struggling with the strange matters of love, a tragedy came to my mountain. Prudence meets me at the door with news. She never meets me at the door. But today, a sick joy glints in her eyes as she rushes to spill news about a girl who has been missing the past few days.

"She's a sinner, trampy and cheap, Brother." She wrinkles her nose. "Surely the Lord had a hand in her dismal fate. She's probably dead in a ditch somewhere."

"You don't know any such thing, Prudence! The Lord doesn't relish a lost soul gone astray. Please don't spread false-hoods whose truths you know nothing about. You should pray for this poor girl's safe return."

Prudence looks at me with such raw hatred that it sucks my breath away. Then she walks to her room, softly closes the door, and locks it. I'm sobered from my convention high, and in that moment, all ties with potential love and happiness I felt in the valley evaporate, and I'm left standing in my sister's poisonous air. I always forget how acrimoni-ous Prudence is until I'm gone and return. I pray for her most fervently.

***

It's Sunday afternoon, two days since I'm back where I belong, even more ill-placed than before. I endured Henry's inap-propriate jokes about love during the days we were together. I stumbled through this morning's lackluster church service. I now know this: love is no laughing matter.

Today Prudence sits by a window and mends socks. I catch

sight of her out of my peripheral view and see her stop and watch me stare out the window.

"You sick?" Her voice holds no sympathy.

I don't know why I don't answer her. It miffs my sister to no end when I don't answer.

"Brother, you hear me? Got cotton in your ears?"

I square my shoulders. This is a new low for me, a rebellion suited for a two-year-old. I stand, pull on my coat and wool scarf, and head to the workshop. I even slam the door behind me for spite, though I will pay for my insolence. I'm guessing Prudence won't fix supper tonight but stay in her room and fume. Or she'll let the woodstove fire die out on purpose, and somehow I don't care—and I'm shocked! I've cared about consequences every moment of every day since I was born. Now I don't.

I haven't been to see Kate since I returned. I've had sitting by the door the penny candy, three used readers, two new magazines holding articles about Loretta Lynn, canned tuna, jars of peaches, and the dog food she ordered. To trudge them to her cabin and leave them at her door is beyond me. If she's there she'll be polite and offer me tea and ask about the convention. I'll have to confess I went to only three one-hour lectures and didn't listen to any of them, and no, I can't remember the topics so we can't talk about them. Then she'll ask if I'm sick, and surely she'll understand when she sees me that I'm not myself. In truth, to explain it all is too much to take in today.

I sit out in my cold workshop among the sawdust and worn sandpaper and unfinished stack of block toys I need to tend to. The frigid wind comes through the opened door that I don't close. My nose runs, and my fingers and toes grow numb. My chest aches like I've got pneumonia. I must be getting very sick. I deserve to get a fever and even more body aches than I already have.

If this is what love feels like, why would anyone seek it out and want to hold on to it? It hurts so much I can't breathe right. Food is tasteless. Sleep has been elusive these recent weeks. To move my arms and legs simultaneously is a weighty chore. When I hear a voice sounding like Kate's call my name, I cringe. *Oh Lord, now I've done it. I'm hallucinating.*

Then the woman who absconded with my thoughts, and who lives behind my eyelids, sticks her head around the edge of the open doorway to my workshop. Her face is flushed healthy, and around her neck she wears a green tartan scarf the color of her eyes. I close mine for a moment because I think she's a mirage.

When I open them, she's still there! The dog stands beside her and whips his tail, and fresh joy floods through my veins like rain in the desert. Kate has her walking stick. She sought me out. She found where I live!

"Well, hello, stranger," she says. "Welcome home."

PRUDENCE PERKINS

*H*ell is being born into a family of preachers named Eli.

A person can't have a thought to herself without some rule taking the starch out of it. From the time I could walk, the path was marked and only a fool would wander. And I won't a fool. I settled for scraps if I wanted something cause Brother got the choice. Being the boy and all. Being another Eli.

Daddy and him sat round the woodstove and talked like equals bout the heavenly plan for salvation and their divine part in it. I was stuck to the ground with thoughts nobody wanted—a girl nailed in a sorry place.

Like today. I wait for that new teacher in the schoolhouse instead of visiting at Fleeta's house with Alice Dickens and Laura June Mayhew, eating molasses cake Fleeta promised to bake. I'm in a bad mood missing cake *and* gossip cause Brother had to preach a funeral and I'm stuck here, and she's late so I wait.

I was six to Eli's eighteen when Daddy got cancer and Brother left home for preacher schooling. I emptied slop buckets and hauled wood, baked biscuits and tended garden. Lye soap cracked the skin open on my fingers when I helped Mama do laundry in yard pots. Everything I did was coated with the Lord's slippery words. I almost drowned in verse. I learned to breathe underwater was what I did, being the daughter of a Eli.

After two years gone, Brother come home a preacher, third generation. Daddy waited till he did and died, and Brother cried cause he was scared. Mama got old fast after that. When she passed on the eve of my thirteenth birthday, only one last Eli needed tending to, and that fell to me. From the outside I stayed pretty much the same after Mama passed. Plain, modest, quiet Prudence.

Then something changed.

Eve's curse come a year later, and blood ran down my skinny legs and stained the very ground I stood on. I kept more thoughts to myself. Course, Brother don't study me like Mama used to. He don't know what ragtime done to the insides of a lone girl without a mama to guide her. Ragtime cramped, and twisted flesh made nothing fit right over tender skin.

God must have hated womankind something terrible to punish her month after month, and leave the mark of blood as her shame.

Jumbled in all the new strange, I had private thoughts bout the boy, thoughts that sprung outta the air when I turned sixteen. Thomas James Slater was his name. Folks called him TJ. Nobody called him Thomas cept me, and that was inside my head and never out loud. He come to church regular. I watched his hair sweep cross his high forehead and curl at the nape of his neck. I wanted so bad to touch one of them curls, pull it open, and watch it spring back and grab holt of my finger.

He was a year ahead of me and already had man's hands— square fingernails with rough palms. One of his fingernails was always bruised from the missed strike of a hammer when he fixed a roof or put down a floor. I wanted to lift that hand and kiss that bruised finger. I wanted to take all his hurt away.

Thomas had a dimple in his right cheek that showed when I caught his eye and made him smile. I did things I never done before to make that dimple come. Cut my eyes down and back up. Glanced over my shoulder to see if he looked my way. I thought that dimple belonged to me.

I lived for Sundays that took me to Thomas Slater cause not much else did. The in-between time I talked to Thomas in my head, and he said nice things back. *What do* you *think, Prudence? You're a good cook. You work hard.*

Once he walked in at the Rusty Nickel for supplies when I was there, and my tongue got tied in a knot. Before it come undone, he tipped his hat and said, "Afternoon, Miss Perkins," flashed his dimple, and was gone. For the life of me I couldn't remember why I come to the store that day. I was such a fool for that boy. I found out how much a fool at the pie auction on Homecoming Sunday.

Thomas Slater's mama let it slip one time at church that he liked apple pie best. I tucked that secret in my heart when pie auction time come, and I made the best, most perfect apple pie for Thomas Slater. I cut out all the brown spots on the apples, put extra butter in the crust, did a lattice weave for the top, and brushed it with a egg white before it baked and turned golden. I even sprinkled sugar on top and watched it careful so it won't burn. I never put this much care in a pie before. I made it for my Thomas. His dimple told me to.

The night before Homecoming Sunday, I washed my hair. Used one of them little bottles of shampoo Brother brought back from convention in the valley. After I rinsed the bubbles

outta my hair, I poured a whole cup of apple vinegar on
for extra shine. My fingers glided through the strands to the
ends, slick as silk. I wanted to smell clean when I stood beside
Thomas tomorrow, when he held my prize pie.

That year I was sixteen, Homecoming Sunday was a blue-
sky day. Planks on sawhorses was set up in the churchyard
and made a table to hold dozens of pies. I held on to mine so
Thomas saw me with my perfect pie. I set it on the table last,
right front corner. Then the auction started.

I stood off to the side so I could watch Thomas out the
corner of my eye. I don't care how many quarters the other pies
brought. I waited for Thomas to declare to the congregation he
had his sights on me. That day, when I waited for love to pick
me, I was happy.

When Thomas raised his hand and called out "fifty cents"
as a high opening bid, I was puzzled. That won't my pie
Burnell Sheets held up for bids. It was some sort of rhubarb
thing, lopsided, with a burnt crust. I thought Thomas made a
mistake or was being kind.

But he paid a whole *dollar* for that rhubarb thing made by
Susie Domer, the little mouse of a girl with limp hair and a
lisp. She carried her ugly pie and placed it in Thomas's bruised,
strong hands, and his dimple turned on and stayed on and
shined down on her scrappy head.

I don't stay to see who got my perfect pie. I don't tell
nobody when I go. I walked home, filled up to the top with
broken hate, working on a plan.

Old memories more than twenty-five years back get more idle time today than they have a right to. Even when your hair turns gray, they don't stay away on this kinda low-cloud day. Thomas Slater never showed his dimple for me again, but I remember what it looked like.

Now this new teacher comes who must not have a watch cause she still ain't here.

The other teachers before Miss Shaw were girls, really. Not what anybody'd call a real teacher. Nervous and jumpy, they won't much good to anybody. I already know this one won't do cause she's old as Brother. Why can't we get somebody in between? Or why can't the valley leave us alone? I heard hope in his voice this morning when he said Miss Kathleen Shaw's name, and that's gotta stop. Brother's a dreamer who's got to wake up. He still believes life in Baines Creek is gonna get better when there's not a speck of proof to show for it. Case in point: this here teacher. She's late by a lot. Said she'd be here at two o'clock, and now it's half past on Mama's watch pinned to my bodice. I'll give her five more minutes.

Now four minutes and I'm outta here.

Three.

Two minutes and I'm gonna leave.

Mixed in the shrill of the rising wind before a storm lets loose, I stand at the open door and hear a car struggle up the road, pull in front of the schoolhouse, and stop. It's gotta be Miss Kathleen Shaw, but it looks like a man inside. The person raises a hand as big as any I've seen, and right then, the rain lets loose and blots out the car behind a wall of water. If that's not a bad omen, I don't know what is.

I close the schoolhouse door to keep out the wet and lean up against it. The empty room and extra time pulls me back to Thomas and my perfect pie. Now the shawl climbs into the story.

Susie Domer, the simple girl Thomas claimed with a lopsided rhubarb pie, was the same age as me back then—sixteen. She always wore the same shawl to church, foggy gray wool with one embroidered red rose that lay between her shoulder blades. After I knew Thomas's dimple was for Susie and not me, I wanted to pick out the threads of that rose, but I did something better.

Susie was careless. She wore her shawl to Mr. Simmons's funeral visitation, and cause the day turned from chilly to warm, she hung that shawl on the back of her chair. I watched it slip into a soft heap as she stood to talk to his widow. Then she walked into the sunshine without a look back. I slid my foot over and pulled the shawl beside my chair, reached down, and bunched it under my sweater. I took my leave and walked home, stitching my plan into place.

That plan was the bend in the river where good God-fearing girls don't go.

Soft grass grew high there. When bodies lay down, the grass stayed down, and the cost to go there was a girl's reputation. I knew the way. Everybody did. On the day it rained too much for anybody to go to the tall grass, I took Susie's vain shawl to the bend in the river. Through the soft, broken grass I threaded her shawl, then backed my way out and went home.

Every day, hope got bigger like a bubble growing in my belly. I could only do this cause Mama was dead. If she was here, she'd see straight into my heart and make me undo it all. With Mama dead, Brother was blind.

In the days to come, the hairs on my body would tingle at the thought of the lost shawl being found. I squeezed my legs together and made a moment of bliss thinking bout that shawl, the tall grass, and the trouble them two would make for Susie Domer.

Next Sunday at church, Susie wore one of her mama's cast-off shawls, and she looked the plainer for it. In the churchyard she stood beside her parents with Thomas off to the side.

"What happened to your shawl, Susie? It's got a pretty rose on the back, don't it?" I asked cause I want her mama and daddy to know everybody knew what her shawl looked like.

"Yeth. I lawthed it," she said in her pitiful, muddled lisp. Her homely face all innocent-like, unafeard, when she should have been scared for her very life.

"Well, it'll turn up, and you'll remember where you left it." I put on my biggest smile, said my farewell, and walked away, surprised to feel my stomach turn sour.

Now the rain that pounded on the roof stops quick as it come, and the quiet makes me leave Thomas and Susie back twenty-five years where they belong. That sour taste stays with remembering. I swallow and open the door as Miss Shaw steps outta her car.

She's a long-legged giant of a woman who's got on man's trousers, for Lord's sake! Her hair's chopped off, too. She's an insult to womankind is what she is. She's a talker, too, and she talks to hear her mouth rattle on bout the ride up the mountain like she done something special. I watch her mouth move but don't listen close. She puts out her hand and I take it, but not really. Miss Kathleen Shaw has got a lot to learn. She come to the right place that'll do the teaching for her.

"I'm sorry, so very sorry you had to wait on me," she says, like two *sorries* will make it stick better. I don't like this big, old person and hope she goes back to the valley quick. Brother's gonna be surprised. He's gonna feel puny beside this one.

I get home from meeting Miss Shaw and got me a headache like I get a time or three a year. It starts small but it's gonna grow, so I take to bed in the late afternoon and put a warm rag over my eyes to block out the harsh light. My world goes small on headache days. Brother knows to fend for himself and leave me be.

I pull up the crazy quilt from the foot of my bed made from scraps of cloth in colors of faded leaves. This won't a hand-me-down. Mama made it just for me. She used pieces of our dresses, Daddy's work shirts, and some of Nana's dresses I never saw her in but know they're hers cause Mama said.

There's one curious piece. It's a sky-blue scrap with red specks. I never saw that color in a dress Mama or me wore. I asked Mama where something that bright come from, and she always spoke in riddles. The first time she said, "From a dress I wore a long while back." Another time she said, "It's from a store-bought dress that got torn." When I needled her too much, she said, "Prudence, you ask too many questions. Let it be and appreciate it cause it's special."

Sometimes I saw her smile when she touched that blue scrap. Once, she cried.

I don't like a mystery in my quilt but I can't rip it out and mess up Mama's fine stitches, so I let it be. She holds me together with her tiny stitches. I feel close to her when I'm under my quilt. It's a comfort is what it is, and my life is sparse of comforts.

Mama used to quilt with the ladies from church till she got sick. She had a fine stitch the others don't, but Mama don't boast. She knew it was a sin, and she was a righteous Christian woman with few blemishes on her soul. She took me quilting with her most of the time, and I stayed right by her side, quiet, while she stitched and the other women gossiped more than they sewed. My stitches won't fine enough to put in, so I sat on the floor when I was little and on a stool when I got bigger. I practiced my stitches on a quilt square nobody wanted.

I heard who had trouble with a husband, whose gout flared up, and whose conscience bothered em. I heard bits bout babies who don't get born, the key to secret recipes, and pieces of meanness nobody had use for. I heard about places I'd never see. Land as flat as a tabletop covered with waves of wheat. A river so wide you can't see the other side. On the way home, Mama said, "Prue, don't believe everything you hear. Folks like to talk, and some like to talk too much, specially when stitching is going on."

When Mama passed, a lot of things left with her. One of em was the answer to the mystery in my quilt. Today, my headache sends me to bed, and like I do sometime when I lay under my quilt, I hope for a clue bout a piece of blue.

I was four when Nana died in this bed I rest in. She lived with us till then and did the cooking. When she won't working in the garden, cooking, or canning, she held me and brushed my hair, singing "Jesus Loves Me" in a shimmy voice. I slept with Nana most nights to keep her warm. I rubbed her cold, knotty feet with my hands, and wrapped em in my scrap of baby blanket, and curled up behind her knobby knees with very close veins.

In the quiet of the night she whispered bits of truth to me. Nobody else said, "They shame to say it was your great-granddaddy gambling that won us this place. They kind of leave that out of the telling, don't they?" She laughed when she said it. Nobody cept Nana ever said a sin brought us to Baines Creek and give us a home.

Another time, she said, "Your mama got two stillborn babies between Brother and you, don't you know. Babies got started, but their little lumps fell out in the chamber pot when your mama's pains come early. They was no bigger than a doe's heart. Your daddy held em in the palm of one hand, they be that small.

"Church said a baby who never breathed on this earth can't be baptized, but Eli done it anyway. He built little coffin boxes for em and buried em in a corner of the cemetery cause your mama cried. Your mama and daddy worried bout them lost babies, and where the good Lord put em since they won't go to heaven."

Another night, she said, "Do you know what *Eli* means, child? Did they never tell you? It means Defender of Men. That's what my Eli and your daddy do. They defend all men."

Even being four, I wondered who defended us girls. I was too shy back then to ask. Now I know—it's nobody.

I smelled Nana's leaving on the night she died. The oil lamp stayed lit so Death could see to take the right one. It was just Nana and me when she pointed to the table Granddaddy built for her when she was young, when she could stay warm on her own. I got out her Bible from the drawer. The old book was falling apart from so much studying. I fit her fingers round it, and she pulled it to her milky eyes to read by the light of the lamp.

I should have been scared by myself to know Death was close, me being four, but Nana's face was peaceful and the smell won't bad. I missed her already and she won't even gone. When she passed, who would tell me the truth bout my people? Who would get the tangles outta my hair without the hurt? Who would sing "Jesus Loves Me" and make me believe?

More than Nana's feet turned cold that night, and me and my blanket couldn't make her warm. When Nana whispered, "Sweet Jesus, I'm ready," I heard him take her, like an open window with a breeze going out stead of in.

I took the news to Mama.

———

I sit up in the evening's gloom, foggy headed, but my headache is gone. I still feel the chill of cold bones against my spine and know Nana's been close. Brother is in the other room peeling potatoes and onions for stone soup cause I hear the peeled ones get throwed in the water bucket. I wonder how many times he cut his finger tonight and leaked blood on potato flesh. He cuts the skin thick and wastes a lotta potato. I keep quiet. Stone soup is his business.

I don't get up yet. I think about my dream and when Nana left, and her old Bible sitting in the drawer. That same table that sits by my bed used to sit by Mama's married bed. Mama often laid her hand on that table and patted it tender like she done a child's head. She never told me why she done such a thing. Now, I run my fingers over the smooth walnut top, and they glide to open the drawer all the way like they got a mind of their own. I take the drawer outta the tracks. I turn it over.

That's when I find it.

On the bottom.

Tacked in place.

A letter.

Mama's name is on it. Not to *Mrs. Eli Perkins Jr.*, like she was on this mountain. Not to *Adelaide Perkins* like she was all my days to family. Not even to *Adelaide Adams*, the name she was before Daddy claimed her for his bride and Brother and me came to be.

The envelope reads: *To Addie.*

My first thinking is *Why's this letter tacked to the bottom of Nana's drawer?*

Then I get me a odd thought about that scrap of blue in my quilt, and my heart beats fast.

I wonder if this letter changes things.

On this day of my finding, I don't pull out the two tacks that hold it in place. Don't lift the letter from its secret spot careful-like so it don't tear. Don't unfold the piece of paper that got folded a long, long time ago. I put the drawer back where it goes, right side up, and I keep Mama's secret safe another day. Now it's my secret, too.

―――――――

That big, old teacher has come to church today, and everybody makes a ruckus about nothing. Everywhere I go the week past, there's a buzz. At the Rusty Nickel, folks who ain't seen her speculate bout her size and her particulars and why she came to be here. Word got around her and me talked, so when I'm out and about, folks pester me.

Timid Alice Dickens asks me, "Do we got a man on the mountain as big as she be?"

Laura June Mayhew, who's usually mealymouthed, asks, "Is it true she wears man's trousers and don't even own a dress?"

Fleeta Wright, who's as big as a house and twice as ugly, whispers the question on everyone's mind: "Prudence, you think she be of immoral persuasion, being like she is and all?"

I do the Christian thing and speak the truth: no, yes, and yes, though I have no proof. Some things just make sense.

Brother's all thumbs this morning. He irks me something fearful, him a man of the Lord who don't pay close mind to what's right in front of him. He sticks his nose in books and looks for answers. He prays with his eyes closed and asks for answers. All he's gotta do is look and use the brain God give him. Case in point: Miss Shaw. Something won't right with that woman.

Miss Shaw's visit to church pulls strangers outta the weeds. Gladys Hicks hasn't been to church since Eli went to convention last and he stayed through a Sunday and we got a traveling preacher who played with fire to make a point. He was plenty entertaining, but he almost burnt down the church.

Today, Gladys marches right on in and steals a seat cause she makes Ellis Dodd squirm and get up. The regulars should be the ones to get the seats. I try to give Gladys a nasty look cause she's pushy, but for spite, she don't look my way.

Her grandchild Sadie Blue slides in the back row and looks like she's been hit with a sack of nickels. That girl had a bad stretch with Gladys's stinginess, then she married that Tupkin boy cause she don't keep her legs together. She should know when you sin against the Lord, punishment comes to the light a day. Her bruises are proof: Sadie Blue got in a family way without a ring on her finger. She's lucky the boy married her, even if he is from the bottom of the barrel.

I won't listening to Brother's sermon cause I got my own thoughts, but nothing prepares me for Miss Shaw to butt in the middle of Brother's talking, stand, and talk to us under the Lord's roof. She's bold-faced is what she is. A brazen hussy. What kind of teacher says to strangers she got fired for doing something shady, then expects a howdy-do and come on in? Miss Shaw will soon be gone by her own hand. The looks on folks' faces say they won't happy one bit. Still, after the service, they line up to shake her hand and tip their heads on the way out.

After Brother washed the soup pot, he gets home from church and says, "I think it went quite well, don't you?"

Even when it comes straight from the horse's mouth, Brother still wears blinders.

Today, I'll read Mama's letter.

It's been a temptation all week tacked under that drawer. Like a piece of chocolate wrapped in foil I saved, today's the day. I close the door to my room—though I'm home alone—and sit on the edge of the bed. I pull out the drawer and turn it over.

The letter's still there. It won't my imagining. I take a butter knife and pry up the two tacks holding it in place. The tacks leave rusty holes and a pressed outline in the paper.

How did this letter come to Mama? Was it slipped to her at church? Left in a special spot? When did Mama tack it under this walnut drawer her daddy made? Did she count on me to find it someday, resting every night two feet from my sleep?

I lift the opened flap and slide out a single folded piece of lined paper and one square photograph. The picture is of a teenage boy and a pretty girl. The sun shines in their eyes so they squint. They stand close together in front of a two-story white house with a mountain behind. The boy's shirtsleeves are rolled up neat, and his arms are strong. His striped tie is loose at the neck of his collared shirt. He's got a dimple like another boy I used to know. Light-colored hair sweeps to the side. The girl has got a satin ribbon in her curly hair. The boy is a full head taller than her, and he's got his arm around her waist like it belongs there. She wears a store-bought dress with puffed sleeves, little buttons down the front, and a thin belt at the waist.

In the black-and-white photograph, the dress could be sky blue with specks of red on it. The girl could be Mama, but that boy won't Daddy. Daddy's hair was dark till he got sick and turned it white. Daddy never was taller than Mama. I never saw the boy in the photograph. I don't think he's from round here.

The letter crinkles loud in the quiet when I unfold it, and I'm glad Brother won't home. The ink is faded so I step to the window for more light to see better. I feel funny is what I feel, cause I know these are Mama's private words she put in a secret place.

That don't stop me. I read the letter that belongs to nobody now but me.

August 21, 1917

My darling Addie,

I have to leave you, sweet girl, to prove I'm the man you deserve. I'll come back. Promise you'll wait. We both have

this picture of a perfect day. We'll have more days like this.
I'll carry this picture over my heart everywhere I go until I'm
with you again. Wait for me? If you do, it'll mean everything.

All my love forever,
David

I read the letter three times real quick, then count the words David wrote long ago. Seventy. That's how many words Mama held on to cause they mattered. *1917* is on the back of the picture like on the letter. That's near the end of the Great War that Daddy don't go to cause his feet was flat. Mama don't marry Daddy till 1918, and the next year Brother come along.

All my love forever, David. No sweeter words have I ever read. David asked her to wait. Mama had a perfect day. She had a picture to prove it, and somebody to wait for who won't a Eli.

Questions swirl in my head. Did David die in the war? Did Daddy know about David? If he did, was he jealous? I never know a boy to write words soft enough to break a heart, or tack to the bottom of a drawer.

I read the letter again and learn it by heart, David's words to Addie in the blue dress. Mama maybe thought she took this secret to her grave. Now it's mine. I put the letter and picture back in the envelope. I press the two tacks back in the holes. I put the letter back on the bottom of the drawer. I slide the drawer closed.

I lay my fingers on the blue cloth in my crazy quilt.

Funny, what started out as one question about this scrap of blue now growed to a long list of questions I'll never get answers for. Every time Mama looked at that blue, it told her what could have been.

Then, I lay my fingers on Susie Domer's rose I cut from her shawl and stitched to my quilt long ago. My stitches won't as neat as Mama's, but they hold okay.

Like I planned that autumn so long ago when Susie and me was sixteen, her shawl—left at the bend in the river where good girls don't go—told a lie her daddy believed. She shamed her family. Her daddy said he couldn't show his face with a daughter who don't know right from wrong. She gave away the milk for free when the cow's the prize. She got beat by her daddy's hand is what she got, then she got sent away for good. She don't take that shawl with her. How could she with all the trouble it brought her? She left it at church on the back pew, like a going-away present for me. I cut out that rose like she cut out my heart.

I remember thinking back then, *The hurt will stop when Susie leaves town. The hurt will stop when Thomas shows me his dimple again*. But Susie left and Thomas turned off his dimple. He stayed in a sour mood over a second-rate girl with a lisp who didn't know how to bake a pie.

For a while, I watched for him at church, but he turned so dull over time, I hardly knew he was there when he come. Then he was gone off the mountain for real. I don't believe it when somebody says he went and married Susie Domer. That thought makes me sick.

That same bad feeling I had with Susie Domer is one I have for Miss Kathleen Shaw. Nobody steals what's mine without payback. That big woman stuck a chunk of ice in my chest when she got Brother to say her name special from the start, her old like him and a jasper to boot. A plan starts private in my head, then digs deep in my brain and takes hold like greenbrier.

Miss Shaw likely got her own kind of shawl—it just looks different. I'll find it and use it against her. She's a slick one though. Said right out loud she was fired from her job so she don't shame easy. How do I lay blame on somebody who don't have the good sense to be guilty? I gotta get close to this one. Brother once preached on *know thine enemy*. This is the right time to do that.

I head to the Rusty Nickel with a short list of supplies scribbled on a scrap of paper. Mooney might be open and he might not, but it's not supplies I need.

I come to the schoolhouse and look in the windows at a odd sight. The children twirl and whirl with their arms up and out, and old Miss Shaw does the same thing. Even through closed windows I hear their voices singsong, *Autumn leaves are falling down, falling down, falling down. Autumn leaves are falling down, yellow, red, orange, and brown!*

At the end, little heads drop from sight as bodies fall to

the floor and giggle. Then the door flies open, and boys and girls with rosy cheeks spill out and swirl past me. I'm shot through with envy at simple joy that won't mine, and anger grabs me so tight I can't breathe. Miss Shaw finds me in the yard with my lungs not working, and I gasp for air. She takes my arm.

"Prudence, please come inside and rest. You look like you'll faint."

Against my will mostly, she pulls me up the steps into the schoolhouse and tells me to sit. I stay put and watch while she crosses the floor, dips me a glass of water from the spring bucket, comes back, and wraps my fingers round the cup. She lifts it to my lips, then sits close to me, looks down on me. Charity pours outta her sad cow eyes.

"You feel better?"

I wanna claw them pity eyes out of their sockets.

"I'm fine, Miss Shaw." I hold it together. Don't want feelings to spill over the edges.

"Kate. Please call me Kate."

I open my mouth to say her name, then close it. Her name don't slide over my lips easy cause my mouth is dry even with the sip of water.

When I stay quiet, she looks at the paper in my hands and says, "You have a list to get at the Rusty Nickel. May I help? Is Mooney even open today?" Miss Shaw stretches her neck out and looks out the window. I see a mole under her chin and a crease of dirt in the fold of skin.

"I manage on my own." I set the line of my lips firm. "If he ain't open, that's okay."

"Looks like you're in luck. The door *is* open. I'll walk over with you. I need to pick up a couple of things myself."

Lord, if that woman don't pull me to my feet and walk me down the steps, gabbing on!

"Never did thank you for your help the day I arrived. Your directions were perfect."

Is she funning me? I made her walk the creek to her cabin on her own that first day, and I been careful not to say a civil word to her since.

She's gonna be a tough nut to crack.

We walk in the Rusty Nickel and Mooney says, "Hello, ladies," and I don't answer. I pick up stuff I don't need and pretend to read my list and wait while Billy Barnhill pays for his dipping snuff and Grapette soda. I stand back cause he stinks. He always looks like he crawled out from under a rock. He's Roy Tupkin's shadow, so seeing him by his self makes him look lost. He leaves without a word or tip of his hat, then Miss Shaw starts yammering to Mooney.

"Thank you for helping with Roy Tupkin the other day."

"No need to say a thing, Kate." Mooney calls her by her familiar name.

"He was outta line is what he was."

"I was surprised he listened to you."

Mooney leans in. "Me, too," he says, and they chuckle too easy for my blood. He adds, "Like I said, that boy better stay under the radar or trouble will rat him out."

"Well, thanks for standing up for me."

"Just don't be alone with him if you can help it. Roy's

a stick of dynamite, and you don't want to be round when something sets him off."

I'm about to leave cause I ain't finding gossip I can use, when Miss Shaw asks, "Any mail?"

Mooney reaches under the counter and hands her a couple of letters and a slick magazine. On top is a small cream-colored envelope with fancy writing. The careless woman leaves her mail on the counter and walks over to the bean bin and asks Mooney the difference between two kinds of beans. He gets off his stool and walks over to her. I scoop up Miss Shaw's top letter, slip it in my pocket, and walk out the door. I remember to say, "I'm fine now. Gotta go. Bye," and put the stuff on the counter I don't need.

My heart thuds like a hammer against my ribs as I hurry cross the clearing, past the church, and outta sight of the store, proud of myself. I can't believe my luck. I don't know what's in the envelope, but I got private words sent to Miss Shaw that I'd never know bout if I won't brave. Like Brother said, "Know thine enemy," and that's what I'm doing.

I hear an odd sound on the walk home and find it's me humming! I *never* hum, but today, I hum "Jesus Loves Me" and I think of Nana and wonder if she's proud of me cause I'm brave.

I pat my pocket to hear the paper crinkle. It's like a Christmas present. I can't figure Miss Shaw has friends who'd write her a letter. If she had friends, why'd she run away from the valley and come here where she's not wanted? How could a body just pick up and go somewhere strange if somebody missed her back there?

All I know is I got a letter today that belongs to Miss Shaw, and she don't know it. What I'm gonna do is steam it open, and she won't hardly know I been inside. If I feel nice, I can get the letter back to her when I'm done. Drop it on the floor at the Rusty Nickel for somebody to find.

If I feel nice.

———

Brother's home when I come in. I say casual-like, "Saw Miss Shaw today at the Rusty Nickel." I inch into enemy territory and make it sound like something I say every day.

"*You* talked to Kate?"

My back is to him so I squeeze my eyes shut, mad at him for playing the fool. I'm the only one who can save him from himself.

"Yep. Saw her at school, too."

"You went to school?"

"Yep." Why is Brother surprised? I go places. I talk to people.

"Tell me about it."

"It won't special. We talked. She thanked me cause I was nice when she come."

"Well, that's good news. You saw her at school. Were students there? Were they happy?"

"Yep."

"Well, that makes me happy, too. Kate makes wonderful progress with our children. I think we've got a teacher who's gonna stay."

That's not the plan, Brother. Miss Shaw's gotta go.

We eat supper, Brother and me, and he talks to himself cause I'm done for the day. When he lights a lantern and heads out to his workshop, grabbing his oilskin against the rain starting, I take Miss Shaw's letter outta my pocket and study it. The front's got spidery writing on it. *In care of general delivery.* When I turn it over, there's a tiny heart drawn at the V of the flap, and my stomach turns queasy. Who'd put a heart on a letter to a big, old woman?

I hold the letter with wooden tongs over the steaming kettle on the woodstove till the flap loosens, keeping an ear out for Brother's footsteps on the porch. I take the opened envelope back to my room and close the door.

What would Miss Kathleen Shaw think if she could look through my window right now and see what I'm doing? Would she be scared? Would she be mad and *tap-tap-tap* on the glass for me to stop? I look out the darkened window and half expect to see Kathleen Shaw's wide face pressed to the windowpane, mist clouding her glasses, the rain flattening her chopped hair.

It serves Miss Shaw right that I do this. If I don't protect what's mine, who will? When Mama left, I got Brother to look after.

It's one piece of paper, so I open it slow to make the thrill last. It's only got a few lines and it starts with:

My dearest K.

Dearest? That word unsettles me. Who in the world calls

that cow of a woman *dearest*? Nobody never said that word to me, and I wouldn't know what to do if they did.

My dearest K,

I miss your company, your wit, your warmth. You've gone off the map to the end of the world to follow your calling, and yet I'm the one who's lost and left without a rudder. When you come off your high mountain, come stay, rest, and BE with me. You are my better half. Now I limp through my days like a worn-out shoe.

Love forever,
R

Is this what I think it is? My belly starts to rumble, and I feel sick something awful. What a bunch of mush for that old hag! David's letter was a sad note, a good note. This one's trash.

I don't know why I do this, but I count the words. I think of em as nails in Miss Shaw's coffin. There's seventy words in her letter, just like the letter to my mama! But this one's got a funny feel to it, and my bowels turn loose. I dash through the rain to the outhouse, quick, sick. When I get back, I don't even wanna touch that letter no more. I don't wanna say out loud what it means. I don't want something like that to even get in my ears and brain and stick cause I know the *R* don't stand for a Robert or a Russell. A man wouldn't have been prissy with his words. Miss Shaw's more than a thought. She's a immoral, wicked sodomite.

And to think she touched my arm and helped me stand up!
I run to the outhouse again.

———

I'm burdened about what to do with this bothersome news. If
Brother won't smitten, he'd do what's right for the good folks of
Baines Creek and drive out the heathen sinner. When it comes
to Miss Shaw, he's useless and under her devil spell. I was right
to take Kathleen Shaw's damning letter and uncover her real
evil. I gotta bide my time to think and do the right thing.

My dearest K…

Sweet Jesus, help me!

Right now I put that nasty letter back in the envelope. I've
never been this close to something unnatural. That's Daddy
and Brother's job. I bow my head to pray like they always
do, squeeze my hands together till my fingers blanche, think
and think, but not a single word comes to mind. I want this
abomination gone from my mountain. I want her to suffer for
her sins.

People gotta know. Miss Shaw needs to go.

I try to sleep on it but get such a fitful night my body feels
punched. When the sun comes up, I know what to do. More
eyes need to see Miss Shaw's sin. I wrap the letter in a rag and
put it in my pocket. I'll wash this dress when the deed gets done
and the letter's gone. I head to Fleeta Wright's house today for
pie and talk. Alice Dickens and Laura June will be there, too.
Help from those three women will move this along, as this
burden already grows heavy.

When I get there, the pie's been cut. A second pie sits on the side table. Fleeta cooks a lot and most of it goes in her mouth and straight to her hips. Today, it's apple pie. Never eat one without thinking bout Thomas. He ruined my life for a spell. He don't ruin apple pie.

"Prue, glad you could make it. Sit down. I'll cut you a big piece."

"Make mine a small one," I say cause I know she'll give me a big one, which she does.

"You too skinny, girl."

Next to Fleeta, everybody's skinny in Baines Creek cept Mooney.

I let Alice, Fleeta, and Laura June rattle on about recipes and babies and canning while I wait for the right time to bring up the letter.

When I'm about to open my mouth, Laura June says in a tight whisper, "Won't it terrible bout that girl what disappeared? Her folks must be worried sick, not finding a trace of her. We need to have Preacher pray for her. I already keep her in my bedtime prayers."

I know who she talks about. "Pray for her?" I blurt out. "She won't nothing but white trash who don't know the Book of Job from the Book of John. You ask me, praying's a waste of the Lord's time. He's got better things to do than save her sorry soul."

Laura June looks hurt and confused. "Isn't that what praying is for, Prue? To help a sinner return to the fold and know the Lord's forgiveness?"

I guide talk back in my direction when I say, "Y'all can

pray all you want, but we got more to worry about than a tacky lost girl none of us know."

Fleeta puts her fork down. "What worry?" The big woman slides to the front of her chair so she can listen better. The chair creaks unhappy.

I put a bite of pie in my mouth and chew slow and take my time swallowing.

"I come up on something that's powerful bad," I start. "Found it and picked it up as innocent as you please. I never guessed what was inside." I take the letter from my pocket real slow, unwrap the rag around it, and let the letter sit on the table next to the pie.

"What did you find?" each asks in turn, shifting from one worry to mine.

"I don't know… The last thing I wanna do is sully somebody's good name…"

Fleeta reaches over, breaks off a chunk of pastry, and pops it in her mouth. The three lean forward, pulled with the magnet of Miss Kate Shaw's name written on the envelope.

"That's it? That's the bad news? In that little bitty envelope?" Fleeta asks as she chews the crust and smacks her lips.

I nod.

"It was open like that?" she asks.

I nod again and figure if I don't say the lie out loud—if it comes out of Fleeta's mouth and not mine—then it's not a real sin.

"Prudence, would it help you if we read it? See if we think it's bad news, too?" Fleeta asks like I hoped.

I nod.

She wipes her fingers on her apron and slides out the piece of paper, and the three put their heads close. They read, moving their lips, sounding out the words. I watch their faces.

Their eyes float back to the top of the paper, and they read it a second time. Fleeta's eyebrows shoot up and she puffs out her cheeks.

"Oh, merciful Lord in heaven!" she whispers, stunned, and fans her flushed face with a dishrag. Alice and Laura June don't understand yet cause they look puzzled instead of knowing. I think they live more protected days than Fleeta and me. Then Fleeta says, "You explain it, Prue."

Shoot! I don't wanna be the one to poison their minds. However, now's not the time to pull back from the deed.

"I tell you what I *think* we're looking at. This is a love letter to Miss Shaw." I whisper, "From a woman."

Three thuds of my heart, and hands fly to cheeks, eyes flash wide, and lips look like they sucked a lemon. The ladies sit back and stare at the paper like it's a cow patty.

"What you gonna do, Prue? You can't do *nothing*," Alice says.

"What would *you* do?" I ask, needing partners in crime.

"She teaches our children!" Alice wails, ignoring the fact that none of us has children.

"Tell your preacher brother. He helped get her here. He can get rid of her." Laura June always looks for the easy way out. I don't tell em he's a fool for the woman.

"I don't know…"

Like I hoped, Fleeta says, "We don't need men to fix this. Leave that nasty letter with me and I'll pass it round. We get more women knowing her vile nature, Miss Shaw will break under the weight of the righteous and be gone."

"What you mean?" I ask, acting innocent.

"Give me a day to cast more eyes on these damning words. Then we'll go do the deed. We'll be a Christian army of warrior women is what we'll be."

"Tomorrow? Saturday?" I want this done bad.

"Prudence Perkins, you carried this here burden all by yourself. Now we can help you, sister. Right, girls?" She turns to Alice and Laura June, who don't say a word. Thank goodness Fleeta's got a strong way about her. "Let's meet at church at nine in the morning. I'll gather up some other Christian women who live on the right side of the Bible. We don't need the menfolks this time." She puts another slice of pie on her plate and licks her thumb.

Fleeta keeps the letter. I'm glad I don't have to touch it again or put it back in Nana's Bible drawer. Fleeta will put together an army of the righteous, and I'll be one of many.

I'm up early Saturday, get my chores done, and head to church. I don't know how many women Fleeta talked to, but she's not shy, so I think we'll have a virtuous army storming the mountain to Miss Shaw's cabin.

I get to church at nine o'clock and don't see anybody outside, so my heart drops. Then I hear chatter inside and find half a dozen women in the pews along with Alice and Laura June. I nod to em, glad to see Fleeta stands at the front in charge.

"Come right on in, Prue, and join the Crusaders for Moral Fortitude," she says in the loud voice the revival preacher uses. "We good Christian women aim to put a stop today to the evil witch Miss Kate Shaw and get her gone."

I nod in strong agreement and stand in the back outta the way. Two more souls come, and Fleeta says we're ready to face the she-devil. I hoped for more than nine of us, but at least I'm not alone.

I walk at the back of the group and hurry to keep up. I didn't know a stout woman like Fleeta could move up a mountain without stopping, spouting Bible verses against adultery and lust and detestable acts to our stream of *amens*.

We march past the trashy place of Birdie Rocas, who stands at the door, smoking on a pipe.

"Y'all head to Kate's place?" she calls out, snooping. "She know you coming?"

None of us answers. Don't hardly look at her. The biddy's never darkened the church door that I know of. If she did, I won't sit beside her. She's gotta stink something foul under a pile of dresses dragging the ground. Today, she walks right outta her trailer and tags along beside me. She grins and shows rotten nubs. Her pipe smoke smells funny. The wind must blow right cause I don't smell her too much. I keep up with the group; Birdie does too.

The lot of us is sweating and breathing heavy by the time Miss Shaw's cabin comes into view. Fleeta holds up her hand for us to wait so she can lean over and put her hands on her knees to catch her breath. She's wheezing pretty bad. Birdie just puffs on that pipe.

Fleeta straightens up, and when she gets to the door, she pounds on it with the flat of her hand. I don't know why she bothers, cause when we stand on tiptoes, we see in the window nobody's home. Piles of books are on the table, her man clothes hang on pegs, trash sits on her windowsill, and a funny bush stands in the corner. My shoulders sag from disappointment. I've been wound up tight with nerves that want to spring cause I want this done and over.

We look at each other, stumped, and don't know what to do now the steam's out of the day. I think we're gonna leave when Fleeta turns the door handle and finds the door unlocked. I thought Brother fixed the lock but maybe not. Fleeta says, "This place don't belong to her. It belongs to the school and to Baines Creek."

The other women follow her in as natural as you please.

I wait outside cause I can see what they do through that big window, crowding in that little space, sorting through stuff, pulling books off the shelf, fingering her things.

I hear a bark and look up the hill to see Miss Shaw and her stray mongrel coming down. She sees me and raises her hand in greeting, but the dog growls and flattens his ears. I step behind Birdie so it's not just me Miss Shaw sees. Birdie smells ripe up this close, but I stay put.

Right then I hear Fleeta shout, "Found em!" She comes out the door with a look of pride on her face. The other women are right on her heels. She holds up a small stack of cream-colored envelopes tied with a ribbon. I bet they got tiny hearts on the back flaps.

"Ladies." Miss Shaw arrives, cautious, and puts her hand on

the dog's head to make him stay. He could turn wild if she let go. She glances at her open front door.

"What can I do for you?" Her voice is tight, and her face loses its smile cause the Crusaders for Moral Fortitude have been inside her place. She don't know her skin's bout to be ripped off and all her evil drain out.

Fleeta holds out the stack of little cream envelopes like the one I give her two days ago, and she shakes em. "We know what these are, Miss Shaw."

"Do you, now?"

"And we won't put up with your moral ineptitude poisoning our children's minds or squatting on our property."

"Moral ineptitude, you say. Big words."

"Don't you sass me." Fleeta's eyes flash dark, and she puts a pudgy hand on her wide hip.

"What do you think you have in your hand, Fleeta? That's your name, isn't it? Fleeta?"

"You'd know if you come to church more."

Miss Shaw looks down her nose at us. "Ladies, you've come to my home, found me not here, entered without permission, gone through my possessions, and found a stack of letters from my sister. So what is this sin I've committed?"

"From your *sister*!" Fleeta declares with a *humph* and then says even louder, "From your sister! You think we was born in a cabbage patch yesterday and still wet behind the ears?" She steps closer and shakes the letters in Miss Shaw's face. "This here don't sound like sister letters."

We all nod in strong agreement. Some of them got sisters, and I bet nobody never got a letter like the one I found.

Miss Shaw looks at us one at a time, then talks in a calm voice that spooks me.

"My sister, Rachel, wrote those you have in your hand—although I don't know what she has to do with your invasion of my privacy or my moral ineptitude."

I don't expect her to come back at us calm-like. I thought she'd squirm at Fleeta's declaration. Instead, it's us who squirm at her bold-faced lie. What can we do to crack it open?

"I'm not in the mood to offer you tea today, ladies. This visit is over, and you'd best be on your way, for my dog grows weary of his patience. And please…leave my sister's letters with me."

My world tilts sideways. With one little word—*sister*—Miss Shaw might have righted a terrible wrong, but does she tell the truth? I study her face and don't see her flinch. I don't see guilt round her eyes. Don't see her afeard of Judgment Day. She stands there.

Then Fleeta spouts out, "What about them little heart thingies on the back?"

A quiver of hope rises. Why would her sister draw little heart thingies? What's she gonna say bout that? For a moment, I think Miss Shaw won't answer, but then she does.

"Though you have no right to information I would have given freely if asked, I'll tell you this. Long ago, Rachel was in a car accident that left her simpleminded. She is all-loving. She puts hearts on everything. I love her little hearts."

Laura June whispers, "I love little hearts, too," and we glare at her for the traitor she is.

"Now, if you'll excuse me, I need to put my home back

in order after your invasion. You may visit again, but only by invitation."

Miss Shaw looks down at us like we're a bunch a children who've been caught doing something wrong. She steps toward us, and we step back, not wanting to be touched. Some of the ladies act humbled. I know that weak look.

Miss Shaw turns and holds out her hand to Fleeta for the letters. Fleeta don't have a choice. She gives em to her before we even have a chance to read em. On top is the letter I took.

When she closes the door with the wild dog, the letters, and her inside, we take our leave, a bunch of wet hens to tramp down the mountain with the fluff gone out of our feathers. Birdie don't help the mood when she throws her head back and cackles like the witchy woman she is. Nobody talks on the walk down cause we got nothing to say to change things.

I think bout them seventy words and how good they was for Mama, and how bad for Miss Shaw. I never heard a sister write that way. Course, I don't have a sister.

It *could* have been a simpleminded sister, all flowery.

Maybe.

Today don't turn out the way I planned.

Brother don't need to know what we done.

KATE SHAW

I sit in Mr. Poore's Asheville office while he completes my final paperwork. It is a dismal room that strains my enthusiasm to teach at my next post. Everything is coated with nicotine yellow. Even the philodendron with sickly leaves curling in resignation, trailing over the windowsill. Even Mr. Poore, hunched over my paperwork, registering my teaching certificate, transcript, and credentials to my new school district. I pull from my pocket a handkerchief monogrammed *RH* and hold it to my nose for relief against cigarette smoke. The skinny man scribbles and pushes glasses up the sharp bridge of his nose. His worn jacket hangs from gaunt shoulders. Ichabod Crane comes to mind.

He doesn't look up when he says, "Last teacher called it godforsaken where you're going." Mr. Poore's raspy voice is ruined from a million puffs. "Couldn't understand a word they said. Like being in Russia or Africa, she said."

A hairline crack appears in my shell. I've only taught the classics in private schools and have no experience teaching young children. Will I fail miserably? Scare them away? Or will I instinctively know what to do? Outwardly, I stay composed, knowing this appointment is the final step before I climb the mountain before me.

Mr. Poore is one of a dozen worker bees in the Asheville education building, plodding through piles of endless paperwork. Every surface in this office, except the chairs in which we sit, is stacked with papers and folders. A transistor radio is slightly off the dial and plays "Stand by Your Man." The scratch of Mr. Poore's pencil nub on my forms is like mice in the walls. My skin itches. My head hurts. I need a bath. Petty annoyances, truly, when compared to the catastrophic poverty in Appalachia where I am going.

In the last decade, two presidents turned the spotlight on the plight of these forgotten people. Phrases such as *retarded frontier* and *hillbillies* stymie understanding. Disturbing photos of emaciated people, dismal data on teen pregnancies, incest, and genetic deficiencies point to desperate needs in Appalachia. Humanitarians want to save these scraps of Scotch Irish. I am in line as well, turning my back on privileged school life, looking for a place to matter.

My journey toward Appalachia started with an index card. *Wanted: Experienced teacher.* It was tacked to a bulletin board in a church I rushed into for shelter from a sudden storm. Some would call it serendipitous, others fate. Whatever the case, the church gave me more than shelter that day; it gave me direction when I was rudderless.

According to the letter from Preacher Eli Perkins sent in response to my inquiry, his mountain settlement called Baines Creek is barely a crossroads, a dot on a map. It's remote, embraced by natural beauty, and riddled with hardships. He writes that the census, which no one can vouch for, records forty-one children between the ages of six and seventeen in his school district. The preacher's tiny community has had a string of teachers for the one-room schoolhouse. They came but didn't stay. He believes youth and inexperience were to blame, and he asks for someone more seasoned. There is purity in his plea. A tenacity to care for his people. If there is a war to be won in Appalachia, Eli Perkins has lived at the front lines all his life and still fights. He seeks an ally.

I've fought inequities all my life on a different front but have gained little purchase among those who have too much. I want it all to mean more. I need it to mean more. My hope is that I am able to make those I'm leaving behind understand.

"Yep, the locals scared off the other teachers is what I'm told." Mr. Poore giggles like a girl. "Said they got no use for book learning." He mutters, "Dumb suckers," under his breath, then breaks into a coughing fit.

He looks up. "Why in blue blazes do you think you can do any good in that backward place? They don't want to do better."

"Preacher Perkins would disagree." I clutch the letter I've read a dozen times. "He thinks the children on his mountain deserve an education like everyone else." My controlled voice rises a notch. "And just because injustices never end doesn't mean they're not worth fighting against. Women and children have rights. Education is the key." My cheeks flush with familiar heat.

Mr. Poore plops back in his chair and, for the first time, really looks at me.

"You one of them gall-dang liberals, aren't you? Trying to bend the laws. Change the natural order of things." He

tap-tap-taps hard with his finger on one of the papers in my
stack. "Says right here you were fired. Now I know why."

I didn't realize my dismissal was a matter of public record.
I lean forward to see the paper, concerned. "Can just anyone
access that information?"

He ignores me. "Maybe you and that godforsaken place of
losers deserve each other."

I want to shout *You're rude and wrong!* but he's close to
the truth. He strikes another nerve when he adds, "Well, you
being"—he squints at a form—"fifty-one and on the hefty side
may be more to their liking there. They'll have to work extra
hard to run you off."

Mr. Poore crossed the line.

I say softly, "You're not paid much, are you, Mr. Poore?"

"What you say?" His face cocks crooked, and he pinches
his thin lips.

I speak louder. "You're not paid much, are you?"

I could easily strangle Mr. Poore with his skinny tie. Instead
I use words. "Apparently, the pay can't attract a professional
who knows proper protocol."

His eyebrows arch high just as Tammy Wynette belts out,
"Keep giving all the love you caaaan," and Mr. Poore and I
stare at each other. I hold strong, and after a half-dozen heart-
beats, he looks down and says "Well!" and stamps the required
state seal on my paperwork. "May you be happy in Baines
Creek hell, Miss Shaw."

"Proper protocol, Mr. Poore. You really could do with
lessons."

I escape with the smelly documents completed and a

modicum of respect, grateful for fresh air. Mr. Poore was unnerving, but he can't dim the deeper purpose Eli Perkins promised in his letter.

I need an ally to instill hope and possibility in my good people.

We all deserve hope and possibility.

Even me.

———

The calendar reads Friday, August 28, 1970, when I start my climb to the end of the world. I head to a place where only one person may want me, leaving a place where only one person will miss me. I'm surprised the warmth of summer fades quickly this high in clouds that spill over mountaintops, so my car windows are rolled up and the heater works overtime. Wind whips through treetops, and I creep around blind curves with rock walls on one side and drop-offs tumbling into loose air on the other. Gone is this morning's sense of anticipation as my headache tightens. I reach for the bottle of aspirin and swallow two.

On the first patch of level ground, I find the schoolhouse with its rusting roof and unpainted wood. A woman stands in the doorway with her hand raised in flat greeting. I thought Preacher Eli Perkins was to meet me. Just then, the storm unleashes and blots out everything behind a wall of water and I wait, grateful for a reprieve.

I sit in stillness for the first time in a long time, surrounded by boxes of my life. Another hand was raised to me last May, not in greeting, but to put me in my place. I lean my head against the window. Rain pounds around me and obliterates *here* and takes me back to *there*.

"You are dismissed, Miss Shaw."

That verdict had hung in the air of Dr. Virginia Collingwood's ordered office before I even entered. She added, "There's no need for debate. No one stands in your corner on this matter."

I hadn't said a word, yet she raised a small hand in protest. "I'm not interested in your side of the story...how you have been *wronged* or your actions *misunderstood*. Damage has been done, which I must spend precious time undoing, thanks to you."

Dr. Collingwood held out an envelope. "Here is a recommendation of sorts for your years here." She didn't pass it halfway across her expansive desk. She made me reach.

"My words may help you land another post somewhere. In return, you must leave today without further incident. And please, *please* do *not* damage our reputation any further or the consequences will be more severe than dismissal."

Ravenscroft, a century-old boarding school for girls in eastern North Carolina, is conservative and traditional. I am neither. Yet for the ill-fitting years I stayed, a rebel with a friend on the board as buffer, I'd skirted dismissal so often over issues of feminism, liberalism, and our First Amendment rights that I believed I was bulletproof.

I was not.

I stood, interrupting Dr. Collingwood, and walked to the door.

"Miss Shaw! We're not done." She raised her cultured voice in surprise.

The fight had gone out of me. "Yes, we are."

It was easy to put my life in boxes and load them in the deep trunk of my Edsel. I needed to break from this place for many reasons, mostly because I didn't fit. I never fit. I'm always crossing the line; rhetoric is a tedious adversary. My last rebellion was written across the painted wall of my living room in permanent marker. *No woman can call herself free who does not own and control her body.* (Thank you, Ms. Sanger.) How many saw it before it was painted over?

I shut the door to this place I had only borrowed, and the catch of the latch was final. The campus was deserted that Saturday evening, my colleagues off at dinners and movies, so I was spared good-byes. I drove away, numb, windows down, magnolias pungent, the only sound the crunching of tires on gravel. I passed brick buildings and empty sports fields and grazing horses. Then the heady pine woods enveloped me.

I saw lights ahead, like a landing strip. I coasted closer and saw students, my girls, standing on each side of the road, holding lit candles illuminating young faces. Folded notes fluttered through my open car windows. They held the wisdom of Gloria Steinem and Betty Friedan, which we shared in secret, sitting barefoot on the floor of my tiny living room, drinking strong coffee by candlelight until the early hours of day.

Last in line is Jen Carter, a senior on my dorm. She held the bonsai tree that had sat on her windowsill for four years. Her grandfather planted its seed a half century before. Jen loved the tree. It was her peace offering tonight, and a farewell gift I had to accept.

I cried.

The storm abates. I pull a canvas field coat from the backseat and slip it on. The woman is again at the door, waiting. She looks like a woman used to waiting, poor dear. Her age is hard to guess. Like these mountains she calls home, her shoulders are worn down.

I open the door and step over a puddle. "Hello. I'm Kate Shaw."

She screws up her forehead. "You that teacher from down below," she states.

"Kate. Please call me Kate. And, yes, I am she," I say automatically, and then bite my tongue. Judgment slides over the woman's hooded eyes, doubting already my fit for the task. I walk forward with extended hand and she shakes mine limply. She looks up at my height of six feet, two inches and likely questions my inclinations in such a manly frame. I blush when I'm winded or embarrassed. Otherwise, I'm plain as a pikestaff.

When she doesn't answer, I say, "I thought Preacher Eli Perkins was to meet me."

"Had him a funeral."

She doesn't introduce herself, so I ask, "What's your name?"

She stares at me, so I repeat, "Your name, please?" and smile, trying to soften her attitude toward me. She looks off to the side and mumbles. I think I hear "Prudence P…" but don't catch her last name, and don't ask again. She's put me in my place with her insolence.

I make small talk as we step inside the schoolroom. "What nasty weather! I feared the wind would blow me off the road and I'd never be found."

"We'd a looked."

I count eleven scarred desks sitting apart like lonely islands. A woodstove is in the corner, and a blackboard with a diagonal crack is bolted to the wall. A table for the teacher is center front with an oil lamp. A second lamp is on a window ledge. The glass shades are dirty. There's not a book. Not a piece of paper. Not a poster.

When it became clear I was taking this job, Rachel had asked hopefully, "Won't you miss teaching Chaucer and Shakespeare and Virginia Woolf?" I was cavalier, shaking my head. Now, my soul is chilled in this stark space that smells of kerosene and wood ash, with no electric lights or creature comforts against the cold.

"I'm sorry, so sorry you had to wait." My voice sounds out of place in this odd quiet. "I underestimated the time needed. The road was so steep…"

I stop talking and look at the woman. Her face is blank. I've never looked into such a face. The charcoal lids of her eyes are sunken. Her neck is creased with grime, her nails caked to the quick with dirt, her shapeless dress little more than a rag. One shoe is tied with a strip of cloth to keep the sole from flapping. This is poverty the likes of which I've never imagined except in the books of Dickens and the Brontë sisters.

"Do you know how many students will come?"

"Nope." She folds her arms, and I see the face of the enemy, hollow and hard. In the same instant, I realize *I* am the enemy, a threat in this hard and hollow place where she survives and I have yet to prove myself.

I fumble for the right words and sigh. "I come in peace. I simply hope to help."

I think her folded arms relax. Or maybe not.

It's only midafternoon yet night feels close. I'm tired. Tired from the drive. Tired of upheaval, judgment, adjustments.

"I'll get the rest of my supplies from the car tomorrow. Right now, I'd like to go to my quarters. I understand they're close by."

Prudence P drops her arms to her side, turns, and walks toward the door. I follow, thinking we're going to my house. Instead, she says over her shoulder, "Teacher's cottage got burnt down. Your place is up the creek."

"Will you ride with me?"

"No road where you go. Gotta walk the creek. Pass a trailer. You're next."

I dampen the panic in my voice. "I know I made you wait," I say, "but will you walk with me or give me better instructions?"

She won't turn around. She simply jerks her thumb toward the woods behind the schoolhouse. "Thataway. Mile or so. Thirty, forty minutes. All depends," she says and walks across the clearing.

"Depends on what?" I bark to her back in fear.

Prudence P adds, "Watch out for them dogs," then steps down the bank into the mist.

My feet don't move. My mouth is dry. What an awful introduction to my new life. Fear lines my stomach like sour milk and vinegar. It squeezes my lungs. I struggle to breathe. I close my eyes to center myself. My headache is a steel vise.

You can do this, Kate Shaw. No one said teachers got killed up here. Mr. Poore would have happily told you if it was true.

I have no choice but to move. I go to the trunk of the car and fill my backpack and satchel with items I'll need tonight: a change of clothes, raincoat, tea, crackers and cheese, and a flashlight. Last, I grab my walking stick, which feels inadequate for the mountain I'm to climb.

I feel the urge to rush to safety, to a cabin I hope will have a door to bolt against dangers that slither in the underbrush. Or a place to ward off wild dogs that wait to tear me to pieces.

Stop! I order my imagination, and hold tight to the trunk lid for support.

I lock the car, sad to leave its safety, and walk across the clearing, past a store with the name *The Rusty Nickel* painted crudely over the front door. It's a lopsided building with sooty windows. I peer inside and see cans lined up neatly on a shelf, bags of corn or rice stacked on the floor, glass jars of beans, and tools hanging on the walls. Taped to the inside of the window, a scrap of cardboard reads *Open Somtime.*

On one hillside I see the charred remains of a cottage. This must be where the other teachers stayed who came before me, living no more than two hundred paces from school. The sight of its remains chills me even more than Prudence's reception. A scrap of a red curtain flutters in one window like a bloodied flag.

Further up the opposite hillside, a whitewashed church sits

with a wooden cross nailed above the door. Likely Eli Perkins's church. Two small homes on each side of the school are dark, with feed-sack curtains closed. I haven't seen anyone except Prudence P, but that doesn't mean I'm alone.

For the first time in my life, I wish I had a loaded gun. Not the wimpy, pearl-handled pistol my mother kept in her bedside table, but something intimidating. Knowing how to use it would be a plus as well.

I chuckle weakly. Would Rachel even recognize me if she saw me now, cowering?

She'd expect more.

I follow the sound of rushing water that takes me beyond the schoolhouse to a worn path that heads up into the hills. I trust this is where Prudence P wants me to go. I note the time on my watch and start my trek, not sure how far a mile is. The bottoms of my trousers brush wet foliage. When the wind stirs, rain drips from leaves. I whistle weakly. Papa taught me to whistle when I'm nervous. He said relaxed lips help stress dissipate. Today it only helps marginally.

Soaring trees blot out the afternoon so I climb the mountain in twilight. I have to stop often to catch my breath, leaning over, hands on my knees, gulping thin air. I come to a rusting trailer on cinder blocks set back from the creek and see an old, stubby woman wearing layers of dresses, puffing on a pipe, standing in the doorway, watching me.

I stop, curiously comforted by her oddness, and call out, "Hello. I'm Kate Shaw. Is this the way to the teacher's cabin?"

The woman holds me in her gaze. Though ten yards separate us, I see wisdom, not resistance or rebuke, in those squinty eyes wrapped in wrinkles. She nods and points up the path with her pipe. I'm flooded with relief that she understands and answers me.

"Thank you. Thank you so much," I say and continue, on the alert for wild dogs. Plodding slowly, it takes another fifteen minutes before a cabin comes into view. It's planted firmly in the woods, bearing the scars of time, with moss on the shake roof. I knock at the door and peek through glass at simple furniture. I turn the knob. It's unlocked.

"Hello. Anyone here?" I call out, to be on the safe side.

I drop my backpack and satchel on the table. The cabin is one room with a loft, and already night shadows crowd in. There's the strong smell of mildew, a few puddles of water on the plank floor from a leaky roof, and a clammy chill. A sofa the color of dirt sags in the middle and sits under a large window. A field mouse scurries across the plywood counter, looks back at me, then slips through a crack in the corner.

I light a lamp against the gloom, and it throws shadows on log walls. I eat crackers and cheese and lean against the counter, then collect water from the spring to wash up and make a trip by flashlight to the gloomy privy, using my walking stick to knock down spiderwebs. Then I climb to the loft, grateful the mattress is dry, and collapse on my stomach with my boots hanging over the edge.

The next morning, I find I didn't bolt the door against my slithering fears.

The door doesn't even have a lock.

———

Today, the sun is out and the world is washed clean. I raise windows to a breeze carrying remnants of summer and start a fire with the kindling stacked beside the stove. Soon, water boils for a proper cup of tea, and with mug in hand, I open the door.

That's when I see it.

An indigo bunting. A blue bird almost too vivid to be real.

In a wooden matchbox. Chest plump, wings folded in prayer.

Missing its head.

I look around for someone who watches my reaction but don't see anyone. I think about the old woman I passed yesterday on the trek up the hill and instinctively know this isn't her doing. I'm more angry and sad than frightened. This lovely creature didn't have a thing to do with me coming to this place that doesn't want a teacher. He should have soared for years, eating bugs and bits and feeding generations of babies.

But I came. And now this. A small life has been sacrificed, and I haven't been here a day.

I find a rusty spade and dig a hole to bury him, box and all, beside the creek. I mark the spot with a flat stone. This is likely the kind of gruesome prank that scared off the other teachers. Harm on a small scale. Unless you count burning down the teacher's cottage. I may be out of my element, but I'm not easily chased away. Otherwise I'd never have lasted as long at Ravenscroft.

Today is lovely, and beyond my cabin is an expanse of sky. I grab my walking stick and continue on the path that now pulls away from the creek and leads to the summit. I gasp my way to the top, and my reward is wave after wave of mountains that fall away from all sides of a stunning view. Scraps of clouds float in the hollows and blend with woodsmoke. The world looks simple and deceptive from here when I know life is anything but simple, despite its elementary components. A dismissal, an index card, and a letter are all that's needed to chart a new course and end a former life.

I leave the top of the mountain, stop at the cabin for my emptied backpack and satchel, swallow two aspirins with tea gone cold, retrace yesterday's steps, and pass the trailer where only crows sit and watch. The forest holds none of yesterday's slithering fears. This daily walk will come to strengthen and fortify me. Today, I whistle easily.

How many students will come Monday is unknown. The last teacher reported seven showed up on the first day, and then numbers declined. There are no truant officers rounding up dissenters. I make a pact with myself: I will teach what I can to whom I can, and not lament the rest.

I round the corner of the schoolhouse and see a slight, barefoot girl with hair the color of ginger. Her white dress is dingy and the hem is ripped. She sits on the top step, clearly pregnant. Only a child herself. She carries a rolled-up magazine and stares at my muddy car. Her profile is delicate and her skin pale as porcelain with a dash of freckles.

"Hello," I call out. "I'm the new teacher, Kate Shaw." I shift my satchel to my left hand.

The girl stands. Though she's on the top step, I'm still taller. She shakes my hand and looks me in the eye. I like that.

She says, "Name's Sadie Blue," then adds like an after-thought, "Tupkin."

I say, "Hello, Sadie Blue... Tupkin."

She frowns. "Not used to my married name. I come to help if I can."

"Help would be lovely."

She holds out a folded piece of paper. "This here's for you."

"What is it?"

"Preacher Perkins. You won't here when he come by."

I unfold the note and read.

Welcome, Miss Shaw. I apologize for not greeting you yesterday when you arrived. I had a funeral to conduct. I trust my sister, Prudence, made you feel welcomed and led you to your cabin. I look forward to meeting you soon. We're glad you're here.

Respectfully,
Eli Perkins

I'm flummoxed. Could the learned writer of this note possibly be related to glum-faced, monosyllabic Prudence P of yesterday?

"Preacher Perkins brought this by?"

"Yes 'um."

"And Prudence Perkins is his sister?" My tone is incredulous.

"Yes 'um."

I pocket the note and walk to the trunk of my car while Sadie follows. "I met Prudence yesterday after the storm..."

I start to explain, then stop. I'll understand the dichotomy in good time.

I hand Sadie the globe and I carry the heavier box of books and rolled-up posters.

"Found my way up the trail yesterday to the cabin." I chat and unpack the box of supplies at my desk. "Managed to fix a proper cup of tea this morning, so all is right in the world."

I take the globe from Sadie's grasp, set it on the desk, and spin it. Her face opens like a child's.

"This globe represents Earth, the planet we live on. This area"—I outline—"is the United States of America, the country we live in. *Here* is the state of North Carolina, and your mountain"—I point with the tip of a pencil—"would be just about *here*." She leans in close, maybe hoping to see something familiar. I put away the few textbooks, lined paper, and pencils, and Sadie spins the globe.

"What's the magazine you carry?"

She holds it up for me to see and says, "*Country Song Roundup.*"

"It's special to you?"

"Yes 'um. I fancy anything with Miss Loretta Lynn's picture on it."

I don't know who Miss Loretta Lynn is, so I inch into unfamiliar territory. "What do you like about her?"

Sadie isn't fooled.

"You don't know Miss Loretta Lynn?" She sounds more than disappointed in my limited knowledge.

I failed my first test.

"She's only the greatest singer in this whole, wide world," she says, then adds, "I love her so."

"What do you love about her?"

She declares without hesitation, "She got a hard life. Sings hard songs. She found a way up and out of her Kentucky holler. Miss Loretta is a miracle to me."

I didn't expect such an emotional, concise response from this girl about life and its challenges in this remote place. When I pull the desks into a friendly circle, Sadie helps. I drag my teacher's desk into the circle, too. We sit down at desks facing each other.

She hands me her prize magazine. The cover picture features a pretty woman with high cheekbones and stiff hair with curls draped over her shoulder. I thumb through the pages, but the magazine easily falls open to page sixteen, and more pictures of Sadie's hero.

"Tell me what you like most about her."

The girl beams, props her elbows on the desk, and rattles off a string of facts and song titles about a woman who would inspire anyone who appreciates a hard-luck story turned successful. But she concludes by saying, "I don't read but a handful of words."

"Then who reads to you?"

"Preacher Eli, usually. It was him that got me this magazine from the valley two years back. I listen to Miss Loretta singing on the radio."

My heart swells, hearing this tender gift of a hero and mentor Sadie relates to. Eli plants hope and promise in rocky soil that holds little of either. This is a good sign that progress is being made against debilitating odds. I lean in on my desk and put my chin on my fist.

"Do you want to learn to read?"

Sadie bites her lip and looks down at the desktop, suddenly shy. She traces the carved scars with her finger. "Yes 'um, I was sorta hoping, but can't come to school regular."

"If you want to read, you will read."

She says softly with a hint of pride. "I already know me some words to spell. *Stop* and *go*. *Yes* and *no*."

"Those are good words. Do you have a favorite?"

The girl tenderly holds her belly. "*Baby*. B-a-b-y."

I look away as my mind flies back to Ravenscroft and the urgent knock in the night and Jen Carter's frantic face and her falling to her knees to beg.

Jen Carter's favorite word was never *baby*.

There's little to do in the schoolroom except hang posters and stack a few books on a shelf. Sadie follows me back to the car where I refill the backpack and satchel with more things to take to the cabin. I look like a hobo carrying my life's belongings. Last, I pick up the bonsai from the front floorboard.

"That's a puny-looking bush."

"It's a bonsai. A fifty-year-old trident maple tree."

"Bonsai." She tries the word.

"It's an ancient art form," I explain. "This one is quite young."

"What good's it for?"

"You've got a point, Sadie. It's beautiful to some people. A challenge to grow. A gift from a student." I stop, because the concept only has merit in another life.

"Would you like to help me at school?"

"Me?"

I've caught her off guard.

"Yes, you, Sadie Blue. I see potential when I look in your face."

She's puzzled. Few people have likely said she has potential except Eli Perkins. One moment her face glows, the next it closes. "Roy Tupkin don't take to learning."

"Roy's your husband?" I guess.

"Yes 'um. Got married Thursday a week back."

"Ah…and you carry his child."

She nods.

I shift my load. "Teaching doesn't take place only in a schoolhouse. It can happen anywhere and anytime. I'd be honored to teach you to read whenever we meet."

"That'd be nice. But I gotta git," she says quickly, as if remembering an obligation, and leaves. I hope I wasn't too eager with my promise to the girl, not knowing the risk she takes to be my student or friend. But she came to me, and that's a start.

———

September 5

My dear Rachel—

I've been in this hamlet of Baines Creek for a week and am still standing. I promised I'd tell you the truth about this

adventure, and for your sake and mine, I won't hold back.
Already I know accepting this post is what I needed to
do. What I don't know is who will be the more successful
teacher — the mountain or me.

Love,
K

Monday morning, I fortify myself with strong tea, brush
my teeth, then shake wrinkles out of my shirt. Preacher Eli
reminded families at church yesterday that school starts today,
and I'm more excited than I can ever remember being on
opening day. This is a day of firsts for many reasons. I don't
know if anyone will show. I don't have a syllabus or textbooks
but for those I found in a thrift store. I'll be judged by everyone, but the good news is my predecessors left depressing track
records, so I have nowhere to go but up.

I walk down the trail, whistling easily, and get to school
early, all the while nursing the perpetual headache that feeds
on thin air. The desks are separated again into islands, so I pull
them and my desk once more into a circle. The books and
supplies on the shelves have stayed where they belong. Two
bushels of apples that I bought on my way here are in my trunk,
and I put one on each desk along with the word *apple* printed
on an index card. I get the fat-bellied glass jar of penny candy—
Tootsie Rolls, bubble gum, Mary Janes, Black Cows, taffy, and
suckers. The trunk will serve as my lockbox for all things school

related. I write my name on the blackboard—*Miss Shaw*—then I sit at my desk and wait.

When I accepted this teaching post, Rachel was disappointed. She believed I had lost my sanity and was sacrificing my classical education for the rudimentary with little reward in exchange. She said I would quickly tire of the uphill fight. I said my whole life had been an uphill fight. What she chose not to see was how inspired I felt by Eli Perkins's invitation to become his ally for a better cause. In the end, she had no recourse except to wish me good luck and say she was there for me.

I went to the Asheville library to find the backstory on Appalachia and was directed to a pitifully small section in the dusty stacks. In all I found, the message was repetitious: this has always been an isolated community, stretching across parts of thirteen states, a parallel existence, backward from the civilized world that has morphed into the modern day, leaving these people behind. With their isolation come foreign dialects they've held tight to, and that I fear the most. To be understood and to understand is essential to my role here. Without that tool, I'm left powerless to do my job, make friends, ask for help, or offer it.

Printed literature about the Appalachian dialect was difficult to find, but with the help of a historian in Asheville, I found a recent paper by West Virginian Wylene Dial titled "The Dialect of the Appalachian People." I brought a copy with me to help translate. Prudence and I understood enough three days ago to muddle through our meeting. My concern is the children who come through that door and face *different*. My accent, mannerisms, and attitude will be strange. I don't want to build a wall between us.

But students have to show up first.

I'm enveloped in an eerie silence. Minutes pass, and I wonder if my ears still work. I strain to catch the wind passing through and am relieved when it whispers and a crow caws.

It's already nine fifteen. I check my watch every few minutes. Look out the window daydreaming. Study an industrious spider in the corner. Pick up my apple and polish it on my pants when I sense the arrival of little people.

The door opens and five children enter on bare feet, hair in tangles, faces dirty, bodies scrawny beneath thin clothes. They're timid and will bolt if I sneeze. I stay seated, for my height may frighten them.

"Hello." I speak softly. "Come in." They shuffle across the floor with tentative steps.

"My name is Miss Shaw. Please sit." I speak slowly and gesture with my hand.

They crawl up on the seats farthest from me and stare at the apples in front of them. "The apples are yours. While you eat, I'd like to read a story."

The younger ones look at the oldest for permission, and when she picks up her apple and bites, everyone follows suit and licks the juice running down their dirty hands.

Mental note: Remember a wash bucket and soap tomorrow.

I've chosen to read *The Story of the Three Little Pigs* for its fantasy and moral: when you think the odds are stacked against you, preparation can sway the course. Plus, what child can resist the rhythmic line, *I'll huff and I'll puff, and I'll blow your house in!*

Each page I read, I hold the book up so the students can see the pictures. Natural curiosity pulls them forward like sunflowers to the sun. When the book ends, I pick up the round, glass candy jar from the floor and set it on my desk. The children sit up straighter, all eyes on the candy jar. I'm sure it is a mass of sugar treats they've never seen in one place. One of the boys licks his lips.

"Who would like candy?"

Their shoulders sag, and the oldest girl speaks for them. "Got no money, ma'am."

"Oh, my candy isn't for sale. No, you can't buy my candy with money. An *answer* buys my candy, and then you get to pick the piece you like.

"Question one," I ask the girl with long legs and straight hair tucked behind tiny ears. "What is your name?"

She sighs in relief because she knows the answer. "Lucy, ma'am."

"And your surname, your family name?"

"Dillard, ma'am. Lucy Dillard, ma'am."

"Excellent."

"And how old are you?"

"Ten, ma'am. Mostly eleven."

Her name goes in my logbook, and I take the lid off the candy jar. I beckon for Lucy to come forward. "I asked three questions, and you gave three answers, so you get three pieces of candy." I don't rush her. She bites her thumbnail, deliberating. She picks a Tootsie Roll, a Mary Jane, and a red sucker, then sits down. She counted to three on her own.

"Lucy Dillard, ten years old, almost eleven, I'm Miss Shaw. Welcome to school."

On that first day I meet Lucy, and her two younger sisters,

Weeza and Pearl. They wear dresses made of feed sacks. Their cousins, Grady and Petey Snow, in bib overalls, have matching haircuts hacked and shaved and a sprinkle of scabs on their scalps.

I get information and the children get candy. Lunch is another apple, and in the afternoon we go out in the sunshine and sit on a quilt for our lessons.

Near the end of the school day, curious Preacher Perkins arrives as I thought he might. I'm surprised at how nervous I am at him watching me with the children, and I'm a bit ashamed when I sit up straighter and try to impress him. He stands off to the side and leans against a tree, arms folded.

Weeza Dillard, who just found her tiny voice, tells me ways to make poke sallet tasty, and she has my full attention. I think she says, "You soak them leaves in salt water, and you boil em, and you add a piece of pork fat if you got any, and you fry the stalks like okra. You can pickle em, too." She ends with a flourish, "But them berries'll kill you."

"Thank you, Weeza. I look forward to my first taste of poke sallet. And thank you for coming. See you tomorrow." I add as they disperse, "And bring your friends!"

I turn my attention to Eli Perkins. His pin-striped suit is worn to a shine and is sloppy in the sleeves. The trouser cuffs puddle over his scuffed shoes. One lace is tied together where it broke. To look at him, you would not think *smart* and *purposeful*, yet he is that and more.

"You didn't have a full house, but it's a good start, don't you think? That little Weeza's a marvel. I don't think I've ever heard her say so much."

I fold the quilt over my arm and head back inside. He follows.

"It was a good first day," I admit. I put the storybook back on the shelf, proud he saw the children answering questions and feeling at ease. "I want them to see school isn't all work and no joy." I erase the blackboard, pick up the jar of penny candy, and hold it out. Eli chooses a caramel, my favorite, and we walk out together. The candy jar gets locked in the car trunk along with the quilt, and I turn to face the preacher, who looks up at me and grins.

"Miss Shaw. Miss Shaw. Miss Shaw." He shakes his head.

This is awkward, but he's smiling so that's a good sign.

"Yes?"

He leans toward me, up on his toes. "Thank you."

KATE SHAW

The Rusty Nickel, which is *Open Somtime*, is open today.

At lunchtime, I leave school with students in tow, cross the clearing, and enter to meet the proprietor, Mooney. I hope the children will open social doors for me that might be closed because I'm the outsider who hasn't paid her dues yet. Mooney is another short man, but as wide around as he is high. He chews on a licorice stick that stains his lips black. Wild hairs shoot out of his ears, eyebrows, and bulbous nose and give him a look of perpetual surprise.

"Are you Mr. Mooney?" I ask.

His laugh rolls up and out and shakes his belly. "Name's Mooney. Only the po-lice call me *Mister* Mooney. You that teacher lady. Got you a bunch of scallywags with you today, I see." He reaches his hand across the scarred counter and takes mine with limp, pudgy fingers. He studies me while the children study the shelves in the dim light. A couple of them pull pieces of penny candy from their pockets and unwrap them slowly. Makes me wonder if they're taunting Mooney with their good bounty that didn't cost precious pennies.

"Heard you was a big 'un. And up in years. Won't exaggerating, was they?"

Mooney scrutinizes me but not in a mean way, and I smile, for my smile is the loveliest thing about me.

"Good to meet you, Mooney. I'm Kate Shaw. Preacher Perkins said you're the man I need to know because you have all the answers. When are you open?"

"Well, when the door is unlocked, I'm open." He chuckles at his direct answer. "Otherwise, it depends on the day. And what somebody needs. Things open here pretty regular cept when the road's closed, or it rains a lot, or snows, or it's time to hunt, or my knee's gone out. You need something, talk to me. I get it when I can. Always do."

"I'd like to order a bag of dog food, please."

———

For the rest of the week, more children come to school and find apples on their desks. Penny candy is just reward for answers. Potatoes in their jackets bake in the coals of the woodstove. Word spreads that school isn't all bad and bellies don't stay empty. I keep a list of mountain words I struggle with and consult my book when I get home. Pearl said, "It's startin to get arish," and that means it's getting chilly. Petey Snow said, "I brung in a cathead for lunch," and that's a large biscuit. The most helpful phrase—*Was you born in a barn?*—is thrown at anyone who forgets to shut the door. My initial expectation remains simple: pique their curiosity. Once joy is instilled, we can roll up our sleeves and go to work.

———

September 11

My dear Rachel—

I had a run-in with a dangerous man today—Roy Tupkin, Sadie Blue's husband. I had just left the Rusty Nickel across from school when Roy staggered out into the clearing, drunk, and locked me in his hard gaze. He's a leather strip of a man with a cocky swagger, and insecure as all cocky men are. He stared at me from beneath the brim of his hat and shouted unoriginal obscenities—"Hey, bitch cow, you even a woman in that big body of yours? Got any titties under that man shirt?"

Mooney, the proprietor, called out to Roy not to make trouble. Said he'd call the sheriff if he did. Roy took three long steps toward me, threw his arms up in the air, and shouted "Boo!" I stood my ground. I knew he was only a bully, plus I had the man by three inches and thirty pounds. He tipped his hat, smiled with dead eyes, and walked off into the woods. I'm truly afraid for the girl Sadie Blue and her unborn child.

———————————

Despite Eli's attempt to put a lock on my door that holds, while I teach, someone comes to my cabin. My books are moved from the window ledge to the table but neatly stacked. My wool sweater moved from one peg to another. The journal that sat on the table when I left in the morning is on the chair in the afternoon. The visits are daily now, and I'm left small gifts: a smooth rock the size and color of a biscuit, an unbroken wishbone, the shell of a robin's egg, the delicate skeleton of what looks like a child's hand.

Someone different and mean-spirited hasn't crossed my threshold but leaves warnings outside, hoping to frighten me. A blue, headless bird was the first. They nailed my privy door shut another day—when I wasn't inside, thank goodness. My tolerance is being tested, and I remain pragmatic as no real danger line has been crossed...*yet*. Rachel has warned me many times that I take chances I shouldn't. So far I've been lucky, and the pranks are dwindling because I choose to ignore them.

I have taken to heart Prudence's warning about wild dogs and, as small defense, always carry my hiking stick when I walk. I even bought a bag of dog food. I'm outside one Saturday, gathering armloads of sticks for the insatiable wood-stove, when I hear the bark of dogs up on the ridge. They're coming this way!

I drop my bundle and run inside, slam the door, and watch through the window while my heart gallops. A deer jumps the creek and darts past, followed by three dogs. Their tails wag. Their tongues loll out of their mouths. They're having fun instead of lusting to kill—they're enjoying the chase. I feel rather silly about the fear I let Prudence Perkins instill.

That afternoon, when I get water from the spring, I see one of the dogs has returned and lies next to the cabin between the door and me. His body is thin, ribs exposed. His mixed breed is the result of a questionable lineage, but he's bits of boxer and terrier. He raises his chunky brown-and-black head when he sees me and beats his whiplike tail on the ground in greeting. I'm cautious and inch toward the cabin door in case he attacks.

I speak softly. "Hey, fella. You okay?" He sits and looks me in the eye. His face shows trust. "Do you belong to somebody and forgot where you came from?"

He walks toward me, wiggles his skinny backside, and lays his lumpy head in my hands. When he pants, his mouth turns up in a grin so delightful I laugh. So much for wild dogs who want to tear me apart. This one seeks a friend.

I go inside and fill a bowl with dog food and bring it outside. He downs the food in three bites, then lifts his leg and pees. I take these as good signs, and we strike a deal: if he stays, he stays, and if he goes, he'll at least have food in his belly before he does.

I confess that the dog with the endearing grin brings comfort I didn't know was missing. He roams by day yet knows when I get home. I'm glad to see him. I call him Dog, and he lets me.

As promised to Eli, I attend church the next Sunday to be neighborly and to meet my students' families, but nothing more. I admit I've never been instilled with burning, blind faith, and I've had no need for it. Other than running into an empty church to escape a storm and finding an index card on a bulletin board carrying my destiny, church has never played a part in my life. I would love to think prayers are answered as Eli professes, but I'm a skeptic.

As predicted, people come today to see me, the newcomer—the *jasper*, I hear some call me—and I'm anxious once more over our differences. The men, in clean bib overalls and ironed shirts buttoned to the top, tip their hats but don't look me in the eye. The women, in plain dresses, hair knotted at their necks, and scraps of hats on their heads, are more skittish and only nod halfheartedly. The doors to the church stay open to accommodate the overflow, and people stand at the back. I look around for my students' faces to tie to parents. Lucy, Weeza, and Pearl are in the seat behind me, and they smile. They look like their mother, who sits with them, stoic, guarded. She holds tight to the smaller girls' hands in her lap. Hers are red raw, and the cracked nails blunt and stained. I clutch my smooth hands together.

Preacher Eli walks to the podium, and everyone grows quiet while he tells a joke, quotes Bible verses, builds up a rhythmic preaching momentum with what I guess is his practiced delivery, then the topic turns to me. His face grows kind. He says I am their blessing. He urges everyone to welcome me.

Then I ask to speak. My stomach is knotted with stress, yet I feel I must own my voice up here. I stand in front of these strangers, choose straightforward words and make the decision to be honest, though Rachel pressed me not to. Mr. Poore read in my file that I was dismissed, so the truth is out there if anyone cares to look.

"I left my last job," I start, then take a deep breath and start again. "No, I *lost* my last job because I helped someone and got into trouble. When I looked for another teaching post, it was Preacher Eli's faith in your children and"—I glance at the preacher in his oversize suit and add—"his faith in me that brought me here to teach. I am happy to be here."

I sit down, surprised my palms are sweating and my heart galloping. My chest is tight so I breathe slowly and deeply, aware I've spoken on erudite topics to groups ten times this size and never broken out in a sweat or elevated my blood pressure. I suddenly know that this primitive place and Eli Perkins and these plain people are important to me for reasons that aren't perfectly clear. That the restlessness I've felt all my life has started to subside and is being replaced by a flutter in my belly of excitement and wonder. Could I be on the right path at last?

Church is finally dismissed, and for the next ten minutes, the onslaught of names and faces meld into a blur. The odd dialect is a jumble to my ears. To the parents, I say kind words about their children, aware my words are as difficult for them to understand as theirs are for me. The overall dynamics are as expected: the giant outsider must earn her place.

Thankfully, the only stone they cast this day is in the soup.

The tragedy of the morning is seeing fresh bruises on Sadie Blue. Practiced at hiding her injuries, she wears oversize clothes. Her hair hangs across the left side of her damaged face. When she smiles, her swollen lips stretch to a grimace. Her aunt Marris drapes a protective arm around Sadie's shoulders, but the old woman's expression says she knows defeat when she sees it. This abuse is nothing new. I clench and unclench my fists by my side and know Sadie sees my concern and the anger in my eyes. She is embarrassed, but I want to lash out at the coward Roy Tupkin who beats a girl carrying his child. Unlike Aunt Marris, I can deliver serious harm.

The next Saturday, while I write to Rachel, Sadie Blue knocks on my cabin door. I haven't seen her this week, and I'm elated she has come by—and equally happy to see her bruises have faded and not been replaced by new ones. I've thought a lot about her, the pregnancy that led to the husband, and possibilities that hold her down by the anchor of poverty. Despite all those strikes, she's spunky. She's exactly the reason I'm here.

"Hi, Sadie. Come on in. I'm having tea. Want some?"

She steps inside, sets the beloved magazine on the table, and says right off, "That ain't good." She points to the pile of sticks I've collected to burn in the woodstove. "Burn quicker than a powder fuse. Need logs for your stove. Gotta be seasoned."

"Where do I get seasoned logs?"

"Jerome Biddle be glad to make a dollar or two chopping wood."

"Lovely. You solve my wood problem, *and* I'll get a new friend."

I pour tea and open a tin of cookies while Sadie walks over to my gifts on the window ledge and studies them.

"It's good you respect em like this," she says, picking up the biscuit rock, then putting it back down.

"What do you mean? Do you know who leaves these things?"

"Birdie. She lives in that trailer you pass coming and going."

"I saw her the day I arrived, but not since."

"She show herself when it's time."

"What can you tell me about her?"

"Anything ails you, she got the cure. Older than dirt. Used to live with a Injun. Got a crow for a friend."

"Why do you think she left the bones of a child's hand? It's so tiny and fragile."

"It's likely tied to a pure spirit, a wise spirit Birdie knows who walks these woods, seeing things, helping. This spirit likely watches over you."

I don't tell the girl I don't believe in the bunk of the supernatural, but it's disturbing to think of a child's grave being robbed or the child never being buried in the first place. I've never held bones like these, intact, delicate, tragic.

Sadie picks up a feather from the window ledge. "Birdie say you brave to stay."

"What tells you that?"

"This here eagle feather."

"She left that yesterday."

Sadie gently puts the feather down and walks back to the table. "Don't never hide it. Don't never let it touch the ground."

———

Sadie made good her promise, and Jerome Biddle, a lop-sided gnome of a man with a wispy beard, has come to cut woodstove-size logs for my woodstove. The day's labor produces a stack four feet high between poplar trees ten feet apart. In my naivety, I think it's enough wood to last a lifetime.

I give Jerome extra money to chop wood for the schoolhouse. Our desks have already been pulled close to the stove, and some mornings there's frost on the insides of the windows, but the mood inside stays warm. I love my time with the children. They're inquisitive and hardworking. They want to please me, and they do. When one of them misses a day of school, I make inquiries and let Preacher Perkins know, but I don't insinuate myself. I'll always be a jasper.

I find a milk supply with Eli's help and add it to the apple and potato diet. Attendance increases to between fifteen and eighteen students. We don't mind sharing desks, and Eli found extra chairs. We graduate from picture books to storybooks. No one knows how to read except simple words, so everyone starts at the beginning. I whistle walking to and from school.

———

The next Saturday, I pass Birdie's trailer and see her.

She waits outside the door, a squat woman with wide hips. As she was the first day I arrived, she wears layers of dull, long dresses that drag the ground, to which she's added a striped sweater, a paisley shawl, and a necklace of beads and bones. She reminds me of a homeless woman I once saw in New York City who wore a dozen layers of clothing—even a bicycle tire around her neck—to keep her possessions safe.

Everything about Birdie is knotted. Arthritic fingers grip a gnarled staff. Lips clamp a twisted pipe. A braided belt hangs from her waist. Cotton-fuzz hair piled helter-skelter on her head has a live crow nesting in it, for heaven's sake! Hygiene is highly questionable.

"Need to talk" is what I think she says before she turns

and ambles up the two steps, lumbering side to side. When she crosses the threshold, the crow lifts off and flies to a branch and perches.

Birdie's door stays open so I must enter or risk rudeness. I worry I'll embarrass myself, or hurt the old woman's feelings when I can't understand her or find her smell too rank. I sense Birdie has been my protector these weeks on the mountain and the giver of gifts, but I'm scared of what I'll find inside.

Still…

I take a breath, stoop low, and step inside.

Every surface—ceiling, walls, table, ledges—is covered with drying herbs, moss, leaves, snake skins, bones, turtle shells, seeds, nuts, and stones. Burlap covers windows and cuts light to a hint. Birdie's trailer smells like the deep throat of a secret cave: rich, earthy, cool, mysterious. It's potent but not unpleasant.

The crone sits regally behind a table made from a tree stump. Old books bound in cracked leather are stacked high. One lies open, and I see writing on parchment paper. A jar of ink and homemade quills from feathers are beside it. Oil lamps and candles light this cave of a place, and I think *magical*, not frightening.

Opposite Birdie is a low stool, and I fold myself down, down low to the ground, until our eyes are level. Then I wait, acutely aware of my breathing.

There's a dry rustling in the walls, and I wonder if the room breathes with me. All the while Birdie sucks on her pipe, squints through blue smoke, and studies me. I vaguely wonder if she has slowed time to a crawl.

Not that I care.

Cocoon.

That's what this place is. A soft cell of heady comfort and wisdom culled from a great student of life. Birdie's home isn't an eerie place. It makes me curious. Feel safe.

"Them things I give. You like?"

I'm pleasantly surprised I understand Birdie's speech perfectly.

"Sadie said they're from you. Thank you." My voice is mellow and easy.

"You even know what you got?"

"Sadie says the eagle feather means you think I'm brave. And the bones of the child's hand represent a spirit who watches over me."

"That girl smart."

"Do you know about the blue bird who lost his head?"

"That indigo bunting give his life for you."

"And blood and guts smeared on my door?"

"They done. Over with."

"How do you know?" My words leave my mouth, thick, and float in the air in front of my eyes.

"I been watching you these weeks. Make sure you was safe."

"You have? How kind." I feel drunk and loose, but I haven't had anything to eat or drink. It's just this lovely, marvelous, blue smoke.

"Did you tell the troublemaker to stop doing those awful things?" I use my little-girl voice I thought I'd lost.

"Kate Shaw, you done passed." Birdie's voice sounds far away. "This here mountain is pleased."

The last thing I hear is the *mountain is pleased*, and the next moment, I wake in my loft, under my blanket, wearing pajamas. I blink against sunshine and wonder if I dreamed the whole thing.

Miraculously, my headache is gone.

September 24

My dear Rachel —

Do you remember all the years I struggled to fit in at other places? How I longed to make a difference but felt I always fell short or was spinning my wheels, fighting futile battles? Do you remember all the self-doubts that plagued me before I came here, and all the fears and headaches that followed me to this end of the world?

They're gone.

Love,
K

On the second Saturday in October, in an iron skillet, venison stew simmers on the woodstove, thanks to Jerome Biddle's generosity. Oil lamps stay lit in the tin, dull day. Rain that won't stop prattles on, and the roof leaks into buckets and bowls I've scattered around the floor to catch the steady plunk of drips. The creek has risen and steadily inches toward my door.

I lay content, warm, and dry on the sofa with my copy of *To Kill A Mockingbird*, and Dog sleeps on the floor, happy to be out of the elements. Out the window, I watch Jerome chop wood in the rain. Then he stops, looks up the hill for something, then chops more wood.

Suddenly, Dog sits at attention and Jerome drops his ax and runs. I jump up too, and spill the book off my lap. Over the ridge, I see Sadie Blue, pale as the mist, make her way through the icy drizzle. She limps and clutches her tummy. I grab the blanket off the back of the sofa, hold it to the woodstove to collect warmth, and watch Jerome and Sadie's final steps. I open the door, and she collapses in the blanket's warmth. I carry her to the sofa.

"Get Birdie," I say.

I tuck the blanket around the girl, put on more water to heat, all the while thinking about Jerome scanning the hills like he knew Sadie needed help on the day the rain wouldn't stop.

In minutes too quick for real time, the door opens, and Birdie and Jerome enter with a sack of herbs and clay pots they stack on the table. Earthy fragrances crowd the air. I step back and watch Birdie probe Sadie's bruised head, arm, belly. She mixes a pungent tea, and while it steeps, she coats the injured arm with a green salve and wraps it in strips of cotton. A hot water bottle made from a deer or goat's stomach goes under the blanket and rests on the girl's mounded belly.

"How far along is she?" I ask.

"Not far enough," Birdie answers.

"My baby..." Sadie murmurs.

"It's Roy, isn't it?" I whisper.

Birdie doesn't have to answer.

Jerome watches from the corner by the door. Water drips off his clothes onto the floor. Dog walks over and licks the puddle at the man's feet. I stay out of the way in a cabin too tight for four people and a dog. Birdie spoons tea between the girl's blanched lips and soothes her swollen face with a compress.

This protracted scene in primitive Appalachia—in the throes of another angry storm that refuses to end, when political assassinations and civil rights battles and the birth control pill change tomorrows down below—is timeless and tiring. Who will keep sweet Sadie safe from harm's way? Not the church, though Eli undoubtedly prays every day for Sadie and those like her. Not the mountain or valley laws, which turn blind eyes to this intimate crime. Not anyone who sees consequences of today but can find no easy recourse.

My anger is focused. I want to dismember Roy Tupkin limb by limb. I'd use a rusty saw.

———————

Dull daylight wanes, and Jerome and I empty pots of water that catch endless leaks in my roof. He refills the woodstove. Now our shadows loom large and crawl up the walls and hover over Sadie in protection. We eat because we should while Sadie fights her fight. She shifts and moans and seeks comfort. Birdie mixes more herbs and steeps more tea and speaks soothing sounds to mend the damage Roy delivered. I sleep fitfully in the loft in hour-long snippets, wake guilty, and climb down the ladder as dawn creeps in.

The storm finally decides to subside, and Sadie opens her eyes.

"Hey," Birdie says. Her voice sounds big in the quiet where the pounding rain has lived for days and has gone away.

Jerome slept standing. He stirs at the woman's word and shakes each leg awake.

"Hey," Sadie says back and pushes herself up. Birdie stuffs pillows behind her for support. Jerome feeds the fire, I make coffee, and the tinge of color seeps into the girl's cheeks. Hope shifts to more solid ground.

"Is she over the danger?" I whisper.

"The day will say," Birdie answers.

The old woman steeps yet another tea that smells more rank than the ones before, so I step outside into the dripping forest with my mug of coffee, and Dog does his business. Jerome is back to splitting wood. He doesn't want to leave. I think he will find wood and cut and split it as long as Sadie stays. His loyalty is pure.

"Jerome Biddle," Birdie calls from the porch. "Come sit with Sadie."

He drops the ax and lopes in with a quick step. Birdie squats on the ground to relieve herself, then stands and lights her pipe. Today's smoke is green. I step closer, inhale deeply, and feel my tired mind clear.

Out of the blue, she says with a sly grin, "You ain't got no simpleminded sister named Rachel, do you?"

I don't hesitate. "No, I don't."

"You smart." Birdie cackles and shakes her head.

I realize, with a quickened pulse, I feel more purposeful, accepted, and liberated in this community than anywhere else. Suddenly I'm famished and go inside with Birdie behind me and fix buckwheat pancakes. We spend the damp day as a family of sorts, united by love for Sadie, who is recovering amazingly well, thanks to herbs and youth's resiliency. By midmorning, the girl stands and sips more rank tea without complaint, her hand tender on her belly, her movements easier, her face calm.

None of us are surprised when Roy Tupkin comes out of the woods in the afternoon, drunk, slipping on slick leaves, stopping short before he reaches my door.

"Sadie Tupkin!" he shouts. "I come to bring you home. You get outta that place with witches and dykes and shitty retards. They *freaks!*" Roy wails and whines and turns in dramatic circles, like a spoiled child onstage.

"You and that baby of mine don't belong in there." Roy howls like a wounded animal. "You're mine, mine, mine."

I look at Sadie looking at Roy, and I see how brave she must be to face the volatile danger of him every day. I watch her face shift, turn to granite, resigned. I want to clutch her arms and shout, *You deserve more! You are more! This is* not *your life!*

"You made me hurt that baby," he rants. "You got me riled is what you done. Made me feel small."

Does she see how pathetic he is? Does she *see* he is a war she can never win?

"Goddamn it, Sadie. Why you gotta ruin everything?" Roy runs down like a windup toy, drops his head to his chest, and sinks to his knees.

In the quiet, Sadie says low, "Him a big baby. I don't need me two babies."

My jaw drops, and Birdie claps and does a little jig. Sadie giggles and covers her mouth with her hands. Laughing, Birdie walks out the door and mumbles chants with outstretched arms and twitchy fingers. We watch little boy Roy back step, and slip and stumble, and his ignorance chases him over the ridge where the weak morning sun breaks through soggy clouds.

Sadie Blue still stands straight with her legs planted wonderfully strong, a warrior newly born. I take a step to hug her, and she grabs her belly, doubles over, and cries out *Oh Lord!* and instantly a tiny creature falls between her legs in a swoosh of crimson that splats on the wooden floor just as Birdie steps back inside. The old woman scoops up the lost hope in one hand and puts it in the empty bag that held healing herbs. Jerome grabs the bag, clutches the remains of a lost soul, and scuttles off into the wet woods.

Emptiness fills the cabin. It stretches thin around Sadie, Birdie, and me, three women who look for the *why* wrapped in grief that numbs us. Hope propelled the last day's efforts but now it evaporates.

All for nothing.

All for everything that matters.

Birdie finds purpose first and reaches for a clean rag. She dips it in the pan of warm water and wrings it out in hands as gnarled as tree roots holding tight to this mountain place. She kneels on swollen knees beside young Sadie Blue and washes away traces of her loss.

I get on my hands and knees and scrub the blood off the floor.

TATTLER SWANN

Like most folks round here, I live on Bentwood Mountain near Baines Creek all my days, and I scrape out a living in the backwoods that suits me fine. I don't need schooling or messing with a jumble of letters and numbers like that fancy teacher from the valley pushes. Mama says Preacher Eli's been by a time or two hoping to change my wandering ways, but I ain't buying what he's selling. He's good-hearted. Even had me try my hand at building a chicken coop for Miz Marris that still stands, but the building life don't take like fishing and hunting do. Truth is, this mountain and Birdie Rocas and them crows she hangs with be teacher enough. My mama Dottie's smarts fills in some more. Then there's my friend, Jerome Biddle.

Jerome Biddle lives at the lonely side of Good Luck Pass in a trailer that leans to the left. That don't bother him none cause his right leg is shorter than the other by two inches. He looks strangely upright when he stands in his little house or walks the right side of the mountain. But he looks off-kilter in the valley where land is flat and people normal.

Nothing's normal bout Jerome Biddle.

Not a single hair grows on his flat, spotted head, and his beard's a foot long, matted with leaves and bits of bone and bird feathers, and it flutters in the breeze. His leather skin is seasoned dark like a Injun's. His blue eyes washed out like a winter sky. You never know if Jerome Biddle looks at you or through you. He don't mind looking odd, but it scares the bejeezus outta me when I come up on him in the woods. I be hunting or fishing or checking traps and find Jerome Biddle standing so still he's like a tree trunk.

I say, "Jerome Biddle, why you standing like that? You got nothing better to do?"

And the odd man answers real careful so only his mouth moves and words slide sideways through the crack of his lips. "I plant this tree to tie me to eternity."

Or he says, "I listen to the moaning of time and take it to the borderline."

Jerome Biddle calls his self a poet. I say he speaks in riddles, and stuff like that don't do a body good. I know what I talk bout cause Saturday brings trouble neither of us is ready for—least of all Jerome Biddle.

The river is worrisome high after six days rain. My lucky fishing spot on the riverbank is underwater, and I finally take to scooting out on a sycamore tree felled over thick water and drop a line. I know no fish will likely pay attention to my worm in the churning water. I'm more gambler than Mama likes. Plus I got me a streak of lazy. She sometime says, "Tattler Swann, you waste more time than is good for a soul that's gotta feed and clothe his self."

I say with a smile that always turns her soft, "Mama, don't worry none. Life's too short to work all day. I got time enough to do the necessary."

So, Saturday late afternoon, I sit on a tree that fell across water rushing so loud I can't hear nothing but the rushing. While I dangle a fishing line with weak hope in the strong-willed water, I look and spy Jerome Biddle downstream two hundred paces on the rocky bank. The man's got a burlap sack throwed over his crooked shoulder, and the bottom of the poke looks bloody. Black blood drips down his shirttail, down the back of his pants, and into the heels of his moccasins. He looks back to the woods like something fearful is coming. He's crying, too, wiping his nose on his raggedy sleeve. I forget fishing and turn curious bout my friend's blubbering and that bloody sack.

So I scoot back cross the log to the bank and think to follow Jerome when I hear over the water's din coonhounds coming along the ridge, hot on a trail. They make a racket, and I can tell them owners hold tight to the leashes to keep em from running free just yet. I look back downstream and see Jerome Biddle, chest high in the tangled river, battling the current. He holds tight to the poke that's mostly underwater now. He works his way round a big boulder with a crack in the side, then ducks down and don't come up.

My friend crawled into the rock the weight of water and time wore out hollow. It's got air enough on a regular day to last for a good while, cept this won't no regular day with the water high. The seed of worry gets planted in the back of my mind. Few folk know the hiding spot cept me and Jerome Biddle and the Stoner boys from Rock Hall who hid from revenuers one night and caused a bunch of head scratching.

I look back up the hill as three men and a pack of dogs

swoop down my way. I still clutch my fishing pole when the strangers slap up against my space with their sweaty heat.

Boss Man carries a rifle on his shoulder, a wad of chew in his cheek, and a mean edge. He looks vaguely like my daddy I see once when he come by the house to see Mama. She blocked the door and won't let him in, but he was coming in anyway till he caught sight of me and stopped. Raised his eyebrow at my five-year-old self. Stared at me and saw responsibility he can't handle and ownership he won't claim. He turned round and marched off that porch without a glance back or a fare-the-well.

Without looking my way, Mama held out one arm, and I walked into her comfort and leaned into her warm side while she leaned into the hard doorframe. We watched the man cross the yard and head down the road. I remember him chewing tobacco and his jaw working. His hair was clipped short enough to see his scalp. His ears stuck out like mine. Most of all, I remember his mean edge.

"That's your daddy, Tattler. You won't never see him again."

My mouth goes dry looking at Boss Man who won't my daddy but could be. The big man raises his voice over the stirred-up water and the racket the dogs make.

"What's your name, boy?"

I raise my voice, too. "Tattler Swann, sir." Mama taught me to be mindful of my elders.

"You from round here?"

"Over a couple of ridges thataway, sir." I point.

"What's your folks' names?"

"Dottie Swann's my mama. Got no daddy to speak of."

"You been here long?"

"All my life."

At my sass, Boss Man's lips draw a stingy line cross his pocked face. "Don't get smart-assed with me, boy. I ask if you been here at the river long." His black eyes hold a puny soul.

"Long enough, sir."

He cocks his head to the dangerous side. "You itching for a whipping? What kind of answer's that?"

"Long enough to get tired of fishing. Ain't caught nary a one."

Boss Man stares at me hard. Tries to make me squirm.

I stay put. I can wait out the best of em when I aim to.

Finally the man says, "Did you see a odd-looking man come this way?"

"What kinda odd?"

"Bald head. Straggly beard. Carrying a poke."

I size up the posse and know they ain't in no talking mood. They shoot Jerome Biddle in the back and never think to ask questions till too late. I vex em for spite.

"That depends."

"On what?"

"What day you mean."

"What day? What *day*?"

The veins on Boss Man's neck bulge like fat night crawlers I want to stick a fishhook through, but don't think a fish would even take the bait.

"Today, you little snot-nosed bastard! *Now!* We know we're on his trail. I'm trying to pinpoint his lead time on us. Have you seen him or not?"

I don't know most of these men. They ain't from round here. One feller I know from Roy's moonshine business I come up on in the woods awhile back. I hightailed it outta there before they see me cause I don't borrow trouble if I can help it.

Before I answer, my belly squirms. Lying does that to me. So I say, "I don't see no odd-looking man. Maybe he come to the river in a different place than here," and my belly calms down cause it's true; Jerome Biddle won't odd looking to me no more. When I look at the little man, I see goodness and a tender soul.

The first time Jerome Biddle saved me, I was seven and fell down a old well shaft, mostly dry. Landed in soft mud and scattered bones of critters who fell in and can't get out. The scariest was finding a human skull bashed in. I thought I was a goner for sure. I twisted my ankle and don't have a prayer for climbing up the slick walls. Still, I yelled and cried and screamed till my voice quit on me, thinking this might be my bones' final resting place, too. Then I prayed real hard for a real live miracle, and Jerome Biddle's head leaned over the well.

He say, "Tattler Swann, hang on to hope, gonna tie me a knot and throw you my rope."

And he did.

Jerome Biddle looped his end of the rope round a tree

trunk and pulled till I popped out the top of that well, muddy and wore out. I fainted is what I done. My friend carried me home to Mama.

The next time he saved me I was ten and broke my leg when I fell through a rotten tree stand, hunting on Scooter's Ridge. The end of my broken shin shot clear through my britches. The sight of it made me want to faint and got me to bawling like a sissy girl. It was shameful is what I remember most.

Along come Jerome Biddle like my savior-in-waiting again. He don't pay no mind to my crying. Just went to work tying my broke leg to a straight branch, made me a crutch from another branch, and then hobbled with me all the way back home cause I was already too heavy for him to carry.

When Mama saw us, she said, "Jerome Biddle, you done it again. My boy used up one more of his nine lives, and you the one to bring him back to safety. You a angel and that's a fact."

Mama got a soft spot for Jerome Biddle, and when he shows up at mealtime, he's got a place. The next day or two she finds rabbit or possum or a mess of pigeons hanging from the nail on the porch post, and she knows Jerome looks after us. He's the best kind of friend.

The three men turn to leave and head to the riverbank when I think to ask, "What he do?"

Boss Man spit a sharp stream of tobacky juice toward my shoe. He misses by a foot. "You not worth the breath I waste on you." He shakes his head sorrowful-like. "Come on, boys. Let's catch us a baby killer."

They head on downriver where the dogs lead, determined, and I drop to my haunches and watch em go.

Baby killer? Jerome Biddle don't have a baby. He don't even have a hunting dog. He's got friends like me, Birdie, and Miss Sadie, and that teacher lady...and the Stoner boys who keep him in moonshine. The only thing he can call his own is a trailer that leans to the left, and a leg too short for normal.

The pack of hounds get to where Jerome Biddle waded in, and they beat up on top of one another when the scent runs out at water's edge. I can tell none of the posse wants to enter the rolling river from the way they back away from the water. They point fingers and flap arms that go on for a minute or two with nary a foot put in the water. I glance at the heartless rock that holds Jerome Biddle and his bloody sack, and wonder how much air is left for him to breathe. I look back at the men who don't know how close they are to Jerome Biddle. God must feel like this all the time—to know more than regular folks do and keep it to his self.

The men are in a fix. Boss Man grabs two dog leashes from one of the fellas' hands and pushes him into the water. He must be the one who can swim. He holds his hands high—to keep em dry, I guess—and makes it to the middle before he gets bowled over by the current and floats downstream with his head dancing like a bobber.

Boss Man don't look happy. He spits tobacky and walks on down the riverbank and looks for a easy place to cross. Him and the other men go, dragging the yelping dogs. They don't look happy neither. Their ruckus echoes off the stone walls of the mountainsides. A heap of frustration is pulled down that riverbank. They take their sweet time. I watch, hunkered down on my heels. I lean on my fishing pole to keep from tumbling downhill.

Soon, the sun falls behind the ridge and cold crawls out the ground, and the three layers of cardboard in my shoes go damp clean through. The posse's still in sight when my knees cramp and make me stand and lean on a poplar tree. Even when the hoot owl calls out close and a slice of moon climbs overhead and throws down stingy light, I wait for the men to go home.

They do when night comes.

———————

I'm ready to leave my spot and hurry to the river to pull Jerome out of that heartless rock when a specter floats through the woods in a white dress and pale skin. It heads for that riverbank.

Though I don't believe in spirits, I hang back and watch it. My heartbeat is on the rise, and I lick my lips a time or two cause they dry. The ghost slows its pace when it gets to the rocky shore and wrings its hands. It looks at the rock like it can see the secret buried in the heart of that stone. Then the phantom, with arms and legs as white as bone, wades into those whirling waters. Sheer cloth rides on the surface, and long hair streams behind, and thin arms paddle.

Then it sinks outta sight!

I can't help it. I start downhill to get close. I part fall and part slide. A shoe comes off and gets left in the leaves. My sock's got a hole big enough for three toes to come through. Before I know it, I stand on the damp chill of the riverbank and pray in earnest, holding my breath to see what's likely to happen and what's not. When my lungs about burst from worry, a small white head pops up. Then comes Jerome Biddle pulled by its pale arm.

The ghost calls out above the din of the water, "Help me, Tattler."

It shocks me! It knows my name!

"Who are you?" I ask, fearful.

"Sadie. Sadie Blue. Sadie Tupkin." Her teeth rattle from the cold.

I wade in fast and grab holt of Jerome Biddle and Sadie's icy arm. We pull our friend up on the bank away from the strength of the current and lay him down. The poke tied round his waist is flat.

Sadie moves Jerome's soggy beard to the side, puts her ear on his chest and listens, then says, "Build a fire, Tattler. I hear a tiny beat under his ribs."

We get dry twigs and leaves stashed under rocks and logs, and right next to Jerome Biddle's cold body, we coax a little starter blaze. Then some heat comes, then serious comfort. I pack a wall of evergreen branches and moss behind his back to keep the warm from wandering up the hillside. Sadie's lap is Jerome Biddle's pillow. She lays her small hand on his bald head and keeps it there. In the golden flames, she don't look real. She looks like the porcelain doll Mama's got on a shelf to keep away from breaking.

Eyes steady on Jerome Biddle's face, she asks me, "I scare you, Tattler? Think I was a haint?"

I cannot tell a lie. "The thought crossed my mind."

I ain't seen much of Sadie Blue since Roy Tupkin up and married her on a bet back in late summer, her carrying his baby. That's what I hear rumored some months back, and don't believe it's true till I hear it again. Sadie don't belong with Roy and his meanness. I think I see bruises on her skin. It could be from the fire glow casting shadows. I don't wanna look close. Don't wanna know, but I *am* curious; Roy don't seem the kind that would take favorable to his wife running off in the night to save Jerome Biddle. Maybe he's off on mischief of his own.

My head is stuffed with questions that need answers but I bide my time. We won't go nowhere fast. We gotta wait for a froze man to thaw.

I try to think what else Boss Man could have said besides *baby killer*. The churning water made it hard to hear. *Broken tiller. Basic miller.* Nothing makes sense.

When the fire cracks and shifts and a column of sparks flares up in the air like a little celebration, Jerome Biddle flutters his clumpy eyelashes, snorts a little air, and farts. Then he opens his eyes and talks a rhyme that's off. He says "Hey, Miss Sadie, lady. Hey, Tattler, baby" like it's natural for the lot of us to be on a riverbank, in the middle of the night, beside a fire, with his bald head in Sadie's lap.

"Hey, Jerome Biddle," I say, feeling kind of foolish, and wonder why he called me a baby.

He sits up straight and cracks his back and shakes his head

and gets back to his kinda normal fast. Even his matted beard dried and now flutters in a breeze like usual.

He pulls the soggy sack up on his lap and holds it tender. His lips hardly move, and he riddles, "I tried, Miss Sadie, and failed you bad; and now you got nothing and my heart be sad."

"This ain't your fault, Jerome. You my good friend. I'm sad Roy sent them scalawag men after you. He done it for spite, like everything he does. He wanted to scare you and get back at me. I'm sorry for your hurt."

I look back and forth from face to face for clues; I'm bout to pop with curiosity.

"It's a good life I dragged to shore today. With Tattler's help, you was resurrected." She reaches over and pats the back of my hand.

I puff up for no particular reason.

Then Sadie says, "We best get going."

"What? Wait!" I shout louder than I want. I got questions. "How'd you know he was in the heartless rock, Miss Sadie?"

"He told me."

"Nobody knows that secret place."

"*You* know."

"Well, yeah, but how'd you know he was here today?"

"He told me."

She stands and pulls a shaky Jerome Biddle to his feet. He still holds on to that flat sack that's not bloody no more cause the raging river washed it clean. He leans toward the riverside on his short leg.

"You okay?" she asks Jerome Biddle with a tender tone.

The man nods and stares somewhere over her shoulder into

the night. The fire's dying, and our forms are turning darker under the meager light of the moon.

"Where ya'll going?"

"Home. Jerome will walk me part way."

"I wanna go with you."

"You go on home, Tattler. Dottie be fretting."

I can't help myself so I blurt out, "What bout the baby? The one what got killed? Was that your baby?"

"There won't no live baby," Sadie says as she works her way across the stony shore, heading back up the hill. "Just a pile of hope."

"That what's in that sack there? A pile of hope?"

"Not no more."

They move on and get folded into the night.

"Well, tell me this," I shout with a tinge of annoyance that I'm not proud of. "Is Jerome Biddle a baby killer or not?"

"Tattler Swann!" Sadie stops in her tracks, turns, and in the final glow of the fire, I see her put her hands on her hips. She's more grown than I know her to be. It feels like Mama there scolding me, but Sadie is but a handful of years older than me.

"No baby got born today. No baby got killed today."

"Well then, why'd those men hunt after Jerome Biddle and call him a baby killer? Tell me that," I yell to her narrow back as she walks away.

"Roy was being spiteful. There won't no baby to talk of," she says, sad and tired. "It'll grow clear when the sun comes up."

The last thing she say is, "Don't be spreading falsehoods, Tattler. You hear?"

Jerome Biddle and Miss Sadie get swallowed by the inky black. I kick at the coals and make the fire go out.

What started as a regular day of fishing turned into commotion that don't usually live here. Usually things are pretty much like they supposed to be, cept today.

Today, a bloody sack, a posse of mean men, and a friend who almost drowned but come out alive made it different.

Today, I went to catch supper and hooked a mystery.

I head uphill. Gotta find my shoe.

SADIE BLUE

I never knowed a woman like Miss Kate. She's book smart but mountain dumb. If it won't for me and Birdie and Jerome Biddle looking after her, she'd be in a pile of trouble, not knowing seasoned wood from green, a black snake from a copperhead, or buckeyes from chestnuts. She's got her a puny tree she watches over that won't worth the time, and a pile of books that'll take a hundred years to cipher. Found her a wild dog she tamed with a look and a need. She liked me from the first. We gotta good start her teaching me to read.

I go to Miss Kate's place last week when Roy beat me extra and I lose my baby. It was on Saturday, October 10, this happened. I put a little heart on the wall calendar so I never forget. After that day I lose my baby, I find strength enough to save Jerome Biddle from Roy's meanness, then go to the trailer and grieve on my own.

Preacher Eli brung me a Hershey bar from the Rusty Nickel. Miss Kate comes and reads till she stops, then marks the page with a turkey feather. Aunt Marris and Birdie brung soup and tea. They don't talk but brush my hair, wash my face, and change my dress. They wrap me in a blanket like I'm the baby that got lost. Words and doing don't matter to me yet. I'm in a empty place, and bit by bit the days and nights spin, and I start to knit back together.

Roy stays away.

From the first, Miss Kate said, "I see potential when I look in your face, Sadie Blue." I think my baby was my potential, but I don't carry it no more. Now I try to wrap my thinking round something big with only me in it. Miss Kate can help cause she lived for a long spell in the valley, then come up here to live different. I need to know how to live different.

So Sunday morning, when Roy Tupkin is still off somewhere, I get up from my bed, throw on a thick shawl Birdie give me, and walk over to Miss Kate's to talk. Some weeks back she ask a question that buffaloed me. She said, "What do you plan to do with your one special life, Sadie Blue?"

I think it's a trick question. I might *plan* to go to church, or *plan* to go to Granny's, or *plan* to put up jelly. I'm working on a *plan* so Roy don't beat me, but that's a lotta planning things that don't make my life special.

When I get to her cabin, I see through the window Miss Kate sitting at the table, writing in that leather book of hers. She must hear the leaves crunch under my shoes cause she looks up, sees me, and runs to open the door to give me a hug, careful not to squeeze me tight.

I take off my shawl and say kinda quick, "If I got a special life to plan, then I'm in a pickle cause nobody told me and I don't know the first thing bout how."

Her eyebrows shoot up. She laughs and says, "Hello to you, too, Sadie Blue," and goes to fixing tea.

"Hey," I say back, remembering my manners.

She says, "You look stronger today, and that's wonderful. You've even got a little color in your cheeks. Now take a deep breath and we'll sort this out." Miss Kate's face is tender as she takes mugs off the shelf, sets them on the table, then slides her writing book and pen to the side before she sits down.

"So…you want to know how to plan your special life?"

I nod, kinda ashamed to blurt out like that.

"Okay." She shifts her bottom in the chair and holds up a finger. "First truth. Everyone is born with talents, with gifts and the ability to dream."

"Everybody?"

"Yes. Without exception. A person may choose not to use them, or may ignore them, or never even look for them, but they're there. Some talents are obvious. People are born craftsmen and build wonderful furniture and homes. Some women make quilts with exceptional patterns and fine stitches. Someone else may have a beautiful singing voice—"

"Like Miss Loretta."

"Yes, like your Miss Loretta. Or somebody can take squirrel or possum and turn it into a delicious stew. Birdie's talents are unraveling the healing gift of plants. Preacher Eli guides and comforts weary souls. I teach."

"And me?" I say what brings me to my real worry cause I fear I got left out.

"My friend, my friend," Miss Kate says and shakes her head. When she calls me *friend*, my heart flips.

"You have talents you haven't begun to understand. Once you do, the rest will come easily."

Miss Kate's cowlick in front sticks straight up like she's

surprised. There's a deep crease on her cheek. She musta slept on her face funny.

"Name some?" I ask, not to be pushy but cause I can't think of nary a one.

The tea has steeped, and she fills two mugs, drops two sugar cubes in hers and two in mine, and takes a sip. Steam fogs her eyeglasses, then clears when she puts her mug down. She takes her time, puts an elbow on the table, chin on her knuckles, and looks me in the eye like I'm somebody. Nobody ever looks me in the eye this way cept Aunt Marris.

Miss Kate says, "That first day I went to the schoolhouse. You came to see me, an outsider, and you offered to help a stranger from the valley. You do realize no one else came to welcome me except you and Preacher Eli. That was my first hint about your gifts and strong character."

I don't say that I come to ask a favor. I won't just being polite.

Miss Kate looks at her mug and turns it round and round on the table. I wait, and she goes on to say, "You are welcoming. Generous. Unafraid when faced with a goal. You want to learn to read, and the desire to better yourself is a marvelous gift. That talent alone will make you a good student of life. Sad is the person who stops being a student. She misses out on the best parts."

She points to the windowsill. "And you knew how to sort out the mystery of the treasures Birdie left me. I saw *things*, and you saw the *messages*."

She sits back in her chair, easy, and sips more tea, looking pleased with herself. "That's a healthy start, don't you think?"

She don't talk bout my baby. I don't neither. If we do

someday, I'll tell her these first days after don't fit right, like skin too tight and colors gone gray. But nights are worse. Too much time in the dark. Nobody to hear me cry.

I picked names for my baby. *Otis* after Daddy if it was a boy cause I love Daddy and he loves me. *Carly* if it was a girl cause I don't know my mama any other way. Nobody knew my baby names and nobody asked. Not Granny. Not Aunt Marris. Not Miss Kate. It don't matter now cause my baby don't need a name, and I'm getting used to not seeing my baby bump. It's my hands though; they keep reaching to hold that precious bump, hoping to feel a kick that won't never come again.

I pick up my tea to give my hands somewhere to go, and say, "Those things sound awful simple. Helping somebody and wanting to read. They don't sound special to me." Miss Kate hears the sad in my words, and her face folds in like a drying leaf, curling round the edges.

"Please don't underestimate those fantastic gifts. Look deeper. There's more to discover about yourself, and this will become clearer over time." She tops our mugs again from the teapot, but mine's still mostly full.

"At the age of fifty-one, I still discover new things about myself." She opens a tin a sugar biscuits; I take one.

"Like what?" I ask, but really want to talk about me.

Miss Kate scratches her head, and the stand-up cowlick flops to the side. She gazes over my shoulder at some place far away. "Before I came to Baines Creek I lived in a community of five hundred students and teachers. I had two rooms to call my own but I was rarely alone. Rarely ate a meal on my own or took a walk on my own. Until I moved here." Her eyes come back to me. "I find I love my cabin, the challenges, the solitude, the beauty of this place. I lived in a crowd and thought I belonged in a crowd, but—surprise—I'm more content on my own."

We sit still for a minute, then take in a big breath at the same time. Then Miss Kate asks a question out of the blue. "What can you tell me about the teacher's cottage burning down? Do you think it was an accident or on purpose?"

"It be accidentally on purpose is what I think," I say, and dunk my cookie in my tea.

Miss Kate giggles like a girl and shakes her head.

"What's funny?" I say, scared I say something wrong.

She says, "Well, what you said, Sadie. *Accidentally on purpose*. It's what is called an oxymoron. A perfectly executed oxymoron, if I may say so."

"Oxy-what?" I scrunch up my nose.

"Oxymoron. You see"—she sits up taller, getting in that teacher way—"it's one thing for something to be *accidental*—not planned—and entirely another for it to be *on purpose*, planned."

I squirreled those thoughts round, then say, "But *accidentally on purpose* is what I mean."

Miss Kate puts another log in the woodstove and wipes her hand on her britches, then sits back down. The fire pops; the logs shift and settle. "I wasn't criticizing you. And oxymoron isn't wrong words, Sadie; it's a play on *opposite* words, like *alone in a crowd* and *pretty ugly*." Her hands flutter in the air trying to help me see.

"Can you think of another one?" she asks.

She cocks her head to the side but don't rush me. I want to make Miss Kate proud so bad, but now my belly turns sour, and my eyes wander, looking for the answer. I look at the wet marks my mug leaves on the table. Chew on my thumbnail. Watch a line of ants in the corner who wanna get outta the cold and pick here to be safe.

Then, when my head hurts from trying, it comes to me easy, and I say, "Awful good?"

Miss Kate's face lights up like a sunrise. She reaches cross the table and squeezes my hands. "Sadie Blue, *you* are a wonder."

This woman makes me feel good. Granny don't like her but she never saw her cept once at church when we hear Miss Kate got fired and wants us to give her a job. Roy Tupkin don't like her cause she's my friend, so that don't count.

I go to wash our cups in the wash bucket when out the window I see Birdie coming up the trail, huffing. Miss Kate sees her too and opens the door, but Birdie won't come in. She yells, "Come on, you two. Gotta git to the Rusty Nickel," and she whips right round and heads back down the trail. Hips rock to and fro, walking stick jigs, her making good time. I grab my shawl and Miss Kate her sweater, and we head out the door.

"What's happened, Birdie?" Miss Kate calls out while she walks with long legs and I run to catch up. My insides rumble cause none of this can be good.

"Bad news for the Dillards. It's Buck," Birdie says, and a sad wallop hits me square in the chest.

The Dillards is the family me and Aunt Marris been helping through a hard time, and they helped me through my hard time, too. Aunt Marris is smart cause she knows when we bring food and comfort to somebody else, it brings us comfort, too.

I can't stay in bed when hungry babies need tending to. I can't cry for long being round happy ones.

Now this. Something happened to Buck Dillard.

When we get to the Rusty Nickel, we see through the window everybody and his brother is already there. On a good day, Jolene and Horace Dillard and their kids are a spindly lot on the puny side going downhill, needing Aunt Marris and me to feed them. Today, they've got a room full of friends to hold em up in their hour of need. Mooney's behind the counter sitting on his stool; the Dillards are in front near the radio to hear good. We slip inside the door. Aunt Marris stands by the Dillards and she sees me come in and motions for me to come on up with her.

I see Mr. Turner, the mailman, who looks different not riding in his truck, sitting tall, delivering news like I seen him do all my days. I don't figure him for a puny man short as me. I squeeze past Fleeta Wright, who smells like pumpkin pie, and Preacher Eli pats my shoulder, and Jolene Dillard holds out arms to give me a hug. I hug her back, and she whispers in my ear what Birdie said: "It's Buck." Jolene and me hold each other while the man on the radio talks. I can't tell which one of us is shaking more, but we hold each other up and listen.

"…five hours since the explosion rocked this coal town at five thirty this morning, trapping ninety-nine men. It's a sad situation…"

Buck Dillard. He's seventeen like me, and on the shy and quiet side like his daddy, Horace. In my mind, I see a tender picture when Buck was fifteen, two years back. He walked outta church with young Eddie in his arms. Tiny Weeza and

Pearl on each side held to his coattails, coming careful down the steps, them not up to his waist high, and Buck goes slow so the little girls don't fall or have to let go of him. He is a kind soul. I bet this morning he don't plan for his special life to be locked in coal dark, trapped in a mine.

The terrible truth is that paying work in Baines Creek is spotty, and some men go off to work the mines or cut timber. Some men don't come back whole; some don't come back at all. Sometimes paying work costs more than the paycheck.

The radio man goes on. "We've been told two dozen miners escaped right after the explosion before we got here. They're badly burned and have been taken to Morgantown, but we don't know…" Jolene and me squeeze each other and rock back and forth, and hope rises in the crowded room like a bubble of air coming to a gasping man. Bad luck threw Buck a bone, to be burned but not buried. At least there's a sliver of hope.

The telephone shocks us, ringing loud over the radio talk, and everybody stops and looks at it like it's alive and gonna bite us. Mooney turns down the radio and nods for Buck's daddy, Horace Dillard, to pick up the ringing phone, and the poor man trembles and shuffles up to it. On the fourth ring, he lifts the receiver, and nobody makes a sound while Horace listens to a faraway voice, then says *yes*, *yes*, and *bye*. He hangs up, and his shoulders go to trembling, and Jolene hurries to him and takes his crying face in her tender hands, and he whispers, "He's in the hospital."

My empty belly fills with sweet joy I feared won't ever come again, and the Dillard babies run and put arms round their mama and daddy, hugging each other. Buck will come home when he can.

Aunt Marris and me take the Dillards home on a day the sun pokes out from low clouds and shines a little warmth on blessed souls. Jolene and Horace sit in front, and I climb in back with the little ones, and we ride off, waving to Miss Kate and Birdie, who wave back. Preacher Eli does a happy jig in the road to make the children laugh, and they turn young for a minute, giggling at him. Their oldest sister, Lucy, and me hug em extra to keep em warm. By the time we get to the Dillard home, people from church are already there on the porch with food and helping hands. We leave today knowing hope walked in their front door and will stay for a spell.

Heading back to my place, Aunt Marris says, "It don't seem right that beat-down folks gotta get their hearts bruised, too. Buck Dillard's life changed today, but his mama and daddy's gonna take whatever comes home. They got help from folks so they can float awhile."

I'm lucky, too. When I get home, Roy's truck ain't there.

———————

That night, with no sign of Roy, I got the trailer to myself. A wind whips through the trees, and hard rain clacks on the roof like BBs. I sit straight up in bed when a thought flies outta the dark. It's bout when Mama left me behind and went off on her own.

My mama, Carly Hicks Blue, who I don't recollect

these years later, but all the same, we look alike and I carry her blood...

Did Mama go off looking for her special life?

Did she have to leave Baines Creek to find it?

Did she have to leave me behind?

BIRDIE ROCAS

Some folks call me a witch, and that's a good thing when it comes to digging ginseng. They come up on me in my long dress dragging the ground, catching twigs and leaves and stones. Got me a crow nesting in my topknot. I talk a little crazy, and folks back away and turn tail. Those who get forceful to my face got Tattler Swann to deal with. He's scrawny and wiry, but Tattler and me is a pair.

Him and me dug ginseng back in the early days of September, before falling leaves covered the red berries and men turned desperate when the money plant's gone.

When the ginseng was ready for harvest, Tattler showed up at my place at first light that morning with his digging stick. He got leather strips tied below his knees in case of rattlers. I got on three wool dresses so if them snakes strike, they get a mouthful of wool.

"What's seng going for this year, Tattler?"

"Romey's doing seventy dollars a pound."

"That'll do."

The root of ginseng was what we gonna dig that day, hang it to dry, keep some for what ails us, and sell the rest to Romey for big money. Romey sends seng from our mountains all the way to New York City and cross the water to where the

Chinaman lives. Seems rich folks far off got burdens of worry this plant can fix.

That's why Tattler and me headed into danger that day, but when that money plant come in late summer, lazy men turn greedy. They mess with the hardworking. Take what ain't theirs. We got digging sticks and burlap sacks. I got a pistol in my pocket.

There's a honey hole on the north side of Shetland Holler where we headed that belongs to Chilly Dodd. He let me dig on his land cause I plant back what I take. He say he won't shoot if he saw me with my digging stick.

"You a caretaker of the land, Birdie Rocas. I'm pleased to share my seng with you once in a while."

Cause of Chilly Dodd, finding ginseng this year was easy; getting seng home without it getting stole was another matter. Tattler and me got time enough to get to Shetland Holler and back in daylight. We didn't dawdle. Didn't wanna end up in the woods at night with seng poachers.

Tattler always looks like a bundle of twigs, all legs and arms with no meat on his twelve-year-old self. That hunting day last month won't different.

"You eat anything?"

"Had me an egg. Won't near enough," Tattler said, looking like the beggar he was.

"Get you some hardtack and whatever's on the table," I said. Like usual, my crow friend, Samuel, was on a branch outside my door. When he seen me take holt of my digging stick, he glided down easy and settled in my hair, then we three was gone in the shy morning light.

It rained a big one last night, and we waded through mud in the low spots and crossed through the creek to wash it off. It was all the same. When the air stirred that morning, leftover rain dropped on us. We'd dry when the sun popped up.

We got to the top of the first ridge, and I stopped and Tattler stopped. He looked off in the distance while I rubbed my knee and twisted my foot thisaway and thataway. Gout was acting up mean and I got a nasty cramp in my arch. When I walked on, Tattler walked, too. The boy got natural manners.

Been couple of years since I head over Shetland Holler way, but the way don't change. We cut through Old Nate's farm that's stood empty for ten years. We walked under pieces of pale bones hung long ago from a tall tree, dangling and clanking in the breeze.

"Them really damn Yankee soldier bones?" Tattler asked.

"Yep. Nate come up on em in a gully with their flesh rotted off. There was buttons, scraps of uniforms, and musket balls there for the telling. He don't want to bury them bones on his land. Don't want em to poison his dirt so his crops won't never grow again. He strung em up at the edge a his land in insult and disrespect."

I muttered, "Wonder what kinda rope he used that don't rot?"

Tattler don't say, but cut his eyes up at the ribs and hips and leg bones swaying at rope's end, and curled his lips in disgust. He spit to the side to get the taste of *Yankee* outta his mouth.

We passed a shell of Nate's cabin with the door missing. The roof blowed off from strong wind years back but the cockeyed walls still stand. Squatters, who gotta be worse off than most, took up here now and then. Today, it was empty. A barn on the hill leaned to the left like Jerome Biddle and his short leg.

"Birdie, you believe that stuff they say bout Old Nate's ghost who still walks these woods and scares folks to death? You think he's real?"

"Why wouldn't he be?"

"Why wouldn't he be *real*?" Tattler's voice turned high and young. "It's told he scares the bejeezus outta people who walk on his property is what he does. Heard he killed a poacher for shooting a dang turkey in front of his house. You wanna believe that?"

"How'd he kill the poacher if him a spook?"

"The spook stopped that poacher's heart, is what he done. Died right there on the ground next to the dead turkey he killed. Some sorry soul walking by come up on em two dead corpses. Almost had his self a heart attack. If he did"— Tattler stopped and did the math quick—"there'd be *three* dead corpses."

"Bet that sorry soul took that turkey home and cooked it."

"Well, I don't hear that part… I wouldn't pick up a dead turkey on the ground next to a dead man."

"Even if you was hungry?"

"No, ma'am. I would not touch a dead turkey on Old Nate's farm," he said loud enough for Old Nate's spirit to hear him.

"Even if you was starved three days?"

"Well…"

"Even if your innards got tied in a knot so painful you can't stand up straight?"

Tattler chewed on his thumbnail, a worry sign his brain's sorting out killer ghosts and dead turkeys.

"Well…when you put it that way—"

"Uh-huh. *Hungry* changes things."

We walked by Old Nate's weedy apple orchard smelling of hard cider from rotten fruit on the ground. A few wormy apples hung in easy reach. The boy looked, but he don't take. He said, "I don't wanna be on Old Nate's farm come sundown, Birdie. Just in case…you know."

Samuel cawed.

"I hear you."

Crows give me my name Birdie Rocas. Must have been one in another life cause the comfort I feel with them birds is natural. The crow who stays with me most days—now that him and me are getting up in years—is named Samuel. He's smart. He finds things, fixes things, figures out riddles. Like today, Samuel rides on top of my head, like he always does when he gets the notion to warm my brain. All's right in the world when Samuel and his kind are around, soaring on a breeze, nesting in the trees, and strutting on the earth.

Or riding on my head.

I'm midwife, medicine woman, and storywriter for these

parts. For my kind of stories, I don't sit round the fire spinning yarns and giving goose bumps like Tattler's tale bout Old Nate. What I do is collect truth that bends easy if you won't careful, and I write it down in my book where it stays put.

My Books of Truths is bound in soft leather made from the hide of a twelve-point buck I took down with my own bow and arrow. He stopped twenty paces in front of my lean-to when I was a girl learning the ways of the woods from a Injun called Gray Wolf.

That Injun let me glean secrets from him out in the beyond. He had skin the color of tupelo honey, but he was as tough as beef jerky. He went to the woods to die, and I slowed down his leaving cause I had need of him, and he obliged me.

That man's hair glowed silver, and the braid of it lay down his brown back in summer, or over a bearskin in the cold so I could find him in the gloom of the woods. I followed that braid from one season into the next and learned plant magic. Dutchman's pipe helps gas and lung troubles. The leaves of maidenhair ease coughs, and yarrow, the fever.

Gray Wolf was a Cherokee, and his native roots run deep in these mountains, back to the start of time, before Baines Creek got a white man's name. When my kin settled here two hundred years ago, bones—or *baines*, like they was called in the old country—littered the ground. Couldn't turn over a spade of dirt without finding a bit of baine. A war with the Injuns, Brits, Yankees, and settlers made a mess of things way back.

Baines Creek is mostly peaceful since then cept for moonshining, revenuers, ginseng hunters, and jaspers. More bodies been buried since and got turned to bone. That's a fact.

The day in the long-ago woods when I was a girl was a queer one. That buck stood still and looked at me like he knew he would be special in my life for all time. He gave his self to my Books of Truths. Those pages grew thick over time, and when I write, I touch his hide that's turned soft with handling.

I use a quill to put words in my books. Made my first one bout the time I killed the buck. I made it from a turkey feather, stiff and straight. Soaked it overnight in water and cut the tip at a slant. The ink comes from blackberry juice, vinegar, salt, and water. Been using turkey quills and my own ink for sixty years. They lay words neat and honest on paper.

I write down the usual births and deaths, but what makes me pick up the quill and lay down story words is when life don't make sense.

One time, I write bout a swarm of speckled butterflies that come through these hills and stayed two weeks on the ridge they never lived on before. The mountain shimmered them weeks long ago like it was alive. Then the butterflies left with only my words to remember em by.

Then there's the story of the chestnut tree that up and quit long ago and was the scariest thing I ever been witness to. It flummoxed everybody something terrible. Was like the end of the world when those ancient trees decided to die. Chestnuts was here…then they won't.

When the dying started way back when I was a girl, truck-loads of jaspers come to these mountains and scratched their heads. They hauled cameras up steep hillsides to take pictures of the war zone. That's what they called it: the *war zone*. The leaves dropped off early and crunched underfoot when the air was still warm. Age-old limbs shriveled up, then trunks split open showing the heart of em trees was gone. That was one sad story.

The chestnut trees leaving long ago changed mountain life. It left a hardship for every man and every critter to this day. Back then, chestnut wood cut into wide boards made cabins and furniture that don't rot. Chestnuts used to feed folks and four-legged critters with its carrot-tasting nut. And Injuns used them nuts and leaves to tend to whooping cough and heart ailments. Now we dig ginseng for money and a remedy. And shiners make hooch. Money gotta be made some other way with the chestnut tree gone.

Sometimes I feel this old mountain breathing weary. The high, thin air gets sucked deep into her lungs, all the way back to the start of time. I know her secrets and sins. This high place is hard on folks who give in or give up. For those who stay, Baines Creek is enough.

———

We was getting close to the honey hole and nobody messed with us yet, but that don't mean they won't watching. Samuel acted fidgety so I paid attention. The going was steep up that last ridge, and Tattler got in front and hold out his digging stick for me to grab and pull. We made it to the top when I said, "We here."

We stood on the ridge and looked down the shade side on Shetland Holler. The shadows under goldenseal and pawpaw trees was blue-green, and red ginseng berries sat on top of the stumpy five-leaf plants.

To get to the seng was steep, so I sat on my fanny and grabbed holt of saplings to ease down the north slope through the seng. On the way down, we dug roots with our sticks and planted the red berries in the holes so they come back. The ground was damp and soaked clear through my three skirts.

Tattler and me was quiet while we worked and listened out for trouble. It don't take long for our sacks to get full of roots, some as big as my hand. We won't greedy, just grateful, and when we got enough for medicine and some to sell for hard times, I gave a short whistle and Tattler come my way. We worked our way up the hill, and it was a struggle I can't hardly manage, and couldn't if it won't for Tattler.

Back at the top, we outta breath, sweaty and muddy from the pull, and we fell back on the ground breathing hard, and Samuel let go my head and flew up to a branch. We was gonna tie them sacks of seng under my skirts for travel, but that got sidetracked.

We heard the cock of a rifle.

We sit up slow and looked behind us. Two men, skinny as hickory sticks, pointed their rifles at us, ready to do us wrong. I won't the cleanest woman, but they was the dirtiest men I seen all year. Up to their elbows was black from digging in the dirt, and their overalls patched twice over. The tall one's bib was tied up with vine.

One said, "I told you, Jed, they was senging, and look it. Ain't we lucky buggers!" That one laughed like a jackass, and there won't a tooth in his nasty mouth.

"Pull me to stand, Tattler," I said, not wanting to sit helpless in front of these ne'er-do-wells.

"Ya'll stay put," Jed ordered, but we stood anyway and he don't shoot.

Tattler was behind me breathing fast and smelling of fear. Off to the side, I saw a scrap of a girl sitting beside bags of their seng they mighta stole from the hardworking. She got remnants of Sadie Blue to her white skin and brown hair, but I think this girl would slit my throat in the dark for a dime.

We in a pickle.

The serious one called Jed pointed at our seng with his rifle. "Grab them pokes, Dooley."

When Dooley reached for my bag, I said, "You don't wanna do that, boy."

He stopped, scrunched up his forehead, and looked back at Jed, then mustered some gumption. "Why not, old woman?"

Samuel flew back and settled on my head for support. "See this bird on top a my head?"

Dooley looked, but he won't scared.

"What's a scrawny bird gonna do?" he asked, sassy. "Peck me on my hand?" He snorted a laugh. "I'd slap him to the ground is what I'd do and shoot his fool head off. And yours, too, for the hell of it."

He done a little dance cause he was crazy on hooch.

"Look over yonder," I said and pointed with my stick to a dozen crows sitting on a low limb close by. Dooley and the girl done like I said, but not Jed. He stared at me and don't blink. He got dead eyes that seen too much. I needed to move his dead eyes off me.

Just in time to help the situation, Samuel stood up, spread his wings, and called out, sharp: *Caw!* Jed cut his eyes up, and I raised my pistol in my skirt pocket and shot.

The bullet hit Jed smack in the knee, and he dropped his rifle and fell screaming and clutching his busted kneecap. Blood run through his dirty fingers. His leg cocked out funny.

I aimed for his foot.

Quick as my stiff body can turn, I pointed the smoking hole in my dress to Dooley, who peed his pants like the chicken he was and raised his hands without being told.

I said, "Get on your knees, and put your hands on your head," and he done it cause he saw Jed was brought down by a old woman with a pistol in her pocket.

I told Tattler, "Get them guns," and he snapped to it, brave, like I hoped.

I added, "Check them pockets, too." He got two rifles and a pistol he fished outta Dooley's stinky pocket, and a knife outta Jed's.

"We don't mean ya'll harm," I said, "but you ain't getting our seng. You getting tied up."

I looked at Dooley on his knees, and add, "Or I can shoot you like I done Jed. Which one you want?"

"Tie me up. Tie me up." Dooley babbled and begged, and Tattler calmed him down and obliged him by cutting some honeysuckle vine close by to use as rope. My boy knowed his knots, and he tied them men's hands behind em and their ankles tight, too.

I already seen up the hillside the girl and their seng's gone, so they got trouble they don't even know bout yet. Don't think she'll come after us now she saw I got a pistol and know how to use it. We picked up our things that day and the outlaws' guns, and hightailed it outta there.

I got new energy, and Tattler and me moved away from Shetland Holler, me hauling one bag of seng and him the rifles and the other bag. I was in front cause I knowed the way, and my long skirts swished back and forth, and my digging stick thumped like a third leg. Samuel clamped down on my head to keep from sliding. Tattler kept up, but I heard him huffing. We don't waste breath on words. I don't think those outlaws was getting out of them vines anytime soon, but I aimed for us to be far away when they do.

Yep. That be the last time I hunt seng—less it decided to grow by my door.

Walking past my door every day be that teacher Kate Shaw. I watch her going and coming, and I study her these weeks she settles in. She got a strong walk. Purpose to her day. She don't rattle easy. Now that we know each other, when she sees my door open, she knocks and calls out, "Birdie, got time for a visit?"

I always do for her.

I put on tea, and Kate picks up another one of my Books of Truths. That's her favorite thing to do when she visits— read my words, cause she's the curious kind. She turns them pages careful, bends over my words, and sounds some of em out loud cause they're different from her spellings. Some of em are Injun words she don't know. Some of em are made-up words I need for my story. Her finger slides along from side to side.

"Birdie, your stories are treasures," she says, sips her tea, and goes back to studying.

I never let nobody read my words before Kate Shaw. Nobody before would understand or care like she does.

"You capture this community of people beautifully, and their pioneering independence. Your message is raw and powerful. Where did you learn to write like this?"

Kate gets flowery with her words, and she's got surprise in her voice. I light my pipe and blow lavender smoke. "You think *you* the only teacher to come?"

Kate takes it like the part tease it is.

"Of course not. However, I think your writing is more than words on a page. You spin them into living history. What *you're* recording is different from what *others* write about this place. Outsiders see Appalachian poverty as something to be cut out. The good with the bad. They send volunteers to save you from yourselves."

Kate don't say she's one of them volunteers.

"Do you know the saying, 'Don't throw the baby out with the bathwater'?"

The teacher in her don't give me time to say so, when she adds, "Well, you write about the baby while everyone else is writing about the bathwater."

I nod and puff on my pipe. "You smart."

In that first week of October when frost come most mornings, Roy Tupkin and his shenanigans make my crow friends grow curiouser. The fool's leaving a trail, and the crows bring me bits of his messy life. They put em in a box I got outside my door just for Roy's stuff. I'm shuffling through that box when Kate comes by.

"What's this?" She steps in close and looks over my shoulder, nosy as all get out.

"Roy Tupkin's stuff. The crows bring it to me."

"Roy Tupkin's? These are specifically *his* things?"

"Yep."

"A box only for Roy Tupkin's things…"

"What's wrong with your hearing?"

"I hear you, Birdie, although I find it impossible to believe the crows know what belongs to Roy. You have to admit, it sounds far-fetched."

"Far-fetched or close-fetched, these here things is Roy's things, and the crows bring em."

I don't like to raise my voice to her, but she's got too much valley thinking left in her. She edges closer and looks over my shoulder at what I lay out on the stump. A chewed toothpick. A white shirt button. A strand of red ribbon. A gold necklace. A plastic comb.

"And all of these things came from Roy Tupkin. For certain." Kate's got that uppity teacher tone in her voice.

"Kate, you what Preacher Eli calls a *doubting Thomas*. You wanna see Roy drop that there toothpick, a crow pick it up and bring it to this box, but that ain't gonna happen. And you don't know jack squat bout crows. Take Samuel there."

My friend rests on the low branch, watches, and puts up with doubting Kate.

"I've been friends with that *rocas* going on twenty years."

"Twenty years?"

"Yep."

She blinks twice and says, "Did you say 'rocas'? That's *your* last name."

"Yep."

I light my pipe and give Kate time to think. She's turned addlebrained today.

"Does 'rocas' mean 'crow'?"

"Yep. Rocas *is* crow, and crow is rocas." Everybody knows that.

"In what language?"

"Gerlac."

"You mean Gaelic?"

"That's what I say."

"And you've known *this* rocas"—she points to Samuel—"*this* crow for twenty years?"

I look at her like she needs to grow an extra head cause the one she's got don't work. I don't insult Samuel and answer. I head inside and pull out one of the Books of Truths.

She follows me in. I say, "Sit. Read." I leave her.

———

My story starts with a mean winter. It snowed to beat all, with drifts up to the roof and low clouds dropping ice steady. Felt like you had to stoop to get under those clouds. I've got snowshoes on and wear Gray Wolf's bearskin that hooks in front with wire and trails behind. I head out to check traps cause the larder is bout empty.

Pickings was slim that story day, and I only had one hare to show for it. Had one more trap to check before I head back home when I hear a gunshot from up on the ridge.

They shot *me*! Shot me in the *back*!

I stood for a odd second, then fell in the snow. The wind went quiet like it knowed something bad just happened, and the fire pain in my back made me suck air in little bites. Bodies come running, crunching through the icy snow, then they come up beside me. One of em said, "Shit, Elton, I told you it won't no bear. You kilt a old woman, is what you done. Get her hare. Least we got something to eat out of this. You want the bearskin?"

They pulled on Gray Wolf's bearskin but it stayed hooked, then they flipped me over. When I opened my eyes clumpy with snow stuck to my lashes, they jumped back.

A different voice said, "Lord, she ain't dead. What we gonna do now?"

Elton said, "She's a goner for sure, losing all that blood. I'm not wasting another bullet when the deed's mostly done."

Just like that, them scalawags walked off with my hare and left me for dead.

I looked up at the sky and gotta decide: Am I gonna die today or another day?

I picked another day.

I started the crawl to the tall hemlock to get outta the sleet coming down hard. I was a worm inching along, a snail leaving a trail. I got to the tree weaker than a body got a right to be and call itself alive. Scooted under the branches up against the trunk. Pulled the bearskin over my head. The pain in my back's gone numb. Home's far off. The hunters who shot me long gone. The snow has already covered my tracks. I wanna sleep. I heard the crows. I sleep.

I woke up cause something like BBs was falling. I pulled back the fur and saw juniper berries. They don't grow here, but I ate some, slept some. The sun went down. The sun come up.

When I wake next time, I hear a rustling through the branches, and a man's voice said, "There you is," like he was looking for me. He picked me up, bearskin and all, and put me on his dogsled, and off we went over the snow.

I woke up in a teepee, warm and weak. Got no clothes on under the furs. Got a strip of cloth running round my middle holding medicine of comfrey root and honey from the smell of it.

The man in his underclothes sat on his heels and stirred stew over a fire. Wet clothes hung on a line. He saw me come to and poured black tea in a wood cup. "Drink this."

I drink tea, sleep, and wake through daylight, then dark, then day. Day and night got turned upside down, and I don't care.

One day I opened my eyes and sat up and ate his stew. The man said his name was Abraham. He said the crows saved me, and I said, "I know."

"How come you know that?" Abraham asked, curious.

"I was a crow in another life. You believe that?"

"I believe you," that man said.

"How come?"

"Cause you said so."

Abraham had been coming through that stretch of valley where I was shot, and he saw a dozen crows circling a hemlock. He said he would have passed it by if it was vultures, but crows is different. They dipped in front of his sled, then flew back to that hemlock. He paid attention. He looked under that tree and thought he saw a starved bear, but it was me. He said I would have been a goner in another day if it won't for them crows.

———

Kate comes out the trailer when she finishes my crow story. I'm quiet. I sort the box, but not really, and make her talk. She takes her time and I don't blame her. She's finding out she don't know much, and that's gonna make her feel lost for a spell. All her book smarts is worth a handful of nothing when it comes to real truths.

"I don't know what to say," she starts.

That's good.

"Did you see Abraham again?"

That's safe.

"No. Him a rover. Don't stay in one place."

"How long did you stay with him?"

"Nigh on two weeks to heal, then he brought me home, got in wood, built my fire, hunted, and filled my larder. Then he left. But something come home with me."

"What?"

"Samuel."

"Samuel?"

I nod my head toward the branch.

"Samuel, the crow? *That* crow?"

Kate looks at him sitting on his branch. He looks off a ways, but he listens. He don't mind being talked bout but you gotta be respectful.

"He come home with me and stayed."

"When was that?"

"Like I say. Twenty years now, or near bout."

I puff on my pipe and wait cause Kate's got a cloudy look in her eyes.

"*That* crow came twenty years ago?" she mumbles. "Don't they all look alike?"

I blow out a stream of pink smoke, and it circles Kate's muddled head.

"If you don't know what you looking for."

We don't talk for a spell. Just stand side by side in front of the box of Roy's stuff. The top of my head is level where her titties should be, but that chest is as flat as a man's.

Kate says, "I'm sorry, Birdie. I'm confused by this story. It's strange and grounded in folklore I can't easily accept. Forgive me if I sound rude."

"You can't help it. You from the valley."

"I'm not trying to be difficult, but…" She steps back from me and Roy's box and slides away from my crow story cause she ain't ready. That's okay.

She asks, "Why do you have a box for Roy Tupkin's things to begin with?"

I wondered when she'd get to that question.

"You hear bout that girl they been looking for?"

"I heard something at the Rusty Nickel, but I wasn't paying attention."

"You know who's tied to that girl gone missing?"

I wait and puff on my pipe, and when Kate's eyes flash wide, I nod.

"Oh Lord." She slumps gainst the side of the trailer.

"Uh-huh. Roy and her was tangled." I cross two fingers as best I can. "Word is he pays for her place. Buys her things."

"My word… Poor, dear Sadie."

"Uh-huh."

I pick up the gold necklace from Roy's box and dangle it from my finger. "Now if this here necklace went round that missing girl's neck, it matters something strong."

"You don't seriously think it's connected to the girl, do you?"

When I don't say, she asks, "When did someone last see her?"

"Seven days back. Tomorrow be eight."

Kate whispers, "Birdie, do you think the girl's dead?"

"Yep. A girl don't up and leave on her own and not tell nobody."

"Well, there're a lot of *ifs* in this discussion: *If* Roy's responsible. *If* she's dead. *If* that's her necklace."

Kate's done talking cause she can't find easy answers. She steps away, waves good-bye, but throws words over her shoulder. "Why don't you ask Samuel where the crows found the necklace? You might find the girl there, too."

Her words might sound regular to some ears, but to Samuel

and me, they say Kate don't think much bout crows. Samuel hears it. He flies off that branch over top of Kate, squawks, and poops on her shoulder, then comes back to his branch.

He's getting old.

Bet he aimed for her head.

Kate don't know how close she is to truth. Lots of folks been looking for the girl called Darlene Simms. I hear from Mooney that Petey Pryor called the law when Darlene don't show at the club. One of em that come to look was Sheriff Loyal Sykes from neighboring Burnsville, and his small posse of men been combing the woods looking for clues or a body, chatting up everybody they can, but they ain't talked to me.

Petey says business at the Midnight Club is off bad cause who wants to see Sheriff Sykes leaning up against his car looking over dark glasses on his nose, him studying on everybody going in and out of the place?

Sadie says Roy Tupkin's come back home most days now, restless. He likely thinks he's safe in his trailer, him with his old routine.

Now Darlene Simms's name is on everybody's lips. This thing could blow over if we don't find the girl or her body.

That don't sit right with me.

It's time I do what I do.

I fetch my shallow bowl the color of blood. Put it in the middle of the tree stump. Pour spring water in the bottom, a finger width deep. The surface goes still as a mirror. I pick up and kiss the horn-shaped stone hanging from a leather cord, and hang it round my neck.

With my thumb, I make a X in the middle of my forehead. Over and over I make a X. Skin oil coats my thumb making that X. When my forehead is tender from the thumb mark, I pick up the necklace from Roy's box. I rub my skin oil all over it and drop the necklace in the middle of the water bowl.

I know what I'll see. The oil moves like swirling clouds, taking shape round the truth. The smell of rotten eggs rises up and grows strong in the air. I wait and watch and wonder.

Why are young girls dumb and men surprised?

What does evil look like to crows from up in the sky?

They're brave to play hide-and-seek with the dead.

BILLY BARNHILL

I always got eyes for Sadie Blue. Long before she up and married my best friend, Roy, I only got eyes for that girl. She sucks the air outta my chest. Makes it hard to breathe. I gotta turn away, sure my eyes are gonna tell on me.

She was but eight years old first time I seen her. So slight a breeze could lift her off her feet and carry her away. Only the paper pokes of supplies in her hands hold her to the ground. She got hair the color of chestnuts and was singing while she walked. Cause I can't help it, I followed her through the woods, walking soft.

She stopped and turned. "Why you come after me?"

I won't walking quiet as I thought.

"Name's Billy. Billy Barnhill," was my peace offering.

She waited and I waited till she said, "Billy Barnhill, you stay away, you hear?" Her voice was down-in-a-well small.

Looking at her stand there that day, I woulda said she was built flimsy with no mind of her own. That the only things she owned was a angel face and long hair. I was a handful of years older, but she put me in my place standing there waiting.

She backed up, then turned round and walked on. I stayed put till she started singing again, far off. I don't think to ask her name that first time, but she already burrowed in my heart.

———————

One day, she walked by the swimming hole me and my bud-
dies was at. I swung out on a vine to drop in the river and make
a big splash so she'd look my way. But I forgot to let go and
crashed back into a tree and broke my arm. It hurt like hell and
made me cry like a sissy.

That girl walked right on without even a glance my way.

Another day she sold apples and jam at a roadside stand.
I squatted down in the bushes and watched her sit on a
crate, straighten her skirt, collect dollars from fancy people
in fancy cars. Sadie said real polite, "Thank you, sir. Thank
you, ma'am."

What I don't know was I was hunkered down on a nest of
nasty chiggers. While I watched Sadie Blue, those little buggers
climbed over my bony ankles and up my legs to the top of my
jeans. Don't know till the next day when the chiggers made me
claw my skin raw. I dug till blood run. Then scabs come, and
I went crazy with a terrible itch. I can't do nothing but scratch
at myself for two weeks.

I don't mind cause I got to see Sadie be normal by herself.

———————

Sadie Blue don't look my way on purpose, but she don't have
to. I settle for crumbs when it come to that girl and don't have
a scrap of pride. She sunk a hook in my heart without paying
attention is what she done. Then Roy up and married her nine
years later. Me and the boys know he don't deserve a angel

like Sadie. He bet he could marry her, and he did. He knew I wanted that girl for myself but he married her anyway. She carries his baby now.

These days, Sadie still makes my heart swell. If Roy catches me pining, he'll deliver punishment cause Roy don't share. I don't cross him, but I ain't proud at what I do instead. I chop away at Sadie's soft side. Snicker when Roy leaves his mark on her so he don't think I'm sweet on his wife. We take all her lightness and snuff it out.

At the end of the day, I leave Roy's place empty. I walk down the worn path through the woods to my trailer and the kudzu what lays heavy on my roof and hangs over the edge and creeps toward my open windows.

———

Thursday morning, I sleep in late on my swaybacked mattress and flat pillow that gives me little comfort. The rain peppers the rusty awning and seeps into my dream bout Sadie Blue, naked and willing. In the half-light of that dream, she wears a odd kinda smile I never seen before. Maybe it's for me. Maybe she's glad she's my girl now. Maybe she forgives me for what I done to her. Maybe she knows it was all for show.

"Billy, you in there?" a man's voice comes from a distance and pulls me back from Sadie's arms. A flat hand hits the window frame near my head. I open my eyes, and Roy looks in on me through the ripped screen. Wet hair sticks to his head like a black helmet.

"Interrupting somethin?" he asks with a crooked grin.

"Gall dang it, Roy!" I sit up and pull my hand outta my britches. I got a wet spot at my crotch. "Ain't nobody here."

Roy's raspy laugh ends in a hacking cough that doubles him over. He hocks up a wad and spits into the weeds. "Come on. We gotta go."

I step in my boots. "Where we going?" I grab a stale donut off the counter and my hat. I don't break my stride walking out the door into the rain. Roy's halfway cross the clearing.

"Where we going?" I ask again and hustle two steps to Roy's long one.

He grunts but don't say.

A loud clap of thunder rattles the trees. Rain comes down hard on the leaves, sounding like buckshot falling outta gunmetal clouds. We trudge single file in quiet through the woods to the truck. He drives and I got thinking time.

I been following Roy Tupkin since we was boys. We was birthed into neighboring hollers with mamas who loved men more than babies. Over the past dozen years, I been Roy's best friend, likely his only friend. I witnessed stuff that shoulda been punished with the heavy hand of the law. Roy snaps quick. Sows wild seeds and dark fear. There was crazy fun, too, but it all had to do with likker and guns and Roy's hot temper.

Roy Tupkin was always bigger than me by a head at least. When he was twelve, he already had hair in his pits and fuzz on his chin. I looked up to him cause he stuck up for me when he don't have to.

It started on a winter night when we was kids and he come up on me bout froze in the front yard, me wearing Mama's slip and my skivvies. I was on the puny side like now, with doughy skin and washed-out eyes that stay runny. One of Mama's boyfriends caught me smelling on her silkies, looking for sweetness. That man made me strip in all my paleness and put that slip on. All the time he laughed and his cagey eyes looked at me hard enough to bruise my heart.

Mama said, "Larry, don't mess with my boy. He don't mean nothin by it."

Larry don't look at Mama. He don't see the pinch between her faded eyes and the pouty cracks in her painted lips. Still, she let him push me into the frosty yard and lock the door.

Roy come up on me bawling. Saw me leaning up against the side of the trailer, me in a baby-blue slip. He don't ask questions. He banged on Mama's door like he had a right to, and when the old man opened it with a huff, Roy beat on him with fists so fast they blurred like a train rushing by inches from your nose. Beat him in the belly. Kicked him in the balls, then broke his nose. Pushed his sorry ass out the door and into the yard where he sprawled facedown in the cold dirt and stayed put.

I run inside and locked the door, bug-eyed and outta breath from the fight, my white skin splotchy red from the cold. Roy laughed easy like it won't nothing. He don't even wash his bloody knuckles.

From then on Roy Tupkin was my bodyguard without me asking. His shadow was long. I don't cast one of my own.

I asked once, "Why you do what you do for me, Roy?"

"Cause we family, you little shit. Besides…now I own your sorry ass."

Well, we won't family, but I don't argue with Roy. I was mostly grateful for Roy. My life's bigger cause of him but not

always better. If I had my rathers, I'd settle down, stop drinking, get a job, and come home to Sadie Blue every night.

I could do that.

If I had a right to.

If things was different.

Roy parks on a old roadbed, grabs a canvas satchel from in back,
and we hike a mile in. Could drive closer, but we don't want
to leave tracks. When we near our still, Roy says, "Somebody's
poking round."

"Who?"

"Don't matter who. Only matters we got warned. Nobody
messes with what's mine."

Roy spits, then spills the contents of the sack. The metal
traps clank at his feet. Dried blood and pieces of skin and fur
are still in the jagged teeth.

"Roy, traps don't make sense. You catch somebody, they
don't die right off. They get caught, they get mad. They stay
right here where you get the blame."

The big man chuckles. "The still ain't staying here. We
moving it. Gonna leave behind some presents for the nosy."

I say, "More than crappy revenuers come this way. What if
Pooter or Earl come by? Or the delivery boy? You want their
pain on your conscience?" My voice goes higher again.

"Sharpen them stakes, Billy. There's gonna be more than
traps when they come back."

The rest of the morning, we plant danger for the

unsuspecting. After noon, we take apart the still, load carts, and move deeper in the mountains. A camouflage tarp gets tied between trees for overhead protection till we build a proper roof. Pipes get connected. Tracks covered. Bush screens set. A new trail remembered. When we're done, we walk the woods by moonlight, make it back to the truck, then Roy drops me off. I stumble home bone weary.

I'm too tired to dream of Sadie.

At fifteen, Roy drove a moonshine getaway car like a pro. It was a 1940 Ford with a Lincoln engine. Black and rusted out along the rocker panel with one hubcap gone. The left rear fender got dented when revenuers got close and almost run Roy off the road. The windshield got cracked when he hit a low-lying limb. The car's got a double gas tank, and one holds the shine. Roy drove with the headlights off in the dark heart of night.

I'd be the one to get the makings for moonshine. I got the secret recipe from old man Hector Hunt for the best hundred-seventy-proof white lightning in the county. He adds a special honey from a holler way off the beaten path, and I found where he got it. When Roy got tired of handing money to Hector, Roy and me helped the old man retire. Ownership changed hands that night, and no one noticed. Customers just want their shine.

There's a lotta money to be made in shine if you do it right. And a lotta ways money gets used up. You gotta build the still and fix the still and pay off the law. At times the mash can go bad on you, if you won't careful. Money flows out as easy as it flows in. Right or wrong, me and Roy never think to save for a rainy day, but we do wanna make the best shine. That takes the best ingredients.

Roy says, "I wanna do something once in my life I'm proud of."

Me, too.

———

Lester Jolly is the king of sweet corn in these parts. The lay of his land makes corn sweeter than most. Other farmers get four dollars a bushel for their corn. Lester gets more. But corn turned into moonshine brings in ten times that. The math's easy to do; Lester is a bottom-line man, cept he's got a four-legged problem that keeps him awake at night.

What happened was over a hundred years back, a grandson of Mr. Vanderbilt, that railroad tycoon with all the money in the world and some pretty stupid ideas, brought Russian wild boars with big tusks into these mountains so the wealthy folk could pretend they was big-game hunters. Before he done that, there won't wild boars in our woods.

If that won't bad enough, a bigger wild pig was brought in—the Eurasian boar, they called it—and they was kept penned up in a game preserve till they busted out, like anybody smart knowed they would.

Some of them boars still roam these mountains. Just a few years back, somebody kilt a seven-hundred-pounder that come from that bad idea. Hungry hunters keep the numbers down, but Lester's got his self a special problem.

"A hog can eat up a quarter acre of corn in one night," Lester complains. "That's a helluva lotta profit gone that won't come back. We need to kill us some hogs."

"We'll trap em for you."

"How you do that?"

"Got a plan. You get ready for bacon," I say and go fetch Roy.

Me and Roy drive before dark to the cornfield where the hogs been eating Lester's corn. I set posts, and Roy nails a spiral wire fence in place. In the heart of that spiral we put a pile of sweet corn hooked to a trip wire. When we come back the next morning, two big hogs pace in the pen and the sweet corn is gone.

Lester pulls up in his pickup. "They don't look happy."

Roy says, "Ain't looking for happy hogs, just dead ones."

He cocks the rifle and puts the barrel through the fence. The first shot kills one hog, but the other gets riled and breaks the fence down. The hog snorts and aims his thick tusks straight for Roy's privates. The hog musk stinks something terrible. Me and Lester run to the truck and I jump in back, but Roy gets cut off and runs into the cornfield. He has his rifle, but he don't have time to turn and take a shot.

Lester starts the truck and yells, "Lord! Hang on, Billy!"

Poor Lester Jolly got no choice but to drive straight into his orderly cornfield on the heels of a wild hog and a moonshiner.

I hold tight to the roof, and we zigzag the hell all over his cornfield followin the sound of wild grunts and breaking stalks.

"Left… Too far… Back to the right… They on your left—"

"Shut up, Billy. You ain't helping!" Lester shouts, mowing down green walls of his prize corn.

Just then, I bang on the truck roof and shout, "Stop! Stop! STOP!"

The truck fishtails and comes to rest within inches of Roy and the hog. The boar has Roy's hunting knife sunk to the hilt in one eye and the rifle stock broke in half cross its head. Roy kicks at the hog with little steam left. Lester pulls his pistol outta the glove box and does the rest, then looks back at the crazy trail his truck made across his field of prime corn and says, "Well, hot damn, I guess I got me a crop circle. Wonder what this looks like from the air?"

That starts us to laughing, and the laughing turns to girlie giggles. When Roy stands and dusts his self off, one of his boots is gone. We try to lift the hog into the truck bed but can't do it, so we tie him to the bumper and drag him. Me and Roy sit on the tailgate, dangle our legs, and look for Roy's boot while the pig plows through the dirt.

The lot of us strings them boars up by their hind legs and guts em. Then Roy and me drive off with the smell of blood drying on our clothes, wore out. We got our corn supplier, and that's good. Roy drives with one arm out the window. His square hand grips the steering wheel, his flat belly caved in. The Possum sings "She Thinks I Still Care" on the radio, and Roy whistles off-key. He looks cool even with one boot on.

———

Roy Tupkin had him lots of women. One he paid for outta curiosity, but the rest he got for free. He's the kinda sweaty danger women love. All of em he treats better than Sadie, and that galls the shit outta me. Still, I sit on horny widows' porches and on back roads where the moss lays thick on the north side of white oaks.

And I wait for him.

Now and again, Roy says, "Don't you get the itch, Billy?" tucking in his shirttail, hitching up his pants, sweeping back his thick hair, and putting on his hat. "Gotta get your hands on a woman's skin? Dip your wick? No? Times I think you a fag, man."

Roy tries to get under my skin. I don't let him. I got me a poker face.

One time I say, "I'm saving myself," and Roy laughed.

I been with a few women, but I don't dream about em.

———

Then comes the night Roy meets Darlene.

She's the new girl at the Midnight Club back in the woods at the end of Danner's Cove. It's a plain place with bare floor, loud music, and cheap likker. The regular girls got dull eyes, dull minds, dull skin bleached out under the glare of lights on the rough stage. Then Darlene appears with skin white as flour, hair as black as raven's feathers, and a attitude wound tight. She don't fool me for a second.

But Roy's smitten. I never seen him act like this. He runs his tongue over his parched lips, dazed. You'd think she was his first. The girl's pretty enough. Fresher than most, cause she's new to the trade and seventeen. I can tell right off Darlene's different from other girls who come to the Midnight Club and stay too long. Behind her dark eyes, she's restless. Itchy. Selfish.

Darlene and me was alone once that I can recollect. Roy sent me ahead when he was gonna be late and told me to get Darlene to wait on him. He handed me a bunch a silly flowers to give her that made me look the fool. When she come out to the parking lot grinning and posing, she looked right through me like I won't here.

"He be along shortly," I say like Roy told me to, and I hold out the stupid flowers. She still acts like she don't see me. She turns her skinny neck and looks round for Roy.

When her eyes decide to find me, she says, "Oh, it's you—*Millie*."

"What you call me?" I get a pinch in my neck and a twitch in my eye.

"Millie, Millie, quite the filly…"

Her lips are slippery and painted outside the lines.

"The way you suck up to Roy and wait in his shadows—*Millie*—you'd think you was his whore. Or a wannabe whore. That what you hope for—*Millie*?"

She come close. Pressed her high titties against my chest. Tried to get me to step back outta my spot. I stay put and blow stinky breath at her till she stepped back and give me my space.

When it's me and him, I ask, "What is it bout that girl, Roy?"

"Don't know" is what he says, being truthful.

I think Darlene sunk a fat hook in Roy's puny heart, and he don't wanna shake it out.

Before long, we stand outside the Midnight Club every night straight for a week, Roy waiting on Darlene. It costs to be inside, plus Roy don't wanna see Darlene with another man. So he waits, runs his fingers through his hair, slouches his wiry body against the poplar tree with his cigarette danglin from full lips, the brim of his hat hidin his eyes. He checks his breath and rubs his front teeth with his stained fingernail to get the film off. He's charged with electricity even standing still. When Darlene comes out the door, Roy says, "Be gone, Billy."

"But we gotta make a run tonight. Get the car loaded. You forget?"

"You do it. You know the way. Git."

I don't know who this Roy is, leaving the business for me to do myself when he never done that before.

What I do know is that when I come by his trailer mornings, he's not home but Sadie is. She comes quiet to the door and holds her round tummy. She says, "Roy ain't here, Billy," and bout takes my breath away. She don't say a word to me since she was eight years old, shy, and traipsing home singing. I don't know how to act when she say my name, so I do the usual. Spit a long stream of tobacky juice and look off into the woods before I walk away. I stand behind the oak tree and wanna go back to her door, step inside, and stay, but I can't find a reason.

When, after a rainy spell, I come upon a mess of chanterelles by some ash trees, I pick em for Sadie. Leave em in a poke on her trailer step, knock, and run away. Don't think she'd eat em if she knew they was from me, even if she loves chanterelles. I bring her ripe persimmons and a mess a black walnuts, too.

One time I knock and don't run away. "Hey, Sadie. Let me know if you need something fixed. I'm kinda handy."

She closed the door on me like I thought she would.

Another time I say, "Hey, Sadie. Can I wash my hands at your sink?" even though they won't dirtier than usual.

She said, "Water tap on the side," and closed the door.

I can tell we working up to a conversation, and that's a good thing. Another good thing is Sadie's bruises go away and her pretty comes back.

———

Roy's crazy about Darlene. He's under a spell like I never seen before. He works hard for this girl. Tries to do right things. The second week they together, he got her that gold flower necklace she asked for. And little slivers of underwear smaller than snot rags. And I don't count the boxes of chocolate-covered cherries wrapped in gold paper he gets. I wonder if Darlene knows the rules. For his money, Roy wants it all.

Roy spends nights down an alley, up the stairs, at Darlene's place. A place I don't go. They stay all night and sometimes all day while I do double chores at the still. When I collect money for the shine, I hand over the roll a dough to Roy, him walkin Darlene to the Midnight Club. He don't count it. Just stuffs it in his pocket. But Darlene's eyes get big as quarters, watchin him stuff the wad in his pocket. She fools Roy, but she don't fool me. I'm ashamed for him. Roy never settled for chickenshit before.

When Roy's busy with Darlene for bout three weeks, the business hits a snag. The ATF snoop like they sometimes do, and sales slow. Suppliers get scared. Buyers back off. By myself, I can't do right, and money stops for a bit. I tell Roy. Darlene hears. Nobody's happy. That's when danger joins trouble.

Darlene gets itchy to move on to somebody else now that her money pot dried up. She don't run cross the parking lot and jump into Roy's arms. She don't wrap her freckled legs round his middle and squeal like a pig, him twirling her round and round like a fool gone loco. She don't stand close to him or put her elbows on the table to catch the words coming outta Roy's mouth. Now, she makes him wait after the club closes. Finds more reasons to make him wait than the desert got sand.

I can tell he gets itchy, too. Keeps score. Counts Darlene's sins. Plans her punishment.

The old Roy's back. Sadie's time off is done.

I find out on a foggy Sunday morning, the last one in September. I stand in my kitchen, drinkin coffee and lookin out the window. Here comes Roy, weaving cross my yard. His clothes are bloody and torn. He turns in circles in the clearing, arms wide, drunk. He falls to his knees, puts his head in his hands, and calls out my name.

I step down into the yard.

"Where that blood come from?" I say, calm-like.

Roy takes his time. Sucks air in deep and fills his chest. On the exhale, he whispers, "Darlene."

At that one word, I shoulda bolted. Shoulda walked off into those foggy woods and left Roy by his sorry self. But truth is, I never bolt from any evil Roy lays at my feet.

I stay calm. Step closer. Watch Roy keen from side to side on his knees, eyes squeezed shut, pained face turned toward the blind sky.

"Where she at?"

He whimpers like a little boy.

"Her place?"

Roy nods, sucks in his bottom lip, closes his eyes tight.

A warm flutter come to my belly when the mighty Roy Tupkin gets on his knees. One of them special flutters cause Roy needs me.

"Where you wanna take her?"

Roy puts his hands flat on the spongy soil, fingers spread wide, and the weight of his body presses em into the wet ground. His spine arches, and his hair hangs limp round his pasty face. Cross the ten paces what separates us, he reeks of weakness. He retches between his hands.

"That shale holler?"

Roy struggles and stands, drained and broken.

"I get my hat."

I get my hat and walk past Roy cause he'll come when he's able. I walk through the woods to his pickup parked on the shoulder of the road and check the truck bed for tarps and shovels. Two tarps are still in wrappers. There's a used one, folded with shovels on top. A gallon jug a bleach and some rags are in a corner; a gas can and cinder blocks are stacked neat along the sides, in case.

I slide in the driver's side, wait for Roy, then drive off. I don't talk but give Roy space to process his situation. Words won't do no good right now anyway. I drive slow in the fog, round the curves, and think about the plastic tarps in the back, the rope, the pointy shovels, and the bloody stories they could tell if anybody listened. Blood's just blood to most folks up here. Roy and me count on that.

Roy only kilt one man on purpose what's buried up where we go. Somebody nosy from clear over McDowell County way that snooped where he won't welcome and paid the price. Roy and me was glad he was a lightweight we could haul pretty far. Another time, a killing was a accident that was only part Roy's fault. Moonshine, knives, and betting don't mix good late at night. There's a bunch more that got hurt for good reasons but not kilt, and we dumped em on some back road so the long walk back gives em thinking time.

Roy and me got secrets.

Darlene's street's empty. The few do-gooders who live in these parts are at Still Water Baptist Church being saved, and the sinners likely sleep the sleep of the dead.

"Pull round to the alley." Roy almost sounds normal. He sits up straighter, and his face is settled. I do like he says, but already know what to do.

I get out and lean the bench seat forward. We don't slam our doors, but leave em open a crack for a quiet coming and quick going. I grab the used tarp from the bed, tuck it under my arm, and put the coiled rope over my shoulder. Roy carries the bleach and rags.

I walk up the steps first, careful that my boots don't come down hard and get heard by somebody who'll remember. Roy does the same. I stop at the top of the stoop and look him in the eye. "You okay?" I whisper.

He nods. A night like he had don't make recovery easy.

"She the only one in there?" I think to ask, to cover my bases.

Roy nods, irritated, and whispers, "I pay for the place."

Shit.

The kitchen table is littered with rib bones gnawed clean, Twinkie wrappers, and an empty bottle of hooch. I walk through the living room, and in three steps, I'm in the bedroom I've never been in before, and she's there. On the bed where I thought she'd be. In a room done up in red and limp lace and that thick perfume smell Darlene wears. She's naked, mostly covered with a sheet with washed-out roses printed on it, eyes open, head turned too far with gray smudges on the sides of her neck, and a blob a dried blood in her dark hair. The back of her head got a gash likely from banging the side table. Blood is pooled and dried on the pink carpet.

The color of her skin is the giveaway her trouble's real. All that glow that filled Roy up for a while got dulled out, like cut-up peaches left in the air too long.

Darlene's used up.

I spread the tarp open, careful not to make more noise than I have to, and whisper, "You ready?"

Roy stands there, and damn if he don't look like he's gonna cry. That pisses me. He can cry over a flighty, nobody girl, and not care what he done to Sadie with his mean fists and meaner words that I bear witness to and wish I had guts to stop. Times like this, I think bout coming between Roy and Sadie. She deserves a lot better than his sorry ass. But this morning won't about Sadie and her heartache that's come back home. This morning we got a dead girl to get rid of.

I don't have time for Roy's breakdown, so I flick back the sheets, take hold of Darlene's tattooed ankles, and shift her to the edge, giving him a pretty big hint we need to move along. Her arms rise up and her long hair trails above like she's cheering. Or fallin down a chute. Or surrendering.

"Roy—*now!*" I whisper sharp, and he moves and takes her by the wrists.

"Wait," he says, and unhooks the gold flower necklace with a fake diamond he give her she never took off. He slips it in his pocket.

"Why you want that? You gonna give it to somebody else? I don't think so."

"Lay off, Billy. I do what I need to do."

I shake my head to tell him he's a fool.

We lay Darlene's body down on the used tarp, put her hands by her sides, strip off the bloody sheets, and throw em on top. Use bleach to wipe blood off the side table and rug, and throw the rags on top of the sheets. Roll her up snug, and I tie the package neat at her head and feet, and make handle grips. Darlene's light and easy to move through her three little rooms.

At the back door, we stop and I check outside for witnesses. The fog is lifting, and safe leaving time is running short. We know the drill. We done it a time or two. We go quiet down the steps to the passenger side of the truck. The bench seat's already forward. Slide body in, pull the old blanket over the package against the curious, get in, hope the truck starts on the first try, hold the doors closed, but don't slam em till we're a ways away.

We're lucky and don't see a soul, sorry or otherwise, when we leave the alley. A dead body behind the seat being carried to its final resting place always feels funny. I think I closed Darlene's eyes. If not, she stares through the tarp at the back of my head and wonders what went wrong. I could have told her she shouldn't mess with Roy's black heart, but I never liked Darlene. She won't as smart as she thought she was. Won't as pretty. She was Roy's plaything for a spell.

What happens to Sadie now, I don't know. It'll be no good.

Roy and me found a new burying spot by accident when we look for a better place for our still. The spot clean over Antler's

Mountain way is so rocky and sharp even settlers don't lay claim to much of it. It's got sour smells and shadows that shift and dankness that throws folks off from staying. Deep slits in the rocks likely drop into the fires of damnation, and that fits our doing this morning.

Good thing Darlene's light cause we got a ways to go on foot, and Roy and me not getting any younger, if you call twenty-six and twenty-five old. Days like this, I feel old. I let him take the lead now that he's come round, and he carries Darlene's head. That's the heavy end, you know.

We walk and climb, and Darlene grows heavier.

We muscle her up through the crotches of boulders, and slide her on dead leaves on the short slopes.

I'm proud to see the tarp stays neat and my knots tight.

ROY TUPKIN

R oy, lift up your end, man. You letting her drag," Billy whines.

I lift up my end so she clears the rocks and stumps, and think on last night that brung us here with me at the head of the rolled tarp and Billy at the feet. We squeeze through a slit in the boulders, cross a tree felled over a stream turned wild after yesterday's storm. We climb above the fog to this slippery shale and stunted trees and smelly sulfur that'll be Darlene's final resting place.

I hold up my hand, stop, and whisper, "You hear that, Billy?"

"What? I don't hear nothing," he says in his regular voice and irks me.

I whisper, "Shh… Somebody's behind us."

We stand still for a full minute, and my ears strain to catch another scattering of shale.

I say, "Be on the lookout. Can't be too careful," and we walk on.

I don't feel right yet. My belly got emptied this morning in Billy's yard, and sour puke coats my teeth. I smell ripe. Head's full of slick thoughts all stuck together and feels lopsided. My skin don't fit right neither. It's stretched too thin. If I reach too far, it'll likely split wide open, and my innards will spill out, and them damn crows sitting low through the branches, quiet as revenuers, will peck at my guts and take scraps of me to the tops of them dying trees.

Crows eat anything.

I stop again, and the head in the tarp bumps my legs.

I hiss, "Goddamn it! You don't hear that?"

"I hear it, Roy, but it's just a rotten limb come loose, or some kind of animal. Nobody's fool enough to come after us."

Billy don't sound sure this time.

We gotta get the deed done today, but I'm nervous and got reason to be. It's high stakes and my ass on the line.

We keep climbing.

———————

In my mind, I still see Darlene's bedroom muddled with hooch and rumpled sheets and plastic beads at the window. Them see-through scarves on lampshades. It always smelled like after-sex, and the perfume of them chunky candles Darlene liked to burn to set the mood, when I don't need nothing to take me over the top but her tight little body glistening slippery.

She made me howl like a wild coyote in the night is what she done.

At the start a month back, Darlene said, "You a man of few words, Mister Roy Tupkin, my super-stud, sweet-sugar-daddy man," and nibbled on my ear, breathed heat at my neck, turned me up when I was already on high.

I don't talk back cause I usually don't, so in the middle of our time together, she said, "How can I know what you think and what you need if you don't say?"

Darlene dipped her chin and puckered her pink painted lips, and all I could do was grin and think, *I've been hungry for special all of my life, and now I got some.*

Till yesterday.

When she wore another man's smell.

———

"Can you move it along, Roy?"

Billy tries to push me faster but only pisses me off.

"You wanna take all day?" he whines.

I turn round sharp and give him the *Don't cross the line, pissant* look, then I go slow for spite cause things in me don't fire right yet. Just cause he come along don't mean he runs the show.

I switch hands and flex my fingers cause they're numb— then hear it again!

Shit! Shit! Shit!

I look back and freeze. Whoever's trailing is close. Out of sight, round the bend.

I reach for my pistol I always got in the waist of my jeans— but crap! It ain't there! Is it in the truck? At home? Did it fall out at Darlene's?

Today won't a good day.

I put down my end real quiet. Billy puts his down quiet, too. We put our boots on the low side so she don't slide and get away from us before it's time. Billy pulls his pistol from his back waistband. I pick up two handfuls of rocks and feel stupid without my gun.

I'm wound as tight as a banjo string waiting to be plucked. I got one arm back, and it quivers, ready to hurl the rocks— when a boar comes round the curve!

A frigging boar!

I never been so happy to see a wild hog in my whole life. I throw the rocks anyway cause my arm wants to, and they hit him on the head. Billy shoots him right between the eyes and kills that old hog with gray in his muzzle, and he drops.

"Why you go and shoot him?" I ask.

"What you mean? It's just a old hog…"

"Yeah, but we could have scared him off. Now it's a old hog kilt on the trail we on carrying Darlene's dead body. You think bout that?"

"No."

"That's your problem. You don't think, Billy. You got shit for brains."

Billy shocks me when he fires back, "You do, too, Roy—cause why else are we carting this girl's body this far cept for your lousy temper. Who's got shit for brains today? Huh? Huh?"

Billy's got a point.

What's done is done. When we come back this way, we'll drag the hog off the trail. At least it's downhill work.

I say, "Let's get this over."

I let my guard down with Darlene is what I done, but I don't beat up on myself. She walked right into my heart cause I don't stop her. I played the kind of fool I don't respect. But truth is, she's the only woman who ever nailed my loose heart in one place.

It sounds queer to say now after what happened to her and all, but for a while she made lightning bolts shoot outta my feet when I laid down in that red room, up the stairs, at that place I paid for. That kind of feeling happens once in a man's life— maybe—and it won't happen again.

One time Billy said Darlene reminded him of my younger mama I hardly remember. I beat the crap outta Billy, and he fessed up to the lie. Said he was just being spiteful. My mama *never* made lightning bolts shoot outta nobody's feet. And it's for damn sure she *never* nailed a man's heart in one place. Every week the name changed, but they was pretty much the same, them smelly men with beer guts hanging over dicks, stained teeth, and a dime in their pockets.

They pay me no mind at first when I crawled in the corner outta the way, hungry, sucking on a sugar-water tit. Then, a few years later, they'd mess with me for the fun of it, and call me *little man*, and rub their hands on my hair buzzed short cause of lice. When I took up too much space and made em call me by name, they beat on me all the way to the back room of that trailer where the door don't lock.

I was smarter than they figured and more spiteful than they guessed. A dead rat under the car hood. A baby rattler in the glove box. A steel trap on the trail they had to walk. I grew up fast with those men going in and outta my mama at ten dollars a pop.

Then I turned tall and got muscle to match my meanness. I bruised ribs and bashed skulls and broke noses. While I beat up on the men, Mama beat up on me, wailing, "Now how am I gonna buy groceries and pay rent if they don't come round, Roy! You ruint everything."

Mamas and mean men shouldn't mess with growing boys.

———

Last time I saw Mama was going on two years back. One morning I woke up with a hangover and a itch in the back of my mind that was tied to her. It was strange cause I never think bout Mama cept if Billy be fool enough to say her name out loud and set me in a mood.

No reason for the itch I could think of. No news from that part of the county, but the damn punk itch stayed the next day and turned into a lazy sickness that took the spunk outta me, all in the name of Mama—damn her sorry soul. Maybe it was a warning that the last tie to her might finally be broke. Maybe I needed to drive to that part of the county I stay away from to see nothing got a holt on me no more.

I went back to a place I swore I'd never go again, to lay eyes on a woman I hated more than anybody.

That day, a bank of storm clouds collected dark on the ridge behind her trailer when I come up on it. The wind collected twigs and dead leaves and trash, and whipped em into little twisters that lifted up for a few seconds, then let loose. The place looked empty. A corner of the cinder-block foundation was sunk in the mud, and the metal front door held on by one

hinge and banged in the gusts of wind. The smell of rot met me
by the beat-up mailbox.

I crossed the dirt yard, and dust blew in my eyes and made
em tear up. I wiped em with the back a my hand, but no
amount of strong breeze chased the rank away. I almost turned
round right then and there cause of what I'd find inside, but
death turns me curious. I seen my share.

Mama was on the floor in the narrow hallway, half naked.
Black and purple showed through stretched skin bloated like
the bullfrogs I gig at Peddler Pond when I get a hankering for
frog legs. I guess she died three or four days ago, bout the time
the thought of her started pestering me and won't leave.

From the look of her, she got beat up one time too much.
Her bleached hair with dark roots got bloodied and stuck to
her skull on one side. More dried blood on the carpet spread
out as big as a platter.

With her sass gone and death being a bitch, the only thing
that looked like Mama was the rhinestone earrings she wore
cause they looked almost real. She liked to say one of her
boyfriends give em to her, but she stole em from the pharmacy
rack and forgot I was there when she done it. She liked sparklers on the Fourth of July that blazed up and made her eyes get
big before they sputtered out. Mama liked cheap, sparkly stuff.

One look round her place that day told me everything
that could be took, was. The clock which don't keep time
but always hung on the wall by the sink was broke in pieces
beside her head. The faucet from the kitchen sink was gone,
and it don't make sense why somebody'd take a rusty faucet,
but they did.

In the tin ashtray full of cigarette butts smoked down to the last, I saw my toy fire truck with the wheels off and red paint dotted with cigarette burns. I got that little truck when I was five. It was the only Christmas present I remember, and Mama likely stole that, too.

I blew off the ashes and slipped it in my pocket, then walked back to the truck to fetch the gas can. I stepped over the body and started in the bedroom. I poured gasoline on the stained mattress and on the pile of clothes in the corner, on the sofa with the broke leg, and doused more gas on the rug and bloated body and stack of dog-eared magazines by the toilet.

Then, I stepped outside, lit a cigarette, took a long, deep drag, and held in the smoke till my lungs ached. Then I held it a second more before I exhaled slow. I flicked the cigarette through the open door. It only took a minute for the flames to grow wild and turn hungry.

I stepped away from the heat and listened to the hiss and creak and shuffle of cheap turned to ash. The fire sent cinders into the air like the sparklers Mama woulda liked at her leaving.

That memory of Mama brought back the thought when Billy and me was teenagers and we fished at the riverbank. The summer heat was so sluggish and heavy that day the fish stayed deep in the cool and won't bite.

Cause we was bored, we played a game we made up called The Biggest. What's the biggest *hungry* you ever been? The biggest *surprise, shit, pissed off, happy*, or *tired* you been. We took turns asking and saying, and some of it was funny, a little bit was true, and a lot of it won't.

Now, it won't no surprise when Billy said the biggest *scared* for him was them sneaky, bastard revenuers who hide out in shadows and wait like the boogeyman to pounce on delivery boys. Billy was green to the moonshine business back then at thirteen and as likely to pee his pants as he was to do the job. He won't much good those early years cept as a bottle washer or woodchopper, as he was on the sickly side. Nobody woulda hired him if I won't part of the deal cause I was the muscle and the brains. Billy's nobody without me.

What did surprise me that night on the riverbank was the ass-whopper of a lie Billy told that still sits hard in my gut. He said the biggest *happy day* he remembered was when he was three, and his mama won't drunk, and no man woke up in the trailer and beat on him. He said his mama called out for him cause she don't see him, then found him crawled up under a mountain holly back of the trailer, snagged, and can't get out.

He said she got down on her knees in the dirt and pulled him out by his britches, careful not to hurt him. She talked tender and got cuts on her arms when she pulled him out from under them holly stickers. Then she picked him up by his hands and sang, "Where have you been, Billy boy, Billy boy," and swung him round and round in the yard, and held tight to his little boy arms and made him smile and laugh. She don't let him go. Said he felt like he was flying away from all the bad stuff.

I stood up fast back then and said over and over that long-ago evening, "No, no, no." I was pissed at his lie bout him being happy with his mama. I said, "You made that up cause you want it to be true but it's a lie. A goddamn lie, cause nobody cares bout a little piece a shit like you. Nobody."

On the riverbank, Billy held his bamboo fishing pole and looked away quick so I don't see him turn sissy and cry. But he lied. He had to lie, cause no mama ever looked out for boys like him and me, and took us by the hands, and swung us round and round, singing our name, making us smile.

Billy don't deserve a made-up memory like that.

What's funny now is why I remember it like I do.

I hear more dead branches fall or rocks tumble, but I don't jump so bad like I done before. Billy keeps needling into my daydreaming like he's got somewhere to be when I know there's nothing in his life cept me and my doings.

"Roy, want me to take the front? We gonna make this a all-day job?"

I don't answer, just climb, and he goes quiet on me again.

In life, Darlene don't weigh more than a hundred pounds. In death, she turned heavy after two miles. Or, maybe for me, a couple a nights without sleep, and a killing in between, turned me tired.

The sulfur smell grows stronger and stings my eyes and burns my throat. It's real steep now, and Billy and me got to watch out cause one wrong step could break a leg or snuff out a life. That's what we count on to keep folks away. Darlene's final resting place won't pretty, but she won't pretty no more neither.

From the first, Darlene fit me snug. My hands circled her waist. My fingers touched and made me wonder how there was room in there for her vital organs. I'd listen to her heart beat steady under her sugar tit. Her lungs would rise and lift me with her breath. I'd sink my face in her soft hair when I needed a place to hide. I called her *my treasure*—not out loud, cause I don't wanna sound dumb.

I loved when she put her skull on the flat of my belly. Hair the color of a raven's wing spread out. She warmed my loins with her heat. Traced the dark of my nipple with her finger and stirred the hairs on my chest, going down, down, down. I wanted Darlene touching me. Her touch made the hurt go away.

Petey Pryor owns the Midnight Club and don't loan Darlene out after I claimed her for my own. He gets moonshine from me so he knows to play it smart. I stopped going inside the club when I tagged her. Couldn't stand the smells and sweat pressing on her space. Knew it was her job to get the customers dancing and thirsty and bothered. I got my kicks knowing she excited them hungry bastards, then all they got was frustrated with a hard-on. She was eye candy. She was mine. Till she won't.

Billy rattles on in that whiny voice I can't stand. "…gotta control your temper. We can't keep doing this kinda stuff. The law's already looking…"

I don't listen. I think on that day when I knew Darlene won't different from other lying whores. I tried to keep the light in that girl's eyes. Give her every dollar I got hold of. Give her everything she wanted. I give more, she took more, and then she stopped giving altogether. A smell filled up that red room that won't mine. Darlene's skin turned oily.

Darlene got what she had coming.

———

Billy and me are deep in the holler now. With my free hand, I grab hold of saplings and rocks. *Jesus*, I'm weak, and wonder if I'm sick for real. The sweat stink on me is as bad as the rotten-egg smell.

"Roy, you hear me? Let's stop for a bit."

I stop cause I'm tired, not cause Billy said to. I wedge our burden between rocks so it don't get away. I light up a cigarette and take a deep drag. Billy's hat sets too low to read his face.

My troubles started back with that baby growing inside Sadie Blue when all I wanted was to mess with Billy and the boys. Told em I could get Sadie if I wanted her. They don't believe me so I proved em wrong. Billy was sick sweet on that girl, moon-eyed, tongue-tied. I edged in for the hell of it. She played hard to get, made me take her on, and that part was fun.

Truth is, Billy don't deserve a sweet piece like Sadie. The wimp never said a word when I nailed her. Not a word when she got pregnant. Then I messed up bad having her one more time, feeling a tiny kick, and doing something stupid. I did like showing that wedding license to Billy, Pooter, and Earl.

They bout shit a brick. All of em was in love with Sadie for a spell.

It won't all bad at the start. I don't tell the boys at the start Sadie Blue's pure, like you don't see in this world. She said, "Roy, you gonna be a good daddy to our baby. You gonna take care of us?"

I don't say.

There *was* a patch of time when I think bout a little boy looking like me, looking up to me, and following after me. I smile for no good reason. Then I know I'd ruin it. What the hell do I know bout good daddies or walking straight lines?

When Sadie gave her sweetness to what's growing inside her and let me be myself again, I do what I do. I beat her. I tomcat with Darlene. Then I beat on Sadie again cause I can. She lost my baby. For the hell of it, I sent a bunch of hard-assed moonshine men after that stupid Jerome Biddle fella to teach him a lesson. Now this thing with Darlene gone flat.

I need to turn my bad luck around.

I finish my cigarette and stand. Billy whines, "Ain't this a good enough place? What dang fool's gonna come this far to look for trouble?"

I don't answer. I stand and pick up the package, and Billy does, too. I gotta be *real* picky with this one. Everybody knows Darlene and me been together these weeks, so when she don't come back, they gonna study on me.

Truth is, the law's been gunning for me for a long time. I gotta be careful not to call attention to myself. Don't fight less I got to. Don't speed cept on back roads. Billy does most of the moonshine deliveries now. Without Darlene's body, the law's gonna have a hard time getting me for murder. That's what *hey bus corpses* means—you gotta have a body to prove somebody's dead. Without one, the law gets to scratch its ass in puzzlement and gotta let me walk.

Sheriff Loyal Sykes, stuffed like a sausage in that gray uniform of his, with his spit-polished shoes and slick shaved face, wants me to slip up bad. When he sees me drive down the road and pass his cop car, he chews extra hard on the end of his toothpick and works his jaw. He slides down his black sunglasses on his long nose and stares at me. Swivels his buzzed head like a owl and watches me mosey on by, him frustrated.

We got a chicken game going on for years, him and me. I aim never to drop my guard and lose. I'm too restless a soul to live behind bars.

Sheriff Sykes put me in jail once to make the point he could—it was a lucky break for him that don't happen again. Being sixteen back then, I might have been too high and mighty to get behind the wheel of Boomer's 1940 Ford used for moonshine deliveries, but I won't admit it to nobody that day nor since.

Under the hood, that car had a Lincoln engine, a flathead V-eight out of a ambulance, with twice the power of any sheriff's car. Boomer had outfitted it with a extra gas tank to hold the shine. Extra stiff springs and two shocks in the front carried the extra weight. You could put a hundred and thirty gallons of likker in that car, and it would sit smack level with the road. Billy still talks bout that car today and me going full on. I set speed records in the dark I never could claim in daylight.

I can still feel the fine tune of that fifteen-inch black steering wheel in my hands and the rumble under the gas pedal. That big sloped trunk was sexy as shit. I blackened the wide whitewalls so they don't shine in the dark. Dulled the chrome on the flashy grill and bumpers, too. I thought I knowed it all.

Sheriff Sykes and me was opposites. He followed the straight line happy as a coonhound, and I felt strangled by the straight line. He hated my guts. Back then, Loyal Sykes was a greenhorn deputy like I was a greenhorn runner. He wanted to make a name for his self early on, and he got word of a likker delivery and me part of the deal. Here we was, two hard heads who wanted to make our mark that night, but don't know what's gonna happen.

I did my homework. I studied the delivery route for two solid days cause it crossed two county lines. Knew every dip, curve, and straightaway. Knew the shortcuts I'd use if there was roadblocks. Ate a light supper so nerves didn't upset my constitution. Don't drink much the hours before so I won't need a piss along the way and lose focus.

The good driver gotta have rare skills to drive in the pitch-black on these mountain roads. I knew guys who bailed outta their car in the middle of the chase and let the shine and the car go up in flames rather than get caught. That won't delivering the goods. I got more pride than that.

The night, Sheriff Sykes arrested me for half a minute. I'd

finished my first run and felt smug. I moseyed back on the main
road easy, then the sheriff pulled me over.

I'd forgot to turn on the damn headlights.

The car don't have moonshine in it, and the money was
hid inside the door panels. The sheriff kept eyeing them door
panels and was fixing to pull out his switchblade, ready to cut,
but he needs the judge's signed paper to cut into them door
panels, and he don't get it. The judge is one of ours. I was out
a jail before breakfast, and waved at Sheriff Sykes when I passed
his desk. He won't happy.

I stop, and the body in the tarp bumps into the back of my legs.

"Here'll do," I say.

Here is a crack in the shale wide enough to slide the
bundle in, and deep enough to be outta sight. I lay my end
down gentle. Billy drops his. I'm fixing to smack him. He gets
fatheaded is what happens now and again. My fault cause I give
him too much credit, and then he starts believing it.

"Give me a sec," I say.

Billy looks irked when I stop before I dump Darlene's
body. He backs up a bit and looks off into the woods with a
twitch in his jaw. I don't need him acting pissed.

I reach in my pocket and pull out the gold locket I give
Darlene at the start that hung round her neck till I broke it. A
rose on the front with a sparkly stone in the middle, with the
gold dull on the backside. I kiss that part and think I taste her
perfume, and think to hell with Billy if he sees.

I slip the chain under the tarp rope so it'll go with her to her grave, and it glints in the sunshine like light on creek water.

Damn if my hands don't shake when I reach to push her! I swallow the bile in my throat and push anyway. The bundle drops outta sight, then I hear the cushy thud, and pebbles scatter. She lands in the dark where she needs to stay.

I can hardly breathe my chest hurts so. I scream *"Dar-lene!"* and fling wide my arms, and feel the hurt let loose. Her ghost name flies out into the stinky air and spills into the hollers like lost treasure.

I sit on my haunches and don't wanna look at the crack in the earth where Darlene went, so I look out on the ridge beyond the shale. Old crows sit at the top of a hemlock and stare at me. Every one of them birds looks my way. A breeze ruffles their feathers, but they just stare. Don't even call out.

I stand and hurl a rock at em, which is stupid. Then I throw another and another, till my shoulder hurts, and I feel like a helpless old man.

The nasty crows stay put. I swear them beady eyes lock *right* on me. I stand quick, wipe my snot nose on my shirtsleeve, and head back cross the slippery shale, sure-footed, done with all the lugging and the dead for the day. I won't feel sorry-assed for myself no more.

I move down the hill fast. I want the stink of rotten eggs gone from my nose and skin, and from the back of my throat. I need to scrub with hot water and soap. I need to sleep a long night in my own bed.

I move fast down the mountain to spite Billy. He slips and cusses and falls as he tries to keep up.

SADIE BLUE

It's been seventy-one days since me and Roy bothered a man's liver-and-onion dinner to say *I do*, and Daddy's miffed at me. Him and me don't talk since I lost my baby three weeks back at Miss Kate's, then come back to Roy's trailer. But today I'm gonna change things. I hope Daddy's spirit voice will come back to me then. I miss him.

I still wear my bloody dress from last night's beating and move gimpy slow down the hall this morning, wiggling another loose tooth with my tongue, seeing outta one eye, and holding my side. Roy beat up on me for the last time and don't even know it. He got seventy-one chances to do right by me and messed up every one of em.

This morning he sleeps in his chair in front of the bootleg TV that works some of the time. The floor round him is messy with scraps a food, beer cans, and a half-empty jar of hooch. His head hangs to the side, and drool runs out the corner of his mouth. I click off the TV all fuzzy, pick up trash, put on coffee, wrap a thick sweater round me, and step outside. Frost coats leaves and branches, sparkling in the early light so I have to squint against the bright. I stretch my sore back careful and breathe in gentle cause yesterday's beating makes it hard to do the simple things.

Percy comes outta the bushes, and a line Miss Shaw told me

drifts to the front of my mind. *The fog comes on little cat feet…*
He wraps his silky self round my ankles, and I close my eyes to
feel the softness better. I say, "I see you, little kitty-kitty, but
I'm too sore to bend down and love on you."

"You too sore to bend down for me?"

Roy Tupkin stands in the doorway scratching his crotch
and yawns wide. His spittle's thick and dry on his lips. His
T-shirt stained. When I pay him no mind, his face pulls tight
and turns dangerous.

"Pack two lunches. Me and Billy going hunting," he says,
then he adds with a sneer, "And clean yourself up. You look
like shit."

I go inside and pack two lunches, then stay outta his way
while he downs hardtack, drinks coffee, and grabs his hunting
gear. I see through the window Billy shows up and stands in
the yard, hunched over in his oversize camouflage coat with
the hood up against the morning's cold, smoking a cigarette,
waiting like usual. I don't let myself think long on the trouble
them two get away with, wiggling out from under the law,
but sometimes it come in the yard—stink on shoes, blood on
clothes, and questions pinned lopsided in the air. They been
luckier than their lot deserves.

Billy catches sight of me in the window. When Roy opens
the trailer door, his buddy gets up on tiptoes and looks past him
at me and whistles. "What she do this time?"

Roy don't answer. He don't need a reason.

They leave single file and walk the worn path, Billy at the
rear like always. He cuts a funny look back at me and I turn
away, tired of it all.

I pour a cup of strong coffee and drink it sitting at the table, looking into them woods where Roy and his shadow walked off to hunt on the neighbor's ridge, ignorant.

Roy don't know my backbone's different today, hardened by sorrow and loss.

He don't know I'll take my chances with my Maker but not get beat one more time.

He don't know he's going down for the count of ten, and this time I win.

A song from Miss Loretta Lynn bubbles up soft inside my head. When I figure what she sings, I smile sad. It's her hit with Mr. Ernest Tubb called "Mr. and Mrs. Used To Be." She's singing it slow in my head, and in that song Mr. Tubb sings tender bout his woman leaving and the good at the start that's gone bad. I don't know why Miss Loretta picked that song to bother me by. It don't fit for me and Roy but it's still a pretty tune.

I rinse my chipped coffee cup in the sink and put on Daddy's hunting coat, humming easy with Miss Loretta. The long cuffs hang over my fingertips. I walk to the shed for a shovel with Percy by my side, then down the dirt trail to the ditch where hemlock grows. I hear gunshots and wonder if it'll be rabbit or squirrel coming home for Roy Tupkin's last supper. I push the pointy shovel deep into the soil. Pull out the roots, shake off the dirt, and fill the hole. Drag the shrub home and free the roots with a hatchet and hide the rest in a gully under dead leaves.

"You work smart, girl."

Daddy's back! I clutch at my heart in joy to hear him again.

Daddy, where you been?

"I been close. Watching. Waiting for you to turn brave."

Today's the day. Don't go way.

"I won't miss it for the world. I'm here, sweet girl. Now you be careful of that mousy smell when you boil them hemlock roots. Don't wanna tip him off."

Birdie give me the recipe. Percy's gonna help.

I fill a wash pan to the top with chopped hemlock roots. Then fill the wash pan with water so the poison roots soak. I scrub them roots clean, then scrub em again, rubbing off the purple skin to the white flesh of the root. I dump the lot into my canning pot. Birdie says the secret to good hemlock poison is a eagle's claw dropped into the roiling water. She says, "The hemlock roots gonna turn him mighty sick, but this here eagle's claw tears out the heart of a evil man. Roy Tupkin's gonna die for sure."

Now, back inside the trailer, the water boils and the plan cooks.

———

I go out in the yard, get down on my knees—careful to spring the steel trap under leaves guarding Roy Tupkin's private hooch he don't share with nobody—then carry the jars inside, unscrew the metal tops, and pour a cup from each jar down the drain.

I strain the boiled hemlock root through muslin three times like Birdie said to, then strain it again for luck till the poison is as clear as spring water and the eagle claw sits cooling on the counter. I pour a cup of poison in each jar and swirl it in the likker. To my nose, it smells like hooch, but my hands shake when I screw lids back on the jars and wipe the outside with a rag. It won't do for me to break a jar, so I breathe deep and slow down.

"This gonna work?"

It'll work, Daddy.

It's gotta work.

I put the jars back—alongside the stink of a dead rat Percy brung me—reset the trap, and cover my tracks. Wash up at the sink and scrub the poison pot with extra elbow grease. Put on cabbage to cook to cover the hemlock smell. Change into a clean dress and put on a thick sweater against the chill of the last day of October.

Birdie told me, "Tonight that harvest moon will rise. A watching moon. A blue moon on All Hallows' Eve to turn midnight into daylight. Nights like this, Sadie, don't come but a handful of times. A army of haints is gonna walk these hills in the moonlight. They help you if you ask em to."

It's how come I picked tonight to kill Roy Tupkin.

———

I run a comb through my hair, being careful of the sore knots on my head. Then I sit at the Formica table with my knees together and my backbone straight. Percy sleeps on my lap and warms my empty belly. I wait as light leaks outta the sky, and I hum. When I listen, I find I'm humming Patsy Cline's big hit, "I Fall to Pieces," and I stop and fall silent cause that message won't serve me right today. I can't fall to pieces when I gotta keep it together.

The silence round me feels different from other days. It's peaceful and heavy at first, like a crazy quilt made of all the hurts of my seventy-one days as Roy Tupkin's wife, but now I add worry to the border of silence and can't help myself.

I wonder… When I go to church will sin sit on my skin like scabs? Will Preacher Perkins point a finger at the dark in my heart? Will Miss Shaw shut me outta her days? Will Aunt Marris love me still?

I wonder… Did I get rid of all the pieces of my crime? Did I cover my tracks good? Will Roy know his private hooch got moved and tastes different? Is the trap set right? Did I make a dumb mistake that'll mean the death of me?

Sweet Jesus, help me. I clutch my hands together in desperate prayer. *I promise to be good after this. All I want is to not get beat up. Find my special life. Live up to my potential. Read by myself. Kill Roy Tupkin.*

If I live through this night and days beyond and get Roy buried in the ground, I'll sell jelly at the roadside like I done before. I'll help Miss Kate at school. Tattler can help find me a dog to keep me safe. That dog can stay inside when weather's harsh and I need the beat of a strong heart beside me.

Percy stretches out his hind leg, eyes closed, body soft.

Life's gonna be different, Percy.

Percy likes it when I rub behind his ears.

We won't live scared. Won't watch for the kick of that man's boot. The snap of his temper. The strike of his hand. We'll sing with Miss Loretta every day if we want to.

If we wait a little longer.

If my plan works. Oh, merciful Lord, please make my plan work.

A voice flies outta the air. "Sadie, you in there?"

I jump from the sound. It won't Roy Tupkin *or* Daddy's voice. My heart thumps against hurt ribs. I stand too quick, knock Percy off my lap. My knees give way and I have to push against the table to stand.

"Sadie, come out here," Billy yells louder. "Roy done got shot."

My hand quivers when I reach for the knob and open the door. The harsh setting sun hurts my eyes, and I shield em with trembling fingers to make out shadowy shapes in the yard. I step down from the trailer into the chilled twilight where Roy Tupkin's body lays on a makeshift stretcher of saplings roped together with vines. Over his heart, his camouflage coat has a dark patch the size of a pie.

I circle the body, confused at what I see. All this time I wished the devil would take Roy Tupkin's sorry soul into the hellfires and leave me be. Now this.

"What happened?" I ask in a small voice with arms limp by my sides, eyes on Roy's body.

"I brung him home for you. The rifle went off when…"

Billy's voice fades and my ears listen for scraps of Daddy, but he picked now to be gone again. Every hair on my body itches, and a sick shudder runs through me. I let out a big breath that turns cloudy in the frosty air.

Does this mean I been saved? That I can break the proof against the rocks? That my crime will seep into the soil? That I can tell Miss Shaw my life finally turned into something *awful good*?

Oh my Lord! Did Roy's eyelashes flutter? Did his chest rise under that bloody jacket?

My eyes ache to see what's truth in the waning light, and I press my knuckles to my mouth. What if this is a nasty trick? It'd be like Roy Tupkin to smear deer blood on his coat, then pop up and laugh like a crazy man. Billy would be in on it. He always does what Roy Tupkin says without a thought of his own. I don't understand that kind of unnatural loyalty. But sometimes I think Roy needs Billy more than the other way round.

I inch toward the trailer door and keep my eyes on Roy. "What you say happened?"

When Billy don't say, I look at him for the first time. His face looks loony and dopey. He's *grinning*, for heaven's sake! He steps toward me and reaches out his hand.

He *touches* me!

He drags his stubby finger down my throat where my heartbeat thuds in the hollow.

My legs want to fold under me when his hand grazes my collarbone and slides over the rise of my breast.

Billy leans in and whispers, "I done it for you."

He done what for me? Killed Roy? Roy thought Billy was a nobody. Billy's crazy is what he is.

He walks away, chuckling, and I shudder, watching his weasel body head down the path he'll walk to my door tomorrow. I look down at my dead husband who looks small. I look at this tin can of a trailer that don't look bad in the dusky light. I straighten my back, lift my chin, and call out in a strong, strange voice I claim as mine.

"Hey, Billy."

He turns.

"Why don't you take Roy's moonshine? He won't be needing it now."

READING GROUP GUIDE

1. Life in 1970 Appalachia (and fictional Baines Creek) was undeniably hard and harsh. What did the novel tell you about that historic time and place that you expected? What did you learn that surprised you?

2. Sadie Blue was the principal character in the book, with her story told in three chapters. Did you root for her from the start? What were her key moments of growth? Who were her mentors and supporters? What did they do that helped her grow a stronger backbone?

3. In what ways were Sadie Blue and her grandmother, Gladys Hicks, and Sadie and her mother, Carly, alike? In what ways were they different?

4. Gladys and Marris were best friends. Who needed the other the most? Who gave the greatest purpose to their relationship?

5. Did you think Gladys was oblivious to her mean behavior? Why did she feel entitled to that mean behavior? How do you think she would have described herself?

6. Who were the most lovable or admirable characters? What made them that way? What were their strengths and weaknesses? In what ways were they important to Sadie's salvation?

7. Preacher Eli Perkins never quite believed he was good enough for his job. How did that quality make you feel about him? How do you think he performed his job?

8. Three characters that are hard to love are Prudence Perkins, Roy Tupkin, and Billy Barnhill. Did you find any reasons to empathize with them? What were the pivotal moments in their past that shaped their personalities? How do you think you would have fared if you were born into their families and stations of life?

9. When Kate Shaw arrived in Baines Creek, she expected to be doing the teaching. What were the things she learned instead?

10. Birdie's Books of Truths: What insights did they give you into life in Appalachia and the gifts Birdie possessed?

11. What role did Tattler Swann play in the book? Was he a good spokesman for Jerome Biddle? If so, why?

12. This book is written in first person, present tense. Did that choice by the author make the story more intimate? If so, in what ways?

13. Which characters were most capable of loving? In what ways did they demonstrate that?

14. A number of murders were committed in the book. Do you think any of them were justified? If so, which ones and why?

A Conversation
with the Author

When did you know you wanted to be a writer?

I've always loved pretty words and sentiments, and I got much pleasure writing letters to friends getting married, struggling through a hard time, or celebrating a landmark. Some of those letters were framed by the recipients, so I knew I had a penchant for heartfelt prose that mattered to people. I was well into my fifties when a friend encouraged me to write a book of short stories, and my initial response was *Does the world really need another book?* But his encouragement and support planted a seed that grew roots. The first stories I wrote were about my mom, Lucy, and her life on a tobacco farm in the 1930s. She was one of fifteen children living in an unpainted house without running water or electricity. She and I found a special bond talking about her childhood, which she thought no one cared to remember. I didn't know that in a few months Lucy would die of cancer and I would be left with grief and amazing fodder from those conversations. When the stories tugged at me to do more, I knew I wanted to write them.

Who are your favorite authors and why?

I am a picky reader. I look for a great story written exceptionally well, with the prose highly polished and the deadweight removed from the story line. Because I have a particular love for the southern voice, some of my top choices are obvious: Harper Lee, Rick Bragg, Barbara Kingsolver, Robert Morgan, and Ron Rash rush to the head of the line. Pat Conroy's *The Prince of Tides* was as compelling a read as I've ever had. Even today the images of those sincere, flawed characters Mr. Conroy put to paper burn bright. A more recent book that was a marvelous surprise on all fronts (except it isn't southern) was *The Book Thief* by Markus Zusak. Who would have guessed that Death as the narrator could be so sympathetic and compassionate? Or that a book's format could be so original?

Where did your idea for the book come from, and why is it set in Appalachia?

The inception of this book began in 2011 with a writing contest that had a cap of 1,500 words and an opening prompt of *I struggle to my feet*. From the moment the prompt fell on my page, Sadie appeared in my mind as a complete person and personality, from her slight form and pale skin, to her mountain voice and her birth in Appalachia. Why? That's a mystery I can't explain. Maybe the Appalachia I heard about in my youth resonated in the pain painted in the opening five words. My initial task was to tell Sadie's story in only a few pages. I often wondered what the rest of the story was. Now I know.

Do you have a favorite character? If so, who and why?

Let me preface the answer with the fact that a favorite character for this writer isn't necessarily the lovable one with the kind heart, good teeth, and best intentions. Good characters ground a story and give us someone to worry about and cheer for. The reader in me never likes a book that doesn't have characters I care about. In this book, Marris Jones is about as good a soul as you'll ever find. But the ugly, blackhearted characters, those who manipulate and claw through life, are the most compelling to me as a writer. Prudence and Roy take the cake in that category. Two more self-serving and cruel people I'll be hard-pressed to write about. When I found the courage to walk into the mind-set of these characters (yes, they scared me), their stories floated to the surface like greasy oil, and so did their vulnerabilities. That was the surprise—to discover pivotal moments in their development that formed their life's dismal path and to ask the question: What would I have grown to be if faced with those obstacles?

You talk as if these characters are real, but they're not, are they?

A good writer strives to make her characters complex and flawed and susceptible to all human foibles, and that's what makes them real. But no, this book, the characters, and their settlement are a work of fiction pulled from someplace deep in my psyche and the soup of my life's experiences. Only Preacher Eli Perkins resembles someone I knew, and that was my favorite uncle, who was a Baptist preacher. He could fire off jokes, one after the other, rivaling stand-up comics. He was my inspiration for Eli, but everyone and everything else is fabricated.

What is the most fun part of the writing process?

When the book is 90 percent complete, all the major pieces

are in place, each character has a distinct voice, and the narrative arc is clear—then the fun begins. I call this part of the process "polishing the silver." It is slow going but satisfying to fill in missing pieces and ponder every word to see what stays or goes for the sake of the story. I look for anything that bogs down the story line. Anything that doesn't make sense to the character's behavior or reaction. Then I wander deeper into their background and always discover something new and pertinent I didn't know about them the day before. While it sounds odd, the characters do take on a life of their own—and I miss spending time with them when the story ends.

What is the most challenging part of writing?

For me, it was developing an accurate timeline for the story. I thought I had created one, but it was not tight enough when dealing with ten major characters. Some of my last cleanup efforts were spent fixing it. Until a timeline is clearly established, it is easy to have things happening before they should to people they shouldn't. This part of the process takes patience, research, and copious notes about the time period and the events, large and small, in the lives of each character.

What is the one thing you know now that you wish you had known at the start of your writing career?

I wish I'd known I had to start at the beginning as a writer. Wishful thinking and my love for pretty words didn't give me a shortcut to success. For a while, my ego held me back because I wanted to believe that what fell naturally on the page was good enough. It was when I took down that defensive wall and committed myself to learning this craft from the ground up that progress was made. I could have saved myself a lot of heartache if I'd just enrolled in Writing Kindergarten 101 and started, *In the beginning*—which is the place all good stories start, right?

What advice would you give aspiring writers?

Take to heart the confession above, and believe the world always has room for another good book.

ACKNOWLEDGMENTS

Kudos and heartfelt thanks to my agent, Rebecca Gradinger, for her instant love for this book. She led with a delicate touch and a steady sense of partnership. Her savvy suggestions produced better pacing and greater depth to the characters. Shana Drehs's eagle eye brought more edits and helped the book grow stronger legs. Publicist Lathea Williams came with creative ideas, a quick response, and thorough planning. This trio of professionals left no stone unturned in their quest to get this book out and into the hands of readers.

The idea for the novel's format was born when Sharon McFarland Day, *mon amie* since high school, sent me a signed copy of *Olive Kitteridge*. Its unique short-story structure and the dark character of Olive inspired this book about richly flawed folks.

When *If The Creek Don't Rise* was in a nebulous state, I attended the Roanoke Regional Writers Conference, where author Carrie Brown suggested I sign up for the Wildacres Writers Workshop in North Carolina. I was fortunate my first writing class was under the direction of Luke Whisnant, English professor, author, and poet at East Carolina University. Talented writers in that weeklong short-story class reviewed a shorter version of the *Billy Barnhill* chapter and challenged me to write more fearlessly and go deeper into his unsavory side. I left Wildacres with a clearer vision of where the book was headed.

The next year, between writing and my final year traditionally employed, I researched the history of Appalachia, ginseng, moonshine, healing herbs, Mother Jones, coal mining, the Peace Corps, and exorcisms. No detail was too small to bring authenticity to Baines Creek residents in 1970. For example, in my quest to understand better Preacher Eli Perkins's education, I spoke to Adam Winters, the archivist at Southern Baptist Seminary in Louisville, KY. He emailed me a copy of their 1937 catalog so I could see what courses Eli would have taken, how many men from North Carolina would have been in his class, and what the tuition cost was (free!).

When I was close to submitting the manuscript for an agent's consideration, I had lunch with Marie Colligan, a published author and member of Lynchburg's Hill City Writers. Marie asked to read a chapter, and I gave her one with the request to "bleed ink all over the pages." I had worked in solitude for more than a year, and a fresh and critical eye was welcomed before I hit Send. Marie didn't disappoint. Her editing skills and suggestions were a gift when I needed them most.

The appeal of the story had already been affirmed by early readers, and I thank dear friends Harold and Jenny Beirne, Fran Harker, Sheila Peters, Marti Davis, and Shannon Brennan, who read early drafts and found them compelling enough for me to write on. My nurturing and supportive sister, Glo Swann, has always been my biggest fan. She loves to hear me read my work out loud (and I love to comply). Dan

Smith publicly supported me at every opportunity and was a resource for details from moonshine and hot rods to transistor radios. Kathleen Grissom taught me to give my characters free rein to tell their own stories and to *do the work*. She has shared every exciting step of this publishing journey with me. Her talent and generosity are boundless.

The faith the Virginia Episcopal School community has had in my writing dream is steadfast: the Hanning family, Phil Garmey, Debbie Leake, Liz Parthemore, Mary Stuart Battle, Jen Anderson, Esther Johnson, and Jane Winston followed my progress and cheered me on. Tommy Battle and Sarah Cuccio even bought stock in my future. Cory Anderson, my video guru, took my words and made me look good.

I am forever grateful for the guidance in my early writing years by dear friends Regina Cour, Jill McDonald, and Cheryl McMillan. When I was green at the craft, they were patient beyond measure. And finally, I thank Rolland Smith, who suggested I walk this creative path, and to trust there was room in the world for another book.

ABOUT THE AUTHOR

Photo credit: Ashley Ancheta

Leah Weiss is a Southern writer born in North Carolina and raised in the foothills of Virginia's Blue Ridge Mountains. *If the Creek Don't Rise* is her debut novel. She retired in 2015 from a twenty-four-year career as executive assistant to the headmaster at Virginia Episcopal School. Leah resides in south central Virginia and continues to write. She enjoys speaking to book clubs. You may contact her at leahweiss.com.